# Memories
## of
# Wild Rose
# Bay

BOOKS BY SUSANNE O'LEARY

The Sandy Cove Series
*Secrets of Willow House*
*Sisters of Willow House*
*Dreams of Willow House*
*Daughters of Wild Rose Bay*
*Memories of Wild Rose Bay*

*The Road Trip*
*A Holiday to Remember*

Susanne O'Leary

# Memories
of
# Wild Rose
Bay

bookouture

Published by Bookouture in 2020

An imprint of Storyfire Ltd.
Carmelite House
50 Victoria Embankment
London EC4Y 0DZ

www.bookouture.com

ISBN: 978-1-83888-878-7
eBook ISBN: 978-1-83888-877-0

*For my father*

# Chapter One

The Victorian house, a former rectory, stood in the middle of the village like a monument. It was a reminder to everyone of the old times and traditions that the village was built on. Covered in ivy, it had sash windows and turrets at either end, and was now the surgery and doctor's residence.

Kate stood at the ornate front door and examined the brass plaque that said 'Pat O'Dwyer, GP'. She had heard that Dr O'Dwyer was respected and loved in the community. He had been there 'since forever', or 'about forty years', depending on who you were talking to.

Being away from the rush and stress of an A&E department in one of Dublin's largest hospitals already felt good to Kate. She was relieved to be in Sandy Cove, to begin her training as an assistant GP. A sleepy little village on the edge of the west coast might feel like a bit of a holiday, and she thought it would be interesting, too. A break away from the pressure she had been under lately, both professionally and personally.

Kate had applied for the post on an impulse after a particularly stressful time in the hospital. A time during which she had even come to doubt her choice of medicine as a career. After everything that had happened, she had found herself so shaken that she had asked for some time off, but one of her superiors at the hospital had suggested additional training instead. 'Get out of Dublin,' he had said. 'Try to find some small hospital in the country that doesn't have this kind of pressure.' So here she was, in this small village that she had once planned to visit under different circumstances.

She looked up at the imposing facade of the house and felt a dart of excitement at the thought of living and working here for a while. The house had an old-world charm, but what about the people in it? The doctor she was going to work with and his family who no doubt lived here, too, what would they think of her?

Kate took a deep breath and pressed the doorbell, hearing it chime inside. As she waited for the door to open, she looked down the street at the end of which she could glimpse a beach and the blue glint of the ocean still visible as dusk fell. The air was fresh and clean and full of the plaintive cries of seagulls gliding above her in the sky. Such a maritime feel, Kate thought, and rang the doorbell again, checking the time on her watch.

She touched the face of her dad's old Rolex and remembered how he had given it to her only a week before he'd died, telling her it was the best watch to use to check a patient's pulse rate. A doctor too, her darling father had gone far too soon. He was missed by many, but especially by Kate. She'd always dreamed of walking in her father's footsteps, and here she was, about to spend six months in the village where his side of the family came from. When this position came up, it felt like it had been written in the stars. Sandy Cove in County Kerry, where the O'Rourke clan had lived since time began – a place she had often heard her father talk about but never visited – was now going to become her home and her workplace for a while.

Kate gave a start as the door flew open in front of her, nearly hitting her, and she faced a large woman with a mass of reddish-blonde curls, pale blue eyes and pink cheeks.

'Hello,' the woman said. 'Sorry I took a while to answer, but the doctor's out on a call and I'm here on my own dealing with the phone. Fridays are always like a railway station around here. Everyone seems to suddenly come down with one thing or the other. And they want it to be cured by the weekend.' She spoke without stopping even to take a breath, and Kate stood there stunned. 'But thank God the new doctor is on his way,' the woman continued without waiting for a reply. 'It'll be great to have someone young and fit to run this place when Dr Pat retires.' She stopped for breath and peered at Kate. 'But what can I do for you? Dr Pat will be God knows how long. He's gone up the mountain to see to Mrs Dolan's bad leg.'

'Eh, uh…' Kate blinked. 'Well, I'm… I'm the new doctor.' She held out her hand. 'Kate O'Rourke, actually. You must be Bridget.'

The woman looked at her and then started to laugh. 'Oh, that's a hoot. The new doctor? Kate, you said? And we thought you'd be a man. It said K. O'Rourke on the letter from the HSE. Highly qualified, it said. Worked with that famous heart specialist in Dublin, didn't you?' She paused for breath. 'But how rude I am.' She shook Kate's hand. 'I'm Bridget, nurse and receptionist and mother superior and confessor and all kinds of things you have to be in a place like this.' She backed inside. 'But come in, willya? Let's not stand on the doorstep like two auld women. We didn't expect you until Monday. Maybe you'd like a cup of tea? And something to eat? You look like you could do with a bit of food.'

Kate laughed and grabbed her suitcase. 'That would be lovely,' she said. 'I only managed a cup of tea and a bun in Adare on the way here from Dublin.'

'Holy Mary, that's not enough on such a long drive,' Bridget exclaimed. 'Come in, and I'll see what I can get you.'

They stepped into a large hall, where a sign on one of the doors said 'Surgery' and a sign on the other one said 'Private'.

'Go in through that door,' Bridget said and pointed at the 'Private' door. 'Down the corridor, last door on the left is the kitchen. I'll just put everything away and lock up the surgery and then I'll be with you.' Bridget disappeared through the surgery door, banging it shut behind her. 'And don't trip over the cat,' she shouted.

Kate left her suitcase in the hall and walked down the corridor that smelled faintly of medicine and turf fires. She found a large kitchen at the end of it, where an ancient enamelled green Aga stove emitted a welcome warmth after the chill of the November day outside.

Kate sat down at the scrubbed pine table and looked around at the old kitchen cupboards, the flagstone floor and the window overlooking a small garden. This was a wonderful family kitchen and it seemed strange that she would be living in this old house for six months. Dr O'Dwyer intended to retire once he 'broke her in', as he had said in his introductory letter. She would stay until the spring and then a permanent GP would be appointed. Kate smiled as she remembered they had thought she was a man. Why did this still happen in this day and age? Why did people on hearing the title 'doctor' think of a man first? Sadly, medicine was still a man's world, despite all the highly qualified women doctors. She had even made that mistake herself when she was younger.

Kate had always wanted to be a doctor like her father. When she was small she had played doctors with her dolls and forced her sister to be the patient, wrapping her in long strings of toilet paper and giving her 'injections' with the toy syringe from her doctor set. 'Oh look, how sweet,' her mother had said. 'Kate wants to be a nurse when she grows up.' To which Kate had scowled and declared that she wanted to be a doctor like her daddy. 'A hard job for a girl,' her mother had remarked, and that had certainly proven to be true.

After qualifying at the Royal College of Surgeons, Kate had worked on the teams of different consultants, the most interesting of which was heart surgery. Fascinated, she had watched as the surgeon cut into a patient's chest and proceeded to operate on the human heart, which could help the patient live a longer and better life. Surgery seemed to draw Kate in, but as she spent more time on the wards, watching the consultants deal with patients, she felt there was something missing. There was something cold about the way the specialists treated the patients, as if they were simply numbers or interesting cases, not people with feelings and fears. The consultant never held a patient's hand or asked them about their lives, never told them not to worry or assured them the planned surgery would be successful. They just breezed through the wards, the junior doctors on their teams following like adoring fans, nodding and smiling and sucking up to the consultant as if he were some kind of god. Then the male supremacy among even the junior doctors made it difficult for the few women junior doctors to get promoted even if they were far more talented than the men.

When Kate complained about the politics that went on in the hospitals, her father had shrugged and said that was the reason he had turned to general practice. 'I became a doctor to meet people and make them better,' he'd said. 'In general practice you get to heal more than the body. In any case, I like the detective work of making the correct diagnosis.' Kate had taken this to heart and switched to general practice, which she very quickly realised she was born to do, just like her father. She had worked at the Accident and Emergency department at St Vincent's hospital in Dublin for five years, before she registered for general practice. The work in A&E was exhausting but fascinating, and she quickly built up her diagnostic skills. She had sometimes worked as locum for her father when he wanted to get away for a break, until the day of the car accident.

Being back in a GP's practice already reminded Kate so much of her father. Having lost their mother to cancer five years earlier, she and Tara had known exactly what to do to arrange the funeral, and in a way that had helped them cope with going back to their jobs – Kate to A&E and Tara to New York to pursue fashion photography. But the speed with which they had picked up their lives again had also made Kate feel more alone. Neither she nor Tara had been able to talk about their father's death.

Bridget bustled into the kitchen, pulling Kate out of her daydream. She switched on the kettle and started to rummage around in the cupboards. 'I think I saw a pot of jam here somewhere,' she muttered. 'And there's fresh soda bread in the breadbin.'

'I didn't see your cat,' Kate remarked.

Bridget laughed. 'Oh, I don't have a cat, technically, it's just a stray that comes in from time to time. But he hasn't been here since yesterday.' She picked up a jar. 'Ah, here it is. Plum jam that Mrs O'Dwyer bought in that fancy shop in Killarney.'

'I hope she won't mind me being here in her kitchen,' Kate said.

'Not at all,' Bridget replied. 'She doesn't live here. She recently bought a house in Killarney and is setting it up, leaving Dr Pat to wind up here and break you in, so to speak. He'll be moving into the new house by Christmas. You should be quite used to things by then.'

'I hope so,' Kate said, feeling a pang of nerves as she thought of running the practice on her own in less than two months.

Bridget put one of her large hands on Kate's shoulder. 'Don't worry, girl. I'll be here to help you out. Quite looking forward to running an all-female practice. It feels new and modern. Us women need to show the men we can do without them.'

'Not completely though,' Kate cut in, laughing. 'A world without men wouldn't be that great.'

'Of course not,' Bridget agreed. 'I couldn't manage without my darling husband. He's my rock, really, but then he says I'm his. Been married over thirty years,' she said proudly. 'Four children, all away at university now. Thank God I have this job. I wouldn't know what to do with myself if I had to stay at home all day and wash my husband's socks. He'd love it, though. A woman at home at his beck and call would suit John fine.' Bridget drew breath and put a mug of tea on the table. Then she put bread, butter and the jam beside it and pushed it all towards Kate. 'There you go, girl. Have a bit of my soda bread while you wait for the doctor.'

'Thank you, Bridget.' Kate helped herself to bread and jam, which tasted wonderful after her long drive.

Bridget sat down opposite Kate with her own mug of tea. 'Might as well take the weight off my feet for a bit. I'll check the answering machine in a minute to make sure there isn't anything that needs dealing with. I shouldn't even do that. After hours they have to call South Doc in either Killarney or Kenmare, or go to A&E in the hospital in Killarney if it's urgent.'

'Are there a lot of after-hours calls?'

'Fridays mostly. But only from people who are old and lonely. Dr Pat just phones them back and chats with them for a bit. That's all that's usually needed. Don't worry, you won't have to be on call all the time.'

'That's good to know. Are people generally quite healthy around here?' Kate asked, having finished her first slice of bread and jam.

'Go on, have another slice,' Bridget urged. 'Healthy?' she said and shrugged. 'It comes and goes. Depends on the weather and time of year and such things. No rhyme or reason about that at all. And some folks don't go to the doctor until Cormac has had a go first. He sometimes fixes their ills, sometimes not. A real menace, that lad.'

'Cormac?' Kate asked, intrigued by the look in Bridget's eyes.

'Cormac O'Shea,' Bridget said with a twist to her mouth. 'A healer, he likes to call himself. Just because he happens to be the seventh son of the seventh son. You know that old folk tale, I'm sure.'

'I've heard about it. The seventh son of a seventh son having healing hands or something. Didn't know people still believed in it.'

'I think it's because they're very rare these days, even in Ireland. I mean, how many women do you know with seven sons? Or even that many children. But Cormac's mother did, the poor craythur. Had eight children, the last one a girl. Cormac was the seventh. And her husband was the seventh son in his family as well. Very strange. So of course all the old people around here immediately thought he had to have the gift. They started asking him to touch their wounds and sore limbs when he was just a small boy. Must have been traumatic for the poor little thing. But now he's a strapping lad and works down in the Wellness Centre as a herbalist. He's quite the pet of this village, what with his good looks and charm. But a bit full of himself, if you ask me.'

'Wellness Centre?' Kate asked, wondering if she'd be as charmed by this man as everyone else was. 'Is that like a spa?'

'Not really. It's a place where you go for yoga and that Pilates stuff that I never got my head around. Is it for pilots? Or something biblical?'

Kate laughed. 'No, it's a kind of exercise based on yoga. Quite exhausting, actually.'

'Oh.' Bridget shrugged. 'Doesn't sound like a lot of fun. I get my exercise from housework and gardening. Not glamorous, but then you get a clean house as well as strong legs and arms. Why doesn't anyone talk about that?'

'It's not sexy,' Kate replied with a laugh. 'But of course you're right. Any kind of physical activity is good for you. And housework is productive as well as being a good way to move. I must admit I like going to an exercise class all the same. And I adore hillwalking. Housework could never replace those.'

'And then people are too tired to clean their houses after all the yoga and Pilates nonsense,' Bridget continued. 'So you have all these fit women with messy houses. Doesn't make sense to me.'

'That's true.' Kate felt as if she could sit in this cosy kitchen all day listening to Bridget's take on what was going on in the world.

'But tell me more about the village. My father's family lived here a long time ago.'

'You're not related to Sally O'Rourke, then?' Bridget asked. 'She lives in that house on the hill just off the main street.'

'I might be, but not closely related,' Kate said after a moment's silence. 'All the O'Rourkes around here must be from the same stock originally.'

'Ah sure, this place was overrun by O'Rourkes in the old days. The O'Rourkes and McKennas were the two most important families back then. I mean hundreds of years ago, of course. The O'Rourkes lived in the old village by Wild Rose Bay, but not everyone was able to make a living. The sheep farmers and the fishermen and those who went into local politics stayed. Your lot must have been the ones who had to go and look for work somewhere else, who are scattered all over the country now.'

Kate laughed. 'Yeah, that's what I heard. My dad's family came to Dublin over a hundred years ago. He often told us stories about the village and that little bay and the people who lived there before moving to Dublin. I think some of them worked on the quays and some became policemen. Then my grandfather became a doctor and my father, too. I'm the third O'Rourke who chose medicine.'

'Your lot did well, then. So,' Bridget remarked, getting up from the table, 'I must go and check the answering machine. Then I'll get the doctor's tea ready.'

'Tea?' Kate asked before she realised Bridget meant supper. That old thing of calling the midday meal 'dinner' and supper 'tea' was obviously still alive here.

'That's right,' Bridget said. 'He likes sausages and mash for his tea. How about you?'

'That'd be grand,' Kate said, grateful that she didn't have to cook something for herself the first night.

Bridget nodded. 'I should have said – I organised the back bedroom for you. It has its own bathroom, so it's quite private. You won't be disturbed by the doctor or his son who comes in late.'

'His son?'

'Yes. Mick O'Dwyer. He's quite well known, actually. Ever heard of him?'

Kate stared at Bridget. 'Mick O'Dwyer? The actor?'

Bridget nodded. 'That's the lad. He stays here when he's on a break from the theatre.'

'Here?' Kate said in a near whisper, her heart beating. 'In this house?'

'That's right. But nobody knows, so please don't tell anyone.'

'I won't,' Kate said, knowing she'd be on the phone to Tara in New York as soon as she could.

'I'll be back in a minute,' Bridget said and walked out of the kitchen, leaving Kate staring at the door swinging shut, completely stunned by what she had just heard. Mick O'Dwyer, the award-winning actor who she had seen in numerous plays at the Abbey Theatre in Dublin was old Dr O'Dwyer's son. And he was staying here, in this house.

# Chapter Two

Dr Pat, as everyone seemed to call him, appeared in time for the meal Bridget prepared for them both before she went home. Having installed herself in the small but cosy back bedroom, Kate went downstairs and found a tall man with thick salt-and-and pepper hair sitting at the table, tucking into his sausage and mash. He rose slowly as she entered, smiling and holding out his hand. 'Hello there, Kate,' he said and shook her hand. 'Welcome.'

'Hello, Dr O'Dwyer,' Kate said, returning his smile and shaking his hand. His brown eyes had a kindly look behind his steel-rimmed glasses and Kate immediately liked him, imagining what a wonderful doctor he must be. 'How was Mrs Dolan's bad leg?'

He laughed. 'Not that bad today. A case of varicose veins that had ulcerated. I dressed it and told her she has to have those veins done soon. She has finally agreed, so she'll be going to Tralee to see the specialist in a few weeks. Should improve her life no end.' He gestured at the Aga. 'Bridget put your tea in the oven to keep warm. Do help yourself and sit down. I'm having a glass of wine as I'm off duty. Will you join me?'

'Yes, please,' Kate said and took the plate out of the oven after putting on an oven glove. She looked at the plate of sausages, mashed potatoes, a grilled tomato, fried mushrooms and buttered broad beans. 'Goodness, what a lot of food. Sausage and mash, Bridget said, but there's a lot more than that.'

'She likes to give me a good feed on Friday night,' the doctor said, pouring red wine into a crystal glass for Kate. 'But you look as if—' He stopped. 'Sorry. Didn't mean to comment on your looks. The doctor in me never takes time off, I'm afraid.'

Kate laughed and sat down opposite him. 'I'm not offended,' she said as she grabbed her knife and fork. 'I do have a very healthy appetite despite looking as if I haven't had a square meal in weeks. It's just the way I am.'

'You look more like a dancer than a doctor,' he said. 'Petite and skinny. And please call me Pat. I know I'm ancient but we're colleagues and will be working together.'

'Of course, Pat,' Kate said, smiling at him. 'You're not exactly overweight yourself, if I may say so.'

'You may,' Pat said with a glimmer of a smile. 'I suppose we both have a high metabolism.'

'Yes, I think we must,' Kate said and dug into her meal. 'This looks delicious, and I'm starving.'

Pat nodded. 'Bridget's a good cook.'

'Oh yes, she must be,' Kate replied. 'But why is she doing the cooking here? Isn't that a little above and beyond her duties as a surgery nurse?'

Pat laughed. 'Oh yes, absolutely. But Bridget loves to cook and she's been part of the family ever since she started working for me thirty years ago. It's not something that's in her job description, but that's the way things work round here.' He picked up his fork. 'I must say

I'm pretty peckish myself.' He attacked the food with gusto, and they both ate in silence for a while, taking swigs of wine between bites.

When Kate had cleared her plate, she pushed it away and lifted her glass. 'Very nice wine. Pinot Noir?'

Pat nodded. 'Yes, a nice Morgon I picked up in the supermarket in Waterville. They have good wines there. I'm guessing the golfers who come there from all over the place have very selective tastes.'

'Do you play golf?' Kate asked.

'Indeed I do. And I'm looking forward to retirement when I can play more often. My wife is a fanatic, too. How about you?'

Kate shook her head. 'No. I'm more into hillwalking. I'm looking forward to heading up the mountains here.'

'Not on your own, I hope,' Pat said sternly. 'Never go up the mountains alone, my dear. It's not a good idea. The mountain rescue teams have enough to do with foolish people who go up these mountains without any training whatsoever. We had one death last year. I hope I'll never have to deal with another one.'

'I suppose you're right,' Kate replied, looking at him thoughtfully. 'Is there a hillwalking club in this area?'

'No, the nearest one would be in Killarney. But my son is staying with me at the moment. He's very experienced and knows these mountains like the back of his hand. But even he would never go up alone. He usually goes on hikes with a friend. I'm sure he'd be happy for you to join him and his friend while he's here.'

Kate laughed. 'Really? Mick O'Dwyer taking me on a hike up the mountains? That would be incredible.'

Pat nodded and refilled their glasses. 'Yes, the views from up there are wonderful.'

'I didn't mean the views,' Kate said, trying her best to keep a straight face. 'I'm a huge fan of Mick. I've seen most of the plays he's been in at the Abbey. He's an amazing actor.'

'Oh.' Pat laughed. 'I see. One of his fans, eh? Well, you'll be seeing him up close in a few days.'

'A few days?' Kate said, disappointed. 'He's not here now?'

'No. He's in Limerick at some party in a hotel, I think he said. He'll be back late Sunday night.'

'I see. Well, I'll be very excited to meet him in the flesh,' Kate said, mentally planning a little beauty session in the old-fashioned bathroom over the weekend.

'He'll be equally happy to meet you, I'm sure,' Pat said with a little wink. He drained his glass and got up. 'Now, I'll just put everything in the dishwasher and watch the evening news in the living room. Would you like to join me?'

'I'll help with the clearing up,' Kate offered.

'No need, no need at all,' Pat assured her. 'But maybe you'd like to have a look at the surgery? I'll see you there in a minute.'

'Oh, yes. I'd love to,' Kate said, excited at the thought of seeing her new workplace, even if it was probably very much like any GP surgery she'd ever been in, including her father's.

She made her way down the corridor, glancing in through the open door of the living room. A cosy room with a faded oriental carpet, furnished with a comfortable sofa and two easy chairs covered in worn green velvet. The walls were lined with bookcases crammed with books and two logs smouldered in the fireplace. Very much like the living room of the house she grew up in, Kate thought with a pang of nostalgia as she continued into the hall and through the surgery door. She felt on the wall inside the door, flicked on the light switch and blinked as a rather shabby waiting room came into view.

She sighed as she looked at the sagging chairs, the beige walls and the brown carpet. It all needed serious updating. Such a dreary room would make anyone feel poorly even if they weren't suffering from some ailment when they got here. A door opened into a small windowless box room with a tiny table on which stood a laptop and a phone beside piles of papers. Bridget's office, she assumed. The only other room downstairs was the doctor's office, with the same brown carpet, an examination table, a desk with a computer, shelves of reference books and folders, and a steel cabinet with various medical paraphernalia and an assortment of medicines. The room smelled exactly like her father's, and for a moment Kate was eight years old looking at her father in a white coat as he finished for the day. 'Hello, Katie,' he would say. 'Have you come to help me tidy up?'

Kate closed the door, mentally taking notes on how she would upgrade the doctor's room and smiling at the memories. She gave a start as Dr Pat came in from the hall.

'You've had a look around?' he said, peering at her over his glasses.

'Yes,' Kate replied. 'Nice surgery,' she added politely.

'It's a bit old-fashioned, I know. I'm sure the surgeries in Dublin are lot more modern and shiny.'

'Maybe a little,' Kate had to admit. 'But it wouldn't take much to update this one.'

He shrugged. 'I'm sure it wouldn't. I didn't really feel it was necessary. It's been the same since I started here forty years ago. Nobody's complained yet.'

'Yes, but…' Kate started, but stopped herself before she said anything to hurt his feelings. 'It's not a big deal, really,' she ended lamely.

'No. But if you want to spruce the place up a little, I don't mind. After all, this will be your surgery very soon.'

Kate nodded. 'I know. I'll probably change it just a little bit,' she said, not to seem too critical, itching to rip out the brown carpet for a start as soon as she could.

'Good. Well, let's go next door and we'll watch the news and I'll fill you in on the surgery schedules. And then, tomorrow, you might want to come with me on my rounds.'

'Rounds?' Kate asked. 'At the weekend?'

He nodded. 'Yes. I drive around on Saturdays checking up on some of my older patients who live in remote places. I like to make sure they're following my advice and are improving. Not strictly part of my duties, but that's the way I run things. This is not a nine-to-five job, you know. A country doctor is never really off duty.'

'Of course,' Kate said. She suddenly had a sinking feeling that running this country practice would be a lot more challenging than she'd thought.

Later that night, after watching the news and trying to take in everything Dr Pat told her about the patients and the running of the surgery, Kate said goodnight and went up to her room, where she unpacked her suitcase and hung her clothes in the mahogany wardrobe. The room was lovely, with a comfortable bed covered in a white crocheted bedspread and piled with lacy pillows, and cream velvet curtains drawn across the sash windows. The night table had a cute lamp with a pleated lampshade that cast a soft light on the bed and the sage-green carpet. The walls were covered in watercolours of the Kerry landscape and two little oil paintings, one of a girl in a blue dress sitting on the steps of an old house and the other of a garden where a small dog was half-hidden under a rose bush in full bloom. A bowl with dried rose petals emitted a faint scent. A charming, comfortable room that felt like a cosy nest to Kate. She knew she would be happy to come back here after a hard day at the practice.

But right now she was longing to talk to her sister. She sat on her bed and turned on her laptop after sending a text to Tara to say she wanted to Skype. It didn't take long for the call to be answered and Tara's face came into view.

Kate took in this glossier, more glamorous version of herself on the screen. Tara's dark hair fell like a shiny curtain to her shoulders, her large hazel eyes were expertly made up and her full mouth was a lovely shade of pink. Kate's hair was a similar colour but tied back in a ponytail and her face was devoid of make-up. Tara was the beautiful one, she had always thought, despite them being identical twins. 'Hey there,' she said to the screen image. 'How's the hotshot photographer?'

'A little tired,' Tara replied. 'I've been up since five thirty doing a photo shoot in the park. We had an early snowfall so they decided to do the *Vogue* winter coat feature here instead of flying everyone across to Aspen.' She yawned. 'So yeah, I'm bushed.'

Kate giggled. 'Listen to yourself. You've turned into an American after only a year in New York.'

'It's very easy to fall into, you know,' Tara replied.

'How's it going, anyway? At work?'

Tara grinned. 'It's going incredibly well. I've got jobs with *Vogue* and *Harper's Bazaar* already, and my agent just got a call from *Vanity Fair*. They seem to like my technique over here.'

'That's brilliant, Tara,' Kate said fondly. 'I'm so proud of you.'

Tara blew a kiss at Kate. 'Thank you. I can't believe it myself. I keep thinking they're talking about someone else. But what about you? How are things with you and the country practice?'

'I've just arrived and met the doctor,' Kate replied. 'Nice old guy. Reminds me of Dad in a way. Except he seems to live in the past. Runs a practice that's like something out of that old TV series, *Dr Finlay's Casebook*.'

Tara laughed. 'What did you expect? It's a small village in Kerry. I'd say it's a bit old-fashioned. Like going back to the nineteen fifties.'

'Exactly. But wait till I tell you who's staying here,' Kate continued, barely able to keep the excitement from her voice. 'Only Mick O'Dwyer!'

'Mick O'Dwyer, the Abbey actor?' Tara asked.

'That's him.'

'The guy we used to drool over when we went to the theatre?'

'Yes.'

'He's staying in the village?' Tara asked incredulously.

'Not only the village. In this house. He's the doctor's son.'

'What? You're kidding,' Tara said.

'Nope. Not kidding at all. It's true. I haven't met him yet, but he'll be here on Sunday night.'

'Oooh.' Tara's eyes widened. 'You lucky duck. If I could, I'd fly over straight away. But I have to work over the weekend. All this snow has created great possibilities for winter clothes and Christmas advertising. I'm doing a kids' ski clothing shoot tomorrow. Ten three-year-olds to organise. Can you imagine?'

'Sounds like hard work,' Kate agreed. 'And I'm doing something called "the rounds" tomorrow with Dr Pat. I'm guessing it's just his way to make sure some of the older people are still alive.'

'Sounds like fun.' Tara looked her sister up and down. 'I do hope you'll get a chance to smarten up a little before you meet the hunky actor.'

Kate touched her messy ponytail. 'I'll wash and blow-dry, promise.'

'And you'll put on a little make-up?'

'Just a touch,' Kate replied.

'At least some foundation,' Tara suggested. 'And some of that blusher I gave you. And a coat or two of mascara.'

'Okay,' Kate said. 'But that's all. I'm not a supermodel like you, you know.'

'Can't believe we're twins sometimes,' Tara remarked. 'You're me on a bad hair day.'

'And you're me having been attacked by a team of beauticians at some fancy beauty salon,' Kate countered.

'I'd love to make you up like me. Imagine the fun we'd have going out.'

'For five minutes.' Kate grimaced at the thought. She may have planned to spruce herself up a bit to meet Mick, but she wasn't interested in make-up or fashion and thought it all a waste of time. It was strange that she and Tara were so different in their likes and dislikes. Tara had been the ultimate little princess when they were growing up, and Kate a typical tomboy, preferring to play with boys rather than Tara and her dolls. Kate had been the captain of the girls' hockey team at school while Tara went to ballet. But while they had different interests, they had been as close as most twins and inseparable until they finished school and went to different universities.

Medical school had swallowed Kate up and she found herself spending less time with Tara, until their mother had died the year Kate qualified and they'd both moved back home so their father wouldn't have to live alone. They stayed with him during the first heartbreaking years. It was during that time that they'd heard the terrible news. They had been at home sharing a pizza and planning their birthday party when the doorbell rang and two policemen stood on the doorstep, their faces serious, telling them as tactfully as they could that their father had been in a collision with a truck on the motorway and killed instantly.

'It's been two years,' Tara said.

Kate blinked. 'What? How did you know what I was thinking about?'

'The look in your eyes.' Tara sighed.

'I do feel a little lonely,' Kate admitted, not wanting to delve into their shared grief. 'But it's just because it's all so new.'

'I feel lonely too,' Tara said, her eyes sad. 'Maybe I should chuck this in and come home.'

'Don't you dare,' Kate said sternly. 'You're at the beginning of a great career. Look how well you're doing already. Do you really want to give that up?'

'I suppose not,' Tara replied. 'It's such fun, you know? But if you need me…'

'I'm fine,' Kate interrupted. 'I just felt a little strange here in this old house trying to get used to things. But I'm looking forward to seeing the patients and getting settled in.'

'And meeting Mick O'Dwyer?' Tara teased.

Kate laughed. Tara always managed to cheer her up. 'Yes, of course. Better than queuing in the rain at the stage door for his autograph, like that night a few years ago.'

'And then he never showed up. That was the disappointment of the century.'

'I nearly started to cry,' Kate said, remembering how they had waited in a long queue of other women who were equally disappointed.

'But now he won't be able to get away,' Tara said, laughing. 'Oh, I wish I could be there when he walks in and you get to shake his hand. Promise we'll Skype afterwards.'

'I promise.' Kate stifled a yawn. 'Sorry. I think I'm ready for bed. The drive from Dublin was very tiring.'

'You need lots of beauty sleep,' Tara ordered. 'Go to bed at once.'

'Yes, Mammy,' Kate said, laughing. 'You go on back to work.'

'I must,' Tara agreed. 'Talk again on Sunday night when you'll tell me everything, and I mean *everything*.'

'I will,' Kate promised. 'Bye for now, sis.'

But Tara hadn't finished. 'Wash your hair and wear it down,' she urged. 'Apply a little make-up, especially blusher and mascara. And put on something sexy and…'

'Byeee,' Kate chanted and closed the Skype connection. Tara got carried away at times, especially when she wanted to do a makeover on Kate. The only way to stop it was to walk away, or in this case switch her off.

Kate put the laptop on the old chest of drawers and walked to the window that overlooked the small garden, and the coastline in the far distance. The full moon shone a beam of light across the still water and the stars glimmered in the black sky. It would be a cold night.

Kate shivered, closed the heavy velvet curtains and prepared for bed, not forgetting to put on her wool socks before slipping in under the thick duvet. She felt a hot-water bottle at her feet and smiled, knowing Bridget had put it there. Resting her feet on the hot-water bottle, she snuggled deep, feeling as if she were back in the house she had grown up in and half-expecting her father to come in and kiss her on the forehead like he used to when she was small. But the memory didn't make her sad like before. Coming here was something that was *meant* to happen. It was what her father would have wanted, returning to where their family had lived for so many centuries. She looked forward to her day with Dr Pat and getting to know this village and the countryside that held the history of her family. Delving into it would feel like slowly unwrapping a wonderful gift that had been waiting to be discovered for over a hundred years.

# Chapter Three

The drive through the village and further up the hills on the chilly autumn day was hugely enjoyable for Kate, who hadn't seen much of her surroundings as dusk had fallen when she'd arrived the day before. Bundled up in warm jackets, they set off in Dr Pat's old Ford while he told her about the village and the people who lived there. 'There are a few O'Rourkes around,' he said, gesturing at a shop window full of colourful objects. 'That's Sally O'Rourke's shop, and further down the road above the beach we have The Two Marys', a coffee shop that's run by two cousins with the same name, one of them an O'Rourke. Very popular with the sporty crowd who surf and walk up the hills. It's closed for the season now, but they'll open up for the Christmas holidays.'

'Oh,' Kate said, looking around at the charming mix of old cottages, Victorian houses and the odd modern construction here and there. She could see the pharmacy and the small grocery shop that also housed a newsagent's and a post office.

'Multitasking,' Dr Pat joked as he followed her gaze. 'You'll see a lot of that here. We like to combine our efforts so that all amenities are present in the village. Sadly, we have no Garda station, but it's quite a peaceful place, apart from the odd brawl at the pub on a

Saturday night, or after a hurling match, but we have a few strong lads who'll sort that out in no time. In fact, Sean Óg, who runs the pub, acts as an unofficial Guard at times. He used to play rugby and was a county champion hurler as well. Some of the team work in the pub. So there's no shortage of help should you get into trouble.'

'I can't imagine getting into any kind of trouble here,' Kate said, looking down the peaceful street bathed in late-autumn sunshine.

'Let's hope not,' Dr Pat said and pointed at a long, low building standing at the edge of a small field that led to the beach. 'The Wellness Centre. It's been there two years now. It's run by Sally O'Rourke who also owns the curiosa shop.'

'Another multitasker?' Kate asked.

'You could say that. She manages to make both a huge success, but I think wellness is her real baby. It's very popular. I can't knock it because it makes people feel well to go to yoga and eat organic foods and take some of the herbal remedies. The only problem I have is with Cormac.'

'Cormac?' Kate asked. 'Is he that man Bridget told me about? The seventh son of…'

'That's him. He's a nice lad, and he doesn't really try to push any of his lotions and potions on people. But some of the older people seem to think he's better than any doctor. The old traditions are still so alive here. The mere fact of him being the seventh son of a seventh son is what gives him some kind of star quality in their eyes.'

'Surely you don't believe in that?'

Dr Pat shrugged. 'Not really. But I've heard he has a new ointment that has actually healed wounds that could have scarred badly. That's something I think should be looked into. And I do believe some people have healing powers that we can't explain. I don't think it has anything to do with your place in a family, but in some inherent instinct and understanding of the human body. And perhaps a calming presence that makes a sick person relax. Many doctors have that kind of quality.'

'Does Cormac?' Kate asked.

Dr Pat nodded as he turned into a narrow lane at the end of the street. 'I think he does. He's certainly very charismatic. But you have to get to know him to understand.'

'I'd like to meet him,' Kate said, intrigued.

'It won't take long before you do. It's a small village.'

They continued up the hill and around the bend, across a hump-backed bridge and then through a dense clump of trees covered in white flowers and red berries. Kate regarded the tall trees in awe, surprised to see anything in bloom in November.

'Arbutus trees,' Dr Pat said, noticing Kate's surprise. 'They bloom in November, strangely enough. It's also called the Strawberry tree because of its fruit. They take twelve months to ripen. That's why you see the flowers and berries at the same time.' He slowed the car and stopped under the tallest tree. 'I'll stop for a moment so you can take a look.'

'Amazing,' Kate said, looking up at the beautiful white flowers and the clumps of red berries. 'It doesn't look like a native tree.'

'It isn't really. It's a Mediterranean species, and it's thought to have come over to Ireland from Brittany in ancient times when the two land masses were very close. It only grows in Kerry as the climate is so mild here.'

'Can you eat the berries?' Kate asked.

'I suppose you can. They're not poisonous. But I think they have a rather nasty taste, so it's not something I'd recommend to put in your fruit salad.'

Kate laughed and took out her phone. 'I must take a photo of this. It's so beautiful in this light with the hills in the background.'

'Of course. We're in no hurry. But walk up that field a little bit and take the shot against the coastal view. The ocean is a lovely colour this morning.'

Kate got out of the car and turned to look at the view of the coast. The sea was indeed a beautiful colour, deep blue with turquoise streaks near the beach. The heather-covered slopes of the mountains were a mass of purple and the craggy tops had a light dusting of snow. As Kate walked higher up the field, she saw that the trees with their white blossoms and red berries looked beautiful against the backdrop of the ocean and the blue sky. She took a series of shots from different angles and then stood there taking in all the beauty around her. She spotted a fox running down the hill and watched him make his way further down, round a boulder, disappearing and appearing again as he ran further down towards a tiny bay where the water was a pure turquoise and the dense vegetation had been hacked away to form a path all the way to the beach.

'Wild Rose Bay,' Dr Pat said behind her. 'It's lovely but it's hard to get all the way down there. There are some ruins from an earlier village. The O'Rourke story starts there, I think.'

'Really?' Kate looked down on the little bay with a dart of excitement. Wild Rose Bay. What a beautiful place. She'd go down there as soon as she could. Maybe even tomorrow.

*

They continued on, driving through a windswept plain and up a steep track that led to a small thatched cottage where a column of smoke rose from the chimney. 'Jim and Maura,' Dr Pat said, getting out of the car with his bag. 'Old Jim had a wound on his arm that wouldn't heal, so I want to take a look and change the dressing.'

They walked through the gate and up the gravel path to the red door that opened just as they arrived. A rosy-cheeked woman with a mass of white hair beamed at them. 'Dr Pat! How nice to see you. And is this young girl your niece?'

Pat laughed. 'No, Maura, this is Kate O'Rourke, the new doctor taking over from me in the new year. I think she'll be known as Dr Kate by everyone pretty soon.'

Smiling warmly, Maura held out her hand. 'Hello, Dr Kate. Lovely to meet you. Come in and I'll put the kettle on. Jim's in the sitting room listening to the news. Nothing but misery out there in the world, though. I hope you can cheer him up.'

They walked into the small sitting room where a turf fire blazed in the fireplace and an old man sat with his head cocked to the old-fashioned radio on the dresser that was crammed with framed photos. A white Jack Russell terrier with a black patch over his ear curled up in the old man's lap sat up and looked at them, wagging his little tail. The old man turned and smiled, taking his glasses from the top of his bald head and putting them on.

'Dr Pat,' he said when his eyes had focused on them, 'What are you doing up here in the wild countryside on a Saturday? And you brought a pretty young lady, I see.' Jim rose stiffly, letting the dog onto the floor and held out his gnarled hand for Kate to shake. 'I'm Jim Sullivan, but you can call me Jim. What's your name, pet?'

Feeling like a schoolgirl, Kate shook the old man's hand. 'My name's Kate O'Rourke and I'm the new doctor. I'll be taking over from Dr Pat in the new year.'

'A doctor, eh?' The old man peered at her. 'They get younger and younger these days. Or maybe I'm just getting old.'

'We're both old,' Pat said and put his bag on one of the chairs that stood beside the dresser. 'Sit down and we'll take a look at that wound.'

'It's much better, you'll see,' Jim said and sat down again. 'Maura got some kind of cream from that young man down at the health centre. Worked a treat.' He rolled up the sleeve of his grey cardigan to reveal a bandage on his forearm.

'Really?' Pat started to undo the bandage that had a brownish tint and smelled of something chemical. 'You mean Cormac at the Wellness Centre?'

'That's the lad,' Jim said.

'Hmm,' Pat said, frowning as he removed the bandage. Then he examined the wound and let out a whistle. 'Well, well, well. Take a look at this, Kate.'

Kate leaned forward and looked at the wound that seemed to be healing nicely. 'Looks fine,' she said. 'Looks like there'll be no scarring at all.'

'So it does,' Pat said, peering at old Jim. 'What's in this cream you used?'

Old Jim shrugged. 'I don't know. You'll have to ask Maura, but I'm sure she doesn't know what it's made of.'

'Maybe not.' Pat took a clean bandage from his bag and wound it around Jim's arm. 'No real need to keep it covered for more than another day or two,' he said. 'It's nearly all healed.'

'At last,' Jim said. 'It's been a month since I cut myself on that rusty nail.'

'Yes. That kind of wound is difficult to treat,' Pat remarked. 'And I tried all the creams I could think of to reduce the inflammation. But this one seems to have done the trick.'

'That lad has magic in his hands,' Jim said.

'I'm not sure that's quite true, but he knows a thing or two about herbal remedies. Most of the time they don't work.'

'But this time it did,' Jim said, nodding his head.

'Well, it was probably on its way to healing anyway,' Pat argued. 'I gave you an antibiotic cream to use last time.'

'That one fixed the infection but it was still very red and puckered,' Jim countered. 'Then Maura went to Cormac and got his special remedy. The one he only uses for really bad cases.'

'But I'm not sure…' Pat said, frowning.

He was interrupted by the door opening to admit Maura carrying a tray with tea and buns that she placed on the little table in front of the fire. 'I made a big pot. Help yourselves to tea and those buns I made yesterday. I thought you might be up so I baked the ones you like best, Dr Pat.'

'You spoil me,' Pat said and helped himself to a cup of tea and a bun.

'Please sit down,' Maura said and sat beside Jim, handing him a cup of tea.

Kate took a chair beside the fire and Pat chose an easy chair by the window.

'So, Maura,' Pat said when he had taken a big bite of his bun, 'tell me about this magic ointment you got from the lad at the Wellness Centre.'

Maura looked a little embarrassed. 'Yes, well, it was an accident, really. I was there talking to that nice Sally and then I happened to mention Jim's wound that wouldn't heal. Then Sally said to see if Cormac might have something that could help. And after a little while chatting to him, he told me about a new ointment he had made up that had helped heal a cut on Mrs O'Meara's Labrador, so he said I might try it on Jim.'

Pat shook his head. 'So you used a cream for dogs on a very nasty puncture wound. That could have been dangerous, you know.'

'But it wasn't,' Maura said, beaming at him. 'It worked a treat.'

'Yes, but…' Pat started. Then he gave up and finished his bun. 'I'm going to have a chat with Cormac next week and ask him what's in that ointment.'

'He won't tell you,' Jim muttered into his tea. 'All his formulas are secret.'

'Is this legal?' Kate asked. 'I mean, are you entitled to sell things you've made up like that?'

Pat shrugged. 'I think you can, actually, if you call it natural and not medical. Cormac has studied biology and chemistry at Cork University. So he knows about drugs and medicines. He's applied this knowledge to his own business.'

'I wouldn't call it a business,' Maura cut in. 'He just sells his remedies in that Wellness Centre, not on the line or anything.'

'You mean online?' Kate asked.

Maura nodded her white head. 'Yes, on that internet thing that you get into through a computer. My daughter does our shopping that way. She sends in an order and then the van arrives at our door the next day. It's very strange but who am I to complain?'

'Sure, what would you do without it?' Pat drained his cup and got up. 'We have a few other people to see, so we'd better get going. Thanks for the tea and buns, Maura. Just the ticket on this chilly day.'

'You're welcome, Dr Pat,' Maura said and got up. 'Nice to see you and the lovely girleen. Will you be back next Saturday?'

'I'll drop in to say hello,' Pat replied, putting on his jacket. 'I'm sure Jim's wound will be all healed by then.'

'What's that?' Jim asked, cupping his ear.

'Your wound will be healed by next Saturday,' Pat shouted.

Jim nodded. 'Yes, it will.' He waved his hand. 'Off you go now. Lots of other people to see who need you more. Goodbye, young lady. You'll be a good doctor when you grow up, I'm sure.'

They said goodbye and left, continuing up the steep road to visit other little houses dotted all the way to the top of the hill. They called in to a number of people among whom were a young couple expecting a baby, two elderly sisters who had both been ill with the flu, an old man living alone with his two dogs and a woman recovering from a broken leg. None of these people was strictly speaking ill or even in need of urgent care, but it was good to check up on them all the same, Dr Pat said when they were on their way back. 'A way of making sure nobody was forgotten or had died,' he explained. 'Nothing sadder than those people who are found weeks afterwards because nobody could bother to call in.'

'I know,' Kate said. 'I read stories like that sometimes and it's horrible to think you could die all alone in some remote area. But you can't call in on them every day, though.'

'No, but the postman does, you see. And I do my little round on Saturday, and then on Sundays, our parish priest does his own little spin. We look after our own around here, you see. Nobody is ever forgotten.'

'That's wonderful,' Kate said, thinking she would do the same thing when she was running the practice on her own.

'This is far removed from the exciting life of a heart clinic,' Pat remarked.

'Oh,' Kate replied with a laugh, 'I actually find this more exciting. Surgeons are skilled at saving lives, but they tend to forget about the person whose life they have saved. I mean, they don't see…' She stopped. 'It's hard to explain.'

'You mean that there is very little empathy? Nobody holds hands and asks people about their feelings or even tries to tell them not to be afraid?'

Kate nodded. 'Yes. Something like that.'

'I suspect they don't have much time for that. In any case, general practice is primary care and we should never try to play specialists. That can lead to disaster. You must always hand a patient over to the specialist when you know you can't fix what's wrong yourself. I even tell patients with high blood pressure to get checked by a heart specialist just to make sure there is no underlying cause that I haven't spotted. Better to be safe than sorry, you know.'

'Absolutely,' Kate agreed. Her respect for this sprightly old man had increased steadily through the day, and she realised he was one of those wise old doctors who knew exactly how to treat a patient the moment he saw them. Her dad had been one of them, too. It wasn't something you could learn, it was in the genes.

Maybe Cormac with the magical potions also had it in his genes? Kate was determined to meet him and find out. It seemed to her that he was a bit of a problem for Dr Pat. Superstition was clearly rife around these parts, where the old traditions were still so alive. Would she as a newcomer and a woman be able to overcome all of that? She would have to use a lot of tact and diplomacy with the older generation, she thought. A country practice demanded different skills to an emergency department in a city hospital. This was a challenge she hadn't expected but felt determined to meet. She'd learn how it all worked and get back to Dublin a lot more experienced, ready to take on a city practice. But that was six months away, and she began to look forward to the time here in this nice village, improving her people skills and tackling that faith healer or whatever he was.

*Bring it on*, she thought with a dart of excitement as they rounded the corner and drove into the village that was bathed in the golden light of the setting sun.

# Chapter Four

Sunday was a day of rest, Dr Pat had announced before he set off to Killarney to see his wife and play a round of golf. All alone, Kate wandered around getting to know the old house. It had five bedrooms and two bathrooms upstairs; the surgery, sitting room, dining room, study and kitchen were all downstairs. All the rooms were furnished in a slightly old-fashioned style, with chintzy chairs, mahogany sideboards and chests of drawers. The pictures on the walls were mostly landscapes and the odd portrait or paintings of dogs. It felt a little like a time warp to Kate and reminded her of her childhood home in Dublin.

The garden was not large but a little neglected, with several large rhododendron and camellia bushes that would be in bloom in early spring. There was a small conservatory with wicker furniture and a little terrace with lovely views of the bay and the Skellig Islands beyond. The house felt instantly like home to Kate, even if the surgery was screaming for an update. She'd have to see if she could make a few changes or she'd find it very difficult to work there. But that was for another day.

After breakfast, Kate put on her hiking boots and jacket and walked out of the house and down the main street towards the beach. It was cold and breezy with dark clouds on the horizon, but the rain looked as if it would hold off until the afternoon as forecast. Kate walked onto the beach and stood there for a while watching a man on his windsurfing board disappearing far out into the bay. He looked very experienced and it was a pleasure to watch him expertly dodging the waves and using the sail to get the wind to carry him swiftly out to sea. It must be wonderful to be out there, she thought, battling the elements and feeling the wind and waves carry you where you wanted to go.

When the sail was just a dot on the horizon, Kate resumed her walk, taking the path past a little café with a sign that said 'The Two Marys" and on towards a trail that wound itself along the cliffs all the way to where it divided, one path going down the hill, the other following a long stone fence that went all the way up to the top of the mountain. She could see white dots all over the green slopes which she knew were sheep that had managed to get up the nearly perpendicular fields. It seemed incredible that not only sheep got up there but that people had managed to build these fences to make grazing areas, using stones they had dug out of the earth.

With the wind blowing her hair and the faint smell of turf smoke mixed with the salty tang of the ocean in her nostrils, Kate climbed up the steep slopes, stopping to catch her breath after nearly an hour. She sat down on a rock and gazed out over the view of the coastline all the way to Waterville and beyond. There was a timeless feel to the landscape, and she felt suddenly transported to the days centuries ago when her ancestors had eked out a living from this land, herding sheep and goats, growing potatoes and vegetables and living in the tiny cottages the ruins of which she could glimpse further down the slope. There was a ruined tower on the other side of the hill, and she wondered who had built it and for what purpose. An Arbutus tree full of white flowers stood near the tower and she saw a figure moving around it, digging with a small spade. She wondered if the figure was a man or a woman, but she was too far away to see properly. Then the figure disappeared and she wondered if she had imagined it. How could anyone get to the tower anyway? The slope looked steep, rocky and dangerous. Not a place she'd attempt to get to.

She sat there until dark clouds drifted across the top of the mountain, hiding it from view, and heavy drops of rain plopped on her head and jacket. It was time to leave. She started carefully down the slope, slipping and sliding on the muddy track until she was safely down. The rain increased in strength as she reached the main street and she put up the hood of her jacket and hurried back to the house, nearly falling in through the door as someone opened it at the same time as she pushed.

'Whoa,' a man said as he caught her by the elbow. 'Steady there, or you'll break your nose.'

Kate managed to find her balance. Then she froze. That voice... She nearly stopped breathing as she looked into the face she had seen so many times on stage. 'Oh shit, it's Mick O'Dwyer,' she blurted out, trying to tidy her hair at the same time.

He laughed and let go of her elbow. 'And hello to you too, whoever you are.'

Kate blushed furiously and backed away. 'I'm sorry. I was a little shocked to see you, to be honest. Didn't mean to—'

'Swear?' he said in his deep voice.

'I'm really sorry.'

'That's okay,' he said. 'I get that all the time.'

'People swear when they see you?'

He laughed. 'No, just directors when I get my lines wrong.'

'You're early,' Kate said, thinking of the mini-makeover she had planned according to Tara's instructions. 'I mean, I thought you'd be here tonight.'

He looked at her quizzically. 'You seem to know who I am, but who the heck are you?'

Kate held out her hand while she struggled to get out of her wet jacket. 'I'm Kate O'Rourke. The new doctor,' she added.

He lifted one dark eyebrow. 'Doctor? Are you sure?'

'Of course I'm sure,' she snapped, suddenly annoyed. 'I really am a doctor.'

He laughed and shook her hand. 'I believe you. I was just teasing you. I knew you had arrived. Come on, get out of that wet jacket and I'll make you a cup of tea. I just lit the fire in the living room.'

'Oh,' Kate said, still flustered. 'Great. I mean, I'll just go and dry my hair.'

'Just a minute, young lady.' He pointed at her boots. 'You'd better take those off before you go any further. Bridget won't appreciate muddy footprints on her newly polished floor.'

'Oh. Of course.' Blushing furiously, Kate unlaced her boots, took them off and put them on the mat beside the hallstand. 'I wouldn't want to dirty Bridget's floor.'

'Good plan.'

'Back in a minute,' Kate said, suddenly remembering her dishevelled appearance. Without waiting for a reply, she threw her jacket on the hallstand and raced upstairs and into her room where she looked wildly in the mirror.

Oh, God, she was a mess. Her hair was hanging in wet strands around her face and her damp sweater clung to her chest showing the outline of her bra. Cringing, Kate rubbed her hair with a towel which didn't improve it much but made her feel better. She peeled off her sweater and exchanged it for her blue cashmere polo neck. Then she ran into the bathroom, dabbed on some foundation and blusher and quickly applied some mascara miraculously avoiding stabbing herself in the eye with the wand. After slicking her hair back into a ponytail, she was satisfied that she looked a lot better than earlier and went downstairs to the living room, where Mick had just walked in with two mugs of tea.

'Hi again,' he said and handed her a mug. 'A hot drink to warm you after being out in the rain.'

'Thank you.' Kate sat down on the sofa, wrapped her hands around the warm mug and smiled at him. 'You're very kind. I'm sorry about the swearing, but I was so surprised to see you.'

He laughed and sat beside her. 'Don't worry about that. I've heard a lot worse from girls with sweeter faces than yours.'

'I'm sure you have.' Kate looked at him as she sipped the hot tea. He was more handsome close up than on the stage and she saw now that he was very like his father with the same velvety brown eyes, straight nose and strong chin with a dimple in the middle. His hair was brown with dark blond streaks, curling at the back of his neck. He was clean-shaven and dressed in an Aran sweater, jeans and battered trainers. He regarded her with a twinkle in his eyes and she wondered why he found her so amusing.

'So you're the new doctor?' he said after a moment's awkward silence.

'Well,' she started. 'Not quite. I'm just here for six months and then there'll be someone else. It's all up to the medical board. This is part of my training to qualify as a GP.'

'I see. Then you'll be off to Dublin again, when the six months are up?'

'Yes. I'll be looking for a practice, or maybe going back to A&E in one of the hospitals as head of the department.'

'So you want to be like my dad, huh?'

'Well, I prefer general medicine. I like people and I love that initial search for what's wrong with someone. It's a bit like being a detective.'

He nodded. 'That's what Dad says, too.' He studied her thoughtfully. 'Interesting.'

'What is?' Kate squirmed. She wasn't sure if he was flirting with her; it was more as if he was looking at her like a case study.

'You and Dad. Doctors. People who want to heal. I'm trying to get my head round people who are doctors and healers. I'm working on a play about someone like that.'

'Like the play by Brian Friel?' she asked. '*Faith Healer*?'

'Not really,' he said, looking at her with interest. 'You're well read. Have you seen it?'

'No, but I know most of Brian Friel's work. *Dancing at Lughnasa* is probably my favourite.'

He smiled. 'Mine too. But my play is nothing like his work. This is going to be a kind of black comedy about a snake oil merchant kind of guy who also pretends to have spiritual qualities.'

'Have you given up acting?' Kate asked, thinking what a shame that would be.

'Not for good. But I've taken a year off to write the play. I might even act in it and play the main character. That all depends who buys the play, of course.'

'Does it have a title?'

Mick nodded. 'Yes. I just thought of a great title. It's going to be called *Hotline to Heaven*. What do you think?'

Kate laughed. 'That's a brilliant title. It could even be a movie.'

'You never know.' Mick put his finger to his lips. 'But shhh. That title has to be a secret for now, or someone else will steal it.'

'I won't tell a soul,' Kate promised, flattered he trusted her with this secret.

'Good. So for a start, I'd like to get under the skin of healers, so to speak,' Mick continued. 'Doctors and health workers and even those self-proclaimed ones. There's one in this village.'

'Cormac, you mean?' she asked, forgetting the tea.

'Have you met him?'

'Not yet. I only arrived on Friday. Haven't had much time to meet anyone except Bridget and your dad and some of the patients yesterday.'

'Of course.' Mick paused. 'I haven't met him either. He arrived here only last year and I haven't been home much in the past few years. I worked at a theatre in Edinburgh for a year and then I was in London in a West End production of *Juno and the Paycock*. Very well received, funnily enough.'

'Why would that be strange?'

Mick shrugged. 'Well, considering its content and setting during the Irish Civil War, and all. But the London audiences loved it.'

'It's a good play.'

'That's true.' He checked his watch. 'Hey, it's nearly lunchtime. Why don't we go to the village pub and get ourselves a sandwich or something? I know Bridget made a casserole but that's for tonight when Dad gets back. The pub serves good food. One of those BLTs and a beer seems very enticing right now. What do you say?'

'That would be great,' Kate replied, feeling her stomach rumble. She had intended to look around the surgery but she could do that later.

'Grand.' He got up. 'Then I can continue picking your brains.'

Kate stood up. 'I'll be happy to help.'

As they walked into the hall, she felt like pinching herself. Lunch with Mick O'Dwyer – was this really happening? She couldn't wait to tell Tara. Her sister might have a glamorous job in New York, but this had to be even better. They had swooned over Mick during their student years and used some of their meagre student allowance to see every single one of his plays. And here she was in a small village in the back of beyond having lunch with him. He seemed to be such a nice, unassuming man with a great sense of humour. Friendly and fun. But he was bound to have a girlfriend, she thought, her spirits sinking. Probably some stunning actress or model. But whatever. She'd enjoy his company while she had the chance. No need to imagine anything more.

# Chapter Five

Only twenty minutes later, they sat in the cosy pub on the main street looking at each other across two steaming bowls of potato and leek soup, which had been served with home-made bread still warm from the oven. Kate felt wonderfully warm after the short walk from the house. There was a turf fire at the far end, and the walls were covered in photos of bygone days and postcards with greetings from visitors who had enjoyed pints and good food all through the years. The bar staff consisted of a young man pulling pints and an older woman who welcomed them with a warm smile while she showed them the blackboard with the specials of the day. The soup seemed the best choice for lunch and they both chose that instead of the BLT Mick had mentioned earlier.

'Better than a sandwich,' Mick said as he swallowed his first mouthful. 'Especially on a cold day like this.'

'After a hike up the mountain, this is heaven,' Kate agreed, spreading butter on a slice of bread.

'Where did you go?' Mick asked.

'I went past that little café on the main beach and further up the slope. Lovely views up there. I only walked for an hour or so though. It's a bit steep, and I didn't bring my walking sticks. In any case, I don't want to walk too far on my own.'

'Very wise,' Mick said approvingly. 'But if you're a keen walker, you could join me and my friends next time we go for a hike. We're planning to go up to the MacGillycuddy's.'

'That might be a little too much for me right now,' Kate protested. 'I'd need to get back into shape first, I think.'

'Oh, we're not that fit either,' Mick countered. 'We'll just be going up a bit of the way to try the trails. You'll be fine.'

Kate smiled. 'I'll do my best not to faint on the trail.'

'Much appreciated.' He was about to say something else but was interrupted by the sound of his phone. He frowned and looked at it. 'Excuse me. Got to take this.'

Kate nodded and turned her attention to the delicious soup, trying not to listen to the conversation.

'Fiona?' Mick said. 'Hi, darling. What's up?' He listened to the high-pitched voice for a while. 'Okay. No big deal, then.' The voice carried on while he listened. 'Yes,' he said. Then: 'No, that's not possible. I can't do anything about that, darling. Sorry, but that's not my department. Got to go. I'm in the middle of a meeting here. Bye, darling.' He hung up and looked at Kate. 'That was Fiona,' he said.

'So I gathered. Your girlfriend?' Kate asked, feeling awkward.

'Not really. A young actress who's hoping for her big break. The eternal understudy. You know, the beautiful girl who dreams about the leading lady breaking her leg and getting the chance of a lifetime.'

'And?' Kate asked, intrigued.

He clicked his tongue. 'Not a chance. The leading lady has no intention of breaking anything. If she did, she'd hobble onto the stage and do it anyway. Fiona has to realise that. This time she was asking to be cast in the current play just for a couple of nights. But I'm not in charge of that. She might get a small part in something else if I use all my powers. And if I'm in the mood,' he added with an ironic smile. 'But never mind the histrionics of the theatre. Back to you and healing… I need to know more about you for my play. When did you feel the calling to be a doctor?'

'Oh, there's nothing interesting about that,' Kate protested. 'No calling at all. I just loved to play doctor when I was small. I wanted to be like my dad when I grew up. Then as a teenager, I was so interested in the human body and how it works. Loved watching medical programmes on TV, and so on. It seemed so natural to me to study medicine after school. Nobody pushed me into it or anything. And no voice from above telling me it was my destiny,' she added with a laugh.

'That's disappointing,' he said. 'I had a much more romantic image.'

'Nothing romantic about it at all,' Kate remarked. 'I spent six gruelling years studying the basics and I've been working hard ever since.'

'And you still love it?'

'Oh yes,' Kate replied without hesitation. 'It's a fascinating job.'

'Do you have brothers and sisters?' he asked, pushing away his empty bowl.

'A twin sister.'

'Is she a doctor, too?'

Kate shook her head. 'No. My sister is a photographer and lives in New York. Never had the slightest interest in medicine.'

'Your father must be happy you're following in his footsteps,' Mick remarked as he turned away and waved to the waiter.

'My father died two years ago,' Kate said quietly. 'But yes, he was very happy I studied medicine.'

Mick turned back to Kate. 'I'm so sorry. That's tough.'

Kate looked down at her soup. 'Yes,' she said. 'It is.'

'And your mother?'

'She died eight years ago. Cancer.'

Mick touched Kate's hand. 'How very sad. I'm really sorry, Kate.'

'Thank you,' she said, moved by the kindness in his eyes. 'So,' she said in an attempt to turn the spotlight on him, 'what made you want to become an actor? Some kind of inner voice? Or because, being insecure and shy, you need to hide behind some fictional character? Or you need to escape in some way? Or simply because you enjoy having thousands of people looking at you?'

He laughed. 'Good question. And to go through all the reasons you mentioned… I didn't need to hide behind anything, for a start.'

'Well, my first impression was that you are neither insecure nor shy,' Kate teased.

He grinned back. 'Spot on. But,' he continued, 'it's nice to become someone else sometimes. It's like donning a cloak of invisibility. Suddenly, you are someone else and you walk around being them. It's fun to do. And it's also a kind of escapism into a different world, often the world of the past, which is also fascinating. You have to imagine what it was like to live during the time that particular play was written and try to think like they did. It's like a little time machine sometimes.'

Kate looked at him and nodded. 'I see. Of course it would be. And that's why we, the public, love the theatre and movies and books. To escape the real world.'

'I have this theory that nostalgia for the past is so prevalent these days because the future looks so scary.'

'I'm sure that's true,' Kate agreed.

The waiter arrived at their table and took their bowls. 'Anything else?' he asked.

'Coffee?' Mick asked Kate.

'Lovely,' she replied. 'A latte for me.'

'Americano,' Mick said. 'No sugar.'

'How about some apple pie?' the waiter asked. 'Just out of the oven.'

'Yes, please,' they said in unison.

Mick laughed. 'It's nice to meet a woman who's not afraid to eat.'

'I can't resist apple pie,' Kate confessed. 'Especially if it's home-made.'

'This one will be. And served with a large dollop of whipped cream.'

'Fabulous,' Kate said with a happy sigh. 'That hike made me hungry.'

'I have no such excuse,' Mick declared. 'I just drove from Limerick and that wasn't too much of an effort.' He paused. 'But back to doctors and healing. Especially your line of doctoring. What goes through your mind when you meet a patient for the first time?'

'Oh…' Kate thought for a while. 'I look at the way they hold themselves and the way they look at me. I also look at their skin tone, which can tell me a lot. Like if they smoke, if their diet is healthy, the state of their fitness, and so on. I get all this in a very short time, usually while they tell me who they are and what brought them to the surgery. But that's the same for all doctors, I think.'

'So what does my skin tone and the way I hold myself tell you?' he asked.

Kate studied him for a moment, pretending to assess his general health, even though she already had a very clear picture. 'You don't smoke,' she started. 'And you're quite fit. Apart from the occasional slice of pizza and apple pie, I'd say that your diet is healthy.' She looked at his glass of beer. 'You drink alcohol but not every day and you must be going to the gym quite regularly. So, apart from the way you handle stress, your state of health is good for someone your age.'

'That's good to know.' He stopped. 'The way I handle stress? What do you know about that?'

'When Fiona rang, I noticed that you got quite tense. You were tapping your foot under the table and you were frowning.'

'Bloody hell, *was* I?'

'Yes, you were.'

'That's interesting. I did feel a little cornered by Fiona and her whingeing about not getting a chance to shine. You might be right.'

'That was the good news.'

'You mean… I could have something worse?'

Kate shrugged, trying to keep a straight face. 'I have no idea. I can only tell you what I saw at first glance.'

He laughed. 'You have quite a talent, Dr O'Rourke. Funny how I never got this in-depth analysis from my dad, but I suppose parents don't look at their children in that way. Even doctors. But you were right. That's a sign of a good doctor. I hope people around here will accept you.'

They were interrupted by the waiter bringing a tray with their coffees and two heaped plates of apple pie topped with whipped cream. 'There you go,' he said. 'Mammy's apple pie and cream from the farm up the road.'

'Fantastic,' Mick said and picked up his spoon.

Kate followed his lead and they both ate without speaking for a while. Then Kate looked at him. 'What did you mean when you said you hope they'll accept me?'

Mick put down his spoon. 'A lot of the older people around here might find it difficult to accept a female doctor. And you're – what – twenty-eight or so? Too young to know anything in their eyes.'

'I'm thirty-five,' Kate replied, not knowing if she should be annoyed or flattered. 'Nearly your age, actually.'

'Oh, but I'm a *crusty* thirty-eight-year-old,' Mick said with a glint in his eye. 'I know a lot more about life than you do.'

'So in the three years before I was born, you acquired a huge amount of experience, then?' Kate quipped. 'Amazing.'

Mick laughed. 'Yeah, those three years gave me a head start. I was already eating pizza and drinking beer by the time you were born.'

'I bet,' Kate said, laughing. 'I'm sure you were still a little mammy's boy.'

He shook his head. 'No mammy's boy. My mother was too busy working.' His eyes were suddenly serious. 'My mother thought she couldn't have children. I was an accident.'

'Or a miracle?' Kate suggested.

'I'm not sure. I always got the impression I'd messed up her plans somehow. She runs the family pharmaceutical company that she inherited from her family and she was away working and travelling to international conferences when I was growing up. My father wanted to be a GP in the country, so he was more hands-on than she was and managed to spend a lot of time with me despite his busy practice. He did his best, and Bridget was here most of the time, and then I went to school down the road with all the other kids who often invited me to their houses. In fact, you could say the whole village brought me up between them. It was like living in a very big commune.' He stopped, looking shocked. 'I can't believe I'm telling you all this. We have only just met and here I am sharing the story of my life, telling you stuff that most people don't know. But you have a way of looking at me that makes me want to talk about myself. Is that something you learn at your GP courses?'

'No,' Kate replied, a little taken aback by both his story and the fact that he seemed to have blurted it out without thinking. But this happened to her quite often. People would tell her their deepest thoughts and personal problems, which sometimes felt uncomfortable. But it was a great help during consultations when she tried to assess the cause of illnesses and pain. 'I seem to inspire trust in people for some reason,' she continued.

'You have a very sympathetic way about you,' Mick said after a moment's silence. 'There is a calm about you that is very reassuring.' He nodded. 'Yes, that's it. A calm and caring quality. Must remember that. Could be useful for the part.'

Kate laughed. 'I'll remember that when I see the play. It'll be exciting to see my expression on your face. I hope it fits.'

'I'll stretch it a bit to fit my face,' he joked.

'I'm sure it will.' Kate smiled back at him, the story of his childhood still resonating in her mind. He claimed he was unaffected by it, having been surrounded by people who loved him, especially his father, but Kate could tell he felt neglected by his mother.

Mick looked at his watch. 'It's nearly three o'clock. I have to go back to the house and make some calls. Let's pay and walk back.'

Kate nodded and groped in her jacket for her wallet.

Having paid the bill, they walked out of the pub and down the street towards the house. 'What will you do for the rest of the afternoon?' Mick asked as they reached the front gate.

'I'll continue to unpack and have a look at the surgery and patient records. Then I have to make a call or two myself,' Kate said, thinking of how excited Tara would be when she heard what had happened.

'If you like reading, you might find something in the shelves in the living room,' Mick suggested. 'There's a huge mix of books there. Everything anyone ever read in this house. Anything from my old Enid Blytons to Dickens and Jane Austen, and even some more modern stuff. Dad and I read a lot when I grew up. Especially in the winter.'

'Must have been cosy,' Kate said, imagining him as a young boy reading in front of the fire with his father.

'It was great.' He paused, his hand on the gate. 'Look, what I told you about my mother… It might have sounded as if she was a bad mother or that she didn't care about me. She did, in her own way. My parents' marriage is a little different to the norm of people their age. They live separate lives, always have. But by giving each other all this freedom, they have managed to make their marriage work.'

'Well, I never try to understand what goes on between married people,' Kate replied. 'Or between any couple. In my job, I come across every kind of relationship under the sun. Your mother is probably a free spirit, and maybe that's what your father loves about her?'

'Her pilgrim soul,' Mick said. 'Like in the poem by Yeats. And she never stepped on his dreams. Another Yeats classic.'

'"Cloths of Heaven",' Kate murmured dreamily. 'I love that one.'

'Me too.' He opened the gate and stepped aside to let her pass. 'Thank you for a very nice afternoon, Dr Kate,' he said as they went inside.

'I enjoyed it very much,' Kate said and hung up her jacket.

'I won't be here for dinner,' he announced after a moment's silence. 'I'm driving across to Dingle town for a party. Then I'm off to Dublin for a few days. But I might be back next weekend. If I am, we'll do that hike I mentioned.'

'That would be great,' Kate said.

'Look after Dad, and don't let Bridget scare you. She's a real softie deep down.'

Kate laughed. 'I like her a lot already.'

He nodded generously. 'I think you'll get on with her. Tell her I send my love.'

'I will.'

'Great. Now I have work to do. See you soon, I hope.' He touched her shoulder lightly and then disappeared into the study, closing the door behind him.

Kate stood there, enjoying the afterglow of the past few hours. Meeting Mick O'Dwyer had been a huge thrill, but discovering what a nice man he was and that they had so much in common was an added bonus. She hoped they'd meet again to do that hike he had talked about. The story of his childhood was strange but not as sad as it seemed. He had been surrounded by people who loved him even if his mother had not been around that much. She wondered what she was like.

Kate didn't have to wait long to meet Mick's mother. She appeared that very evening, just as Kate had gone downstairs to the kitchen. She turned round as the door opened and found a tall blonde woman dressed in a grey polo neck and black trousers standing there smiling at her.

'Are you Kate?' she asked.

'Yes,' Kate replied. 'And you must be…'

'Helen O'Dwyer,' the woman said, and held out her hand. 'Pat's wife. A bit of a surprise visit, but I decided to spend the night here before I have to take off for a conference in London.'

Kate shook the woman's hand. 'Hello, nice to meet you,' she said automatically, taken aback by the warm, friendly look in her beautiful blue eyes. In fact, everything about her was beautiful, Kate thought as she watched Helen walk gracefully into the kitchen and take the casserole out of the fridge. She had a wonderful figure and her shiny hair was cut into a short style that suited her heart-shaped face. She was stunning, and must have been even more so when she was younger. No wonder Pat had fallen for her.

'This should take about half an hour to heat up,' Helen said, lifting the lid of the casserole. 'Enough for four, I think, if we bake some potatoes and make a salad. What do you think, Kate?'

'Eh, yes,' Kate replied. 'Four?' she asked. 'But Mick left for Dingle about five o'clock.'

'I know,' Helen said in her melodious voice. 'Pity to have missed him. I invited someone else to join us. A young man who lives in the village. His name's Cormac. He's kind of in the same line of business as me, you see.'

'You mean Cormac from the Wellness Centre?' Kate asked.

'That's right,' Helen said, opening the door to the larder. 'He'll be here in a little while. Now where did Bridget put the potatoes…'

Kate stood rooted to the spot, not only stunned by Mick's mother but also by the fact that she would be meeting the mysterious Cormac. What would he be like, this man who seemed to have the power to heal and the knowledge of natural medicines handed down through the generations? She couldn't wait to find out.

# Chapter Six

Kate was in the living room talking to Pat over a glass of sherry about surgery hours and how to split them up when the door opened.

'Hello. I hope I'm not late,' said a gentle voice with a lilting Kerry accent.

Kate turned around and looked at the man standing in the doorway holding a small bunch of flowers. He was tall with a shock of dark red hair and a handsome face full of freckles. He wasn't really dressed up for dinner, Kate thought, looking at his brown sweater frayed at the cuffs, corduroy trousers and scuffed shoes. But maybe he didn't care. It was the dark green eyes that were the most startling aspect of his appearance. *Green like the slopes of the Kerry hills*, Kate thought as she stepped forward to introduce herself.

'Kate, this is Cormac,' Pat said.

'Hi, Cormac,' she said and held out her hand. 'I'm Kate, the new assistant doctor.'

He grasped her hand in a firm handshake. 'Hi, Kate. Lovely to meet you.'

'I've heard a lot about you,' Kate said, mesmerised by his eyes and his lovely voice.

'I hope they were only positive things,' Cormac said with a laugh as he moved on to greet Pat. 'Hello there, Dr Pat. Hope you're well this fine evening.'

'Very well, thank you,' Pat replied. 'We had a good game of golf in Killarney today despite the bit of rain.'

'I'm sure you're looking forward to playing more often,' Cormac remarked.

'I sure am. But I have to break Kate in first,' Pat joked.

'I'm sure that won't take long,' Cormac replied, smiling at Kate.

'Yes, especially since she's used to a fast pace, having worked in A&E for a long time,' Pat said.

'But I'm not going to be the new GP,' Kate cut in. 'I'll be running the practice until a permanent one is appointed.'

'I see,' Cormac said. 'But you seem to be quite experienced already.'

'She is,' Pat said, holding up the bottle of sherry. 'How about a glass of this old-fashioned stuff?'

'No thanks, Dr Pat. I don't drink anything alcoholic. I'd prefer a glass of orange juice if you have it. Otherwise a glass of water will do.'

Pat put the bottle on the table. 'I'll go and see. Maybe not orange juice, but I think there's a bottle of Bridget's elderflower cordial in the larder. And I'll tell Helen you're here.'

Cormac gave him the flowers. 'These are for her. From my greenhouse.'

'Helen will love them. Excuse me for a moment.' Pat walked out of the room, leaving Cormac and Kate awkwardly looking at each other.

'Maybe we should sit down?' Cormac suggested, pointing at the sofa. 'There's a nice fire there. It's chilly outside. The rain will turn to snow again on the top of the mountain tonight, I think.'

'That'll be lovely to see in the morning.' Kate took her place on the sofa.

Cormac joined her, holding his hands out to the smouldering logs for a moment. Then he turned to Kate. 'A&E, Pat said. In Dublin?'

'Yes. St Vincent's. One of the biggest hospitals there.'

'Must have been a tough job.'

Kate smiled. 'Yes. You don't get much sleep. But it's exciting and very challenging.'

'I can imagine.'

'So this is going to be quite restful by comparison,' Kate remarked.

Cormac looked doubtful. 'Restful? I'd say it will be just as challenging. But in a different way. Especially after Christmas. Everyone gets sick after Christmas.'

'I suppose I'll find out the hard way,' Kate replied.

'You will.' Cormac turned back to the fire and put a log on it, making flames shoot up. 'There,' he said, sounding satisfied. 'That should keep it going for a while. I like the smell of this wood. Must be the old apple tree they cut down last month.'

'Oh.' Kate sniffed the air. 'I don't get anything except the usual smell of wood burning.'

'Your senses aren't as developed as mine,' Cormac replied. 'You have a city person's senses, which are limited because of the pollution.'

'Really?' Kate said, feeling miffed. 'How do you know what my senses are like?'

'Dublin born and bred, aren't you?' he asked.

'Yes,' she had to admit.

'That's how I know,' he stated.

'Can they be improved?' she asked, only to humour him in case she seemed a little sour.

Cormac shrugged. 'I don't know. I'll tell you when you've been here a year or two.'

'But I'm not…' Kate stopped. She had been about to say that she wasn't staying more than six months, but that might result in some other wisdom she wasn't in the mood to hear. She had never met anyone like Cormac before and she kept staring at him, amazed by his unusual good looks of the kind she had only seen in old movies. He was like a throwback to Victorian times and, despite the freckles, there was a Byronesque look to his delicate features and general bearing. He was like an aristocrat who, by some kind of magic, had landed here from another time.

'You're not staying?'

'I don't think so,' she replied, startled out of her musings. 'But I don't like to plan so far ahead.'

'You make it up as you go along?' he asked. 'Is that what you usually do?'

'I suppose,' Kate said, not wanting to go into how she lived her life. He seemed to be looking right into her mind with those luminous green eyes, which unnerved her. 'I mean, who can see into the future?'

'Nobody,' Cormac agreed. 'But you can often see where a person is heading by observing the way they are and their general attitude.

Your path is determined by the choices you make, and those choices depend on your thoughts and feelings and the personality you're born with.'

'It's written in the stars, you mean?'

He laughed. 'No. It's all in your own demeanour. And the people you meet and the circumstances you get thrown into. It's like a giant jigsaw puzzle, but it's up to you to put the pieces in the right places.'

'Oh,' Kate said, oddly fascinated by that idea. 'That sounds very interesting. And complicated.'

'Sure, isn't life complicated?' Cormac said. 'We're all trying to make sense of it all and do the best we can. And sometimes we fail.'

'Or succeed,' Kate filled in. 'I prefer to look on the bright side.'

They were interrupted by Pat and Helen with a glass of cordial and the flowers Cormac had brought, now sitting in a silver vase. 'Hello, Cormac,' Helen said and put the vase on the table. She held out the glass. 'Here. I found a bottle of Bridget's special brew in the larder. Pat, pour me a glass of sherry and we'll drink a welcome toast to Kate.'

They drank the toast and Kate was touched by the gesture and the welcome. 'Thank you,' she said when she had taken a sip. 'You're very kind.'

'I hope you'll be happy here,' Helen said. 'And I'm so glad you came to help Pat and ease his burden a little, now that he's been told to take it easy.'

Alarmed, Kate looked at Pat. 'You have?' She stopped and glanced at Cormac. Maybe it would be better to discuss Pat's health in private. 'Well, perhaps you can tell me tomorrow before we open the surgery.'

'I'll take the morning,' Pat said. 'And then perhaps you can do the afternoon shift so I can take a break.'

'Of course,' Kate said, surreptitiously examining him as he turned to Cormac. What could be wrong? Was it something serious? High blood pressure? Or something to do with his heart? He was in his early seventies, which was when those problems usually cropped up. She'd find out tomorrow.

'The house,' Helen said, interrupting Kate's thoughts. 'We need to discuss the details and the terms for Bridget and her husband moving in.'

'What?' Another thing she hadn't been told. 'Bridget is moving in? With her husband?'

Helen nodded and put her glass on the table. 'Yes. They're doing extensive renovations to their house and we've offered her accommodation while that's being done. We just talked to her about it. Could last several months. You don't mind, I hope? This way we can cut the rent we agreed and you'll have some company while you live here.'

'Oh,' Kate said with a glance at Pat. 'Yes, that's fine. It'll be nice to have some company, actually. It's a big house.'

'It was the rectory before it became the doctor's house,' Helen said. 'My grandfather was the last vicar here. Then he bought it from the Church of Ireland and it stayed in the family. My father let it to the previous GP, who was Pat's father, and then Pat took over when he qualified. I'm still the owner, though.' She walked to the door. 'But we can talk some more over dinner. I laid the table in the kitchen. Much cosier and warmer than the dining room, don't you think?'

'Er, yes,' Kate agreed, wondering what else would be announced that evening. Helen seemed to be the boss in the family, Pat being the mild, gentle soul just going along with whatever his wife decided. The practice seemed to be his domain, though, and she had seen for herself what a wonderful, caring doctor he was. She followed everyone into the kitchen, where Helen had made the table appear both inviting and elegant, with china and crystal that looked as if it had been handed down through the generations all the way from the first vicar's wife way back in the eighteen hundreds.

'My great-great grandmother's dinner service,' Helen said as they sat down. 'A bit too fancy for the kitchen, but I think lovely things should be used as often as possible instead of gathering dust in a cupboard.'

'It looks wonderful,' Cormac said. 'I feel very honoured to be sitting down at such a table.'

Kate wondered if he was being ironic, but he met her gaze levelly without a hint of deceit.

'I mean it,' he said as if answering her question. 'I know I should be all republican and proud, but the vicars in these little villages were good people. Very charitable and kind to everyone who needed help in any way.'

'That's true,' Pat agreed. 'Especially here in the west. Helen's family can be proud of their history.'

'And now we're all in the same boat. All Irish together,' Helen said, as she took the casserole from the oven and put it on the top of the stove. 'Here you are, chicken casserole with vegetables that Bridget made for us on Friday night. Isn't she amazing the way she cooks for us? But she loves cooking, and says it's more like a hobby than work to her. I tried to stop her years ago but she insisted. And now that her children have grown up and left home she enjoys it even more, she says. It smells divine, I have to say. Please take your plates and help yourselves.'

The meal was pleasant and friendly with small talk about the weather and plans for Christmas, which Pat and Helen would be celebrating with her family who lived in Killarney, if Kate wouldn't mind staying behind to take any calls over the holidays.

'Nobody has ever called me on Christmas Day,' Pat said. 'So it's just a matter of being available if anything should crop up. And you can call me at any time, of course.'

'Bridget will be here to help out, too, and I'm sure she and her husband will be delighted if you'd join them for their Christmas dinner,' Helen added in a tone that said it had all been decided. Without waiting for Kate to reply, she turned to Cormac. 'So, tell me, Cormac. I hear you have something special in your bag of tricks? I mean, your array of magic potions, of course.'

Cormac looked at Helen for a moment with a bland expression. 'Oh, nothing special at all,' he said. 'Just a mixture of herbs, as usual. I'm trying to combine them a little differently, that's all.'

Helen's eyes lit up. 'You must tell me about them. I'd be very interested in how they have worked out.'

Cormac shrugged. 'Early days, so I have nothing much to say about that yet. In any case, they are just home remedies that have been used before.'

Helen didn't look convinced. 'I'm sure there's more to all of that than you're letting on. You have a knack with what works for a lot of difficult ills.'

'It's usually very hit-and-miss,' Cormac replied. Then he turned his attention to Kate, changing the subject. 'As you're an O'Rourke, I suppose your family have roots here from way back.'

Kate nodded. 'Oh yes, we do. But I've never really delved into the old family stuff. My father used to talk about this village and said he'd love to come here when he retired to find out more. But he didn't get a chance to do that,' she ended, trying not to let her grief show.

'The O'Rourkes have been here since ancient times,' Cormac said. 'If you study ancient history and folklore, you will even find a connection with the Vikings.'

'Really?' Helen said, having given up pumping Cormac about his potions. 'I had no idea.'

'Oh yes,' Cormac continued. 'I read up about them when I was in college. The O'Rourke family is one of the oldest here. The very first ones came from Iceland.'

Pat looked intrigued. 'How did that happen?'

'Well,' Cormac started, 'it's quite a sad story. It appears that Norwegian Vikings who had settled in Iceland raided Ireland and took Irish women back with them as slaves. The women then became their wives – or concubines – who gave birth to children to whom they spoke Gaelic. But once the children were adults, they came back to Ireland and settled here. The first O'Rourkes in Sandy Cove were the offspring of such Irishmen. They settled here and built that little village you can see above the tiny bay on the other side of the headland.'

'Wild Rose Bay,' Pat said, nodding. 'And some people call that old tower O'Rourke's castle. I had completely forgotten about that.' He turned to Kate. 'Isn't that interesting?'

Kate laughed. 'Amazing. Our very own castle. That's so cool. Can't wait to tell my sister.'

'Well, that's just a local name,' Helen cut in. 'It was never a castle, was it? More like a lookout tower or something.'

'Of course,' Pat replied. 'But it's fun to imagine there might have been one there at some stage in the very distant past.'

'Very distant indeed,' Helen remarked. 'Nearly a thousand years or even more.'

'It's just an old folk saga,' Cormac said. 'But the roots of those sagas must have some truth in them. They began from some event that really happened and then were embroidered over the centuries until there was little left of the original. But they are lovely to read. There is such beauty in the old language.' He smiled at Kate. 'I have a few books on the subject, if you're interested. I'd be happy to lend them to you.'

'Oh yes,' Kate exclaimed. 'That would be great. Thank you.' She was beginning to warm to this unusual young man. He seemed to her like one of those 'old souls' that are said to have lived several lives. Not that she believed in that, but there was something otherworldly in his eyes as he spoke of the old sagas.

'Are they in Irish?' Helen cut in.

Cormac nodded. 'Yes. But not in that old Celtic text that's so hard to read.'

'My Irish is a bit rusty,' Kate confessed, 'but I'll have a go anyway.'

'Cormac can help you if you get stuck,' Pat suggested. 'He's a real Irish scholar.'

'Not really,' Cormac protested. 'But I grew up speaking Irish. My father's family came from Cork, but my mother is an O'Sullivan from the Beara peninsula and they only spoke Irish in her village.'

'A Sullivan Bear?' Kate said. 'Isn't that what they're called?'

'Yes,' Cormac replied. 'And they're very proud of that.'

'The Beara peninsula is very bare,' Helen remarked. 'I always wondered how they could make a living there.'

'Sheep and fish,' Cormac replied. 'And perhaps not being very demanding in what they needed. I always thought they were happy. Content is maybe a better word. Having enough to live on and not wanting much more.'

'And they had the beauty of the landscape all around them,' Pat interjected. 'People in West Cork and Kerry love the place they live in. Always have. Sufficient unto the day, and all that.'

'Sounds wonderful but hard to live up to,' Helen said. 'Anyone for more? Please help yourselves. Kate?'

'I'm fine, thanks,' Kate said.

'Anyone else?' Helen asked.

Cormac shook his head. 'No thank you, Helen. It was delicious, but I don't think I have room for more.'

'Nor me,' Pat said, getting up from the table. 'And if you'll excuse me, I have a few things to go through before surgery tomorrow. A little bit of paperwork for one of my patients who needs a referral. I'd like to do it before it gets too late. Kate, could you come with me so I can show you the list of referrals and some of the contacts I use in various hospitals?'

'Of course,' Kate replied and got up. 'Thanks for dinner, Helen, it was wonderful. I'll help you clear up later.'

'No need,' Helen said, smiling. 'There isn't much to do except load the dishwasher.'

'I'll give you a hand,' Cormac offered.

'Thank you.' Helen rose to her feet and started to collect the plates. 'And we'll have that chat about your remedies. There are one or two I think could be developed to be sold in pharmacies.'

'Ah well, that's not really on the cards,' Cormac countered.

'I might be able to convince you if you'll hear me out,' Helen argued as they walked out.

Pat winked at Kate. 'She's a great negotiator,' he muttered in her ear as they left the kitchen. 'But I think she's met her match in Cormac. She's tried to get her hands on some of his recipes before and never succeeded. He's as stubborn as a mule and tough as nails, despite his choirboy appearance. I tried to ask him about that new ointment. He said he would write down the ingredients when he had the time. I'm guessing I'll be waiting for a long time.'

'You think he wants to keep it secret?'

'I suspect he does. Or he might be worried I'll say it isn't safe or something. But you might have better luck.'

'I doubt it,' Kate replied, feeling that it would be easier to get blood out of a stone. Cormac seemed difficult to manipulate in any way.

They went into the surgery and sat down at the desk together. Pat started the computer and they went through the details of hospital admissions, referral procedures and contacts while Kate tried to concentrate, but her mind was on Cormac and all the things he had talked about. Irish folklore that was linked to the Icelandic sagas, the O'Rourke castle and a whole world of legends and stories that this mysterious, melancholic landscape seemed to hold. Ireland's ancient past that she had never really thought about now looked incredibly fascinating. Then she focused on the computer screen and considered the long list of specialists and hospitals, realising that Pat had an incredible medical network. She suddenly felt a dart of fear, as she wondered how on earth she was going to cope with all this and how these consultants would react to a young female doctor with little experience in general practice.

'You'll learn as you go along,' Pat said as if he was reading her mind. 'And I'll be here for a while anyway while you get the hang of it.'

'I suppose,' Kate said, trying to appear confident. But deep down a little voice kept telling her that this job was going to be a lot more challenging than she had thought.

'Tell me all,' Tara ordered, lying in her bed in her New York apartment, while Kate Skyped her from Sandy Cove. 'I have the day off, so I slept in and then had breakfast in bed. My flatmate went and got us fresh croissants and the Sunday papers and now I'm lazing with a latte reading all the latest gossip.'

Kate sat on her bed and looked at her sister, dressed in a fluffy white bathrobe, propped up by lacy pillows and surrounded by a mess of newspapers and a half-eaten croissant. She looked cute and cuddly there, smiling at Kate, who suddenly longed to have her sister beside her. 'I miss you, sweetie.'

'Me too,' Tara said and blew a kiss at the screen. 'Miss you so much. But hey, back to the hunk you had lunch with.'

'Oh, him,' Kate said, suddenly remembering Mick.

'Him?' Tara asked. 'Was he awful? Smelly? Nasty to women? You don't seem to be floating on a cloud or anything.'

Kate laughed. 'Sorry. I meant to tell you that he was a dream come true and we fell instantly in love and then we drove off into the sunset in his white Ferrari to get married in a romantic little church while the music of angels played.'

'You're being sarcastic,' Tara said.

'Sorry again.' Kate sat up and organised a pile of cushions under her head. 'I'm tired. It's been a long day with a lot happening, and I have just gone through a lot of stuff I have to remember for my first day in the surgery tomorrow.' She paused. 'But okay, I'll tell you how I came to have lunch with Mick O'Dwyer.' She told Tara what had happened and gave a rough outline of the conversation they had. 'He was lovely, actually,' she concluded. 'Very interesting to talk to. He's writing a play at the moment and has taken a year off acting.'

'Oh great,' Tara said. 'But did you two… you know…'

'We hit it off,' Kate said. 'And he's invited me to go on a hike with him and some friends next weekend.'

'Sounds lovely.' Tara sounded envious. 'What does he look like close up?'

'Very good-looking,' Kate said, her mind drifting to the dinner and Cormac.

'What did he wear?'

'A brown sweater and baggy corduroys,' Kate replied.

'What?' Tara exclaimed. 'That sounds horrible! You're having me on.'

'Sorry,' Kate said, laughing. 'I meant a white Aran sweater, jeans and trainers.'

'That's better,' Tara said. 'I bet he looked good.'

'Yes, he did.' Kate had to agree as the image of Mick at lunch popped into her mind. He was a very good-looking man with impeccable manners and a lovely smile. 'He has beautiful eyes,' she added. 'And he was very good company.'

'You're so lucky.'

'It was a nice afternoon. But dinner was even more interesting.'

'He stayed for dinner?' Tara asked.

'No, he left. But Dr Pat, my boss, arrived with his wife, who's very beautiful.'

'That's where Mick gets his looks, I bet,' Tara suggested.

'No, he looks more like his father. But anyway,' Kate continued, 'they have a very strange marriage. They've been married over forty years but have never really lived together.'

'Sounds like the ideal relationship,' Tara remarked. 'I mean, that way she got to have her cake and eat it. Freedom but a husband as well.'

'And he seems to have brought up their son while she was off on conferences and doing stuff for the company she runs.'

'What a perfect husband,' Tara said with a giggle. 'I think I'd love him.'

'You would,' Kate replied. 'Everyone does. And then there was another guest. Cormac, who is some kind of healer around here. Makes up lotions and sometimes they even heal wounds that conventional medicines have failed to fix.'

'Oh,' Tara said, looking disappointed. 'Sounds strange.'

'He's a bit unusual,' Kate agreed. 'He's a fluent Irish speaker and knows a lot about the O'Rourkes and how they came here. And listen to this: there's an old ruined tower here they call O'Rourke's castle.'

Tara's eyes lit up. 'Really? You must send me a picture so I can post it on Instagram. That'd be so cool.'

'I will,' Kate promised.

'Brilliant.'

'I want to find out more about the O'Rourkes and their history. It's amazing to be here where they lived so many centuries ago.'

'I'm sure you'll enjoy that. History was never my thing.'

'But this is about our family,' Kate insisted. 'Dad used to talk about it a lot, remember?'

Tara looked away. 'Yeah, I know. But do we have to talk about this now?'

'Maybe we should,' Kate said. 'Would it not be good to remember instead of trying to push it away?'

'Maybe. But not now, not today.'

Kate sighed, knowing it was no use. Tara was still in some kind of denial while Kate was beginning to be able to face the memories and think about their father. What Cormac had told her about the history of this place had awakened a need inside to find out more and connect with the past that seemed captivating to her. 'Okay,' she said softly. 'Perhaps not today.'

'Thanks. I knew you'd understand.' Tara stretched her arms over her head. 'But now I have to get up. It's three o'clock in the afternoon here. You must think me such a slob to be still in bed. But I worked all day yesterday until the light went and then we all went to a party in someone's loft in Tribeca and then we ended up in a club listening to jazz until four in the morning.'

'God, you have a horrible life,' Kate said, laughing.

'It's quite nice really,' Tara admitted, grinning at Kate. 'But exhausting.' She yawned. 'I have to go. I'm meeting the gang from the shoot for an early dinner at an Italian place in the theatre district. But first I have to go for a run, then shower, then do my make-up and find something to wear.'

'That sounds exhausting all right,' Kate agreed. 'But you love it.'

'I totally do,' Tara said with a grin. 'We'll talk soon, okay? Let me know how you get on with Mick.'

'My job is more important,' Kate said sternly. 'I've come here to work, not flirt with actors.'

But Tara had switched off and Kate found herself talking to a blank screen. She closed the laptop. It was true. Her job – and this new experience – was so important. There were new challenges here that would be invaluable for her future career in medicine. In a big city hospital, she had the back-up of modern technology and close proximity to specialist medicine should she need it. Here, in this remote rural area, she only had her own knowledge and resources to fall back on. She would have to think on her feet and use her judgement and instinct to the max. It would be nerve-racking but incredibly stimulating at the same time. And of course, she would have Pat by her side during the first two months. After that, she would be on her own.

She suddenly remembered what Pat had said about having to take it easy. Was there something seriously wrong with him? He looked fine, if a little pale and frail. But when they had been on their rounds, he had seemed energetic and enthusiastic. He loved his job, Kate realised. If he had to give it up, it must be because of something serious, even life-threatening. She would have to find out what it was.

# Chapter Seven

Kate woke up early the next morning, and lay there listening to the wind in the trees outside. It was pitch-black in the room and not even a chink of light showed under the curtains. The room was cold and she snuggled deeper under the duvet, waiting for the heating to come on at seven thirty like Pat had told her. She felt snug and warm and oddly safe in the cosy little room, similar to her own room in her childhood home. Funny, she thought, how Pat was very like her father in a strange way. The same generation and the same dedication to their work and their patients. They probably had more of that 'calling' Mick had talked about, something that had got lost with time, making medicine a career rather than something you felt in your heart and soul. She had fallen into that way of thinking herself during her training. How to get up the medical career ladder and make money seemed more important these days. She realised she would learn more here about the true meaning of being a doctor and how to deal with people than she had during the years working in big city hospitals.

She pricked up her ears as she heard voices and footsteps in the corridor outside.

'I'll be in touch tonight,' Helen said. 'I'll let you know how the work on the house is progressing.'

'Fine, but shh, I think the lassie is still asleep,' Pat replied.

'Nice girl,' Helen said in a more hushed tone. 'But is she up to the work here? I mean, she has to step into your shoes when you're gone. She doesn't look very strong.'

'I'm sure she'll be fine,' Pat said. 'But she's...' the voices drifted away as the couple went down the stairs and Kate didn't catch what they were saying. She felt butterflies in her stomach as she thought of taking over the practice. But that was two months away, and she'd be more clued up on how everything worked by then. The patients would be used to her, she hoped, remembering what Mick had said. She sighed and got out of bed, feeling restless. A walk in the cold, fresh air would be better than staying in bed fretting.

There was nobody in the kitchen, and Kate quickly made herself tea and toast and then headed outside, into the main street, as the sun rose over the mountain in the east, casting a rosy light over the rooftops. The street was busy as shopkeepers were opening their stores and delivery vans arrived with supplies.

Kate went into the little grocery shop that also sold newspapers and had a post office counter on the far side. She was amazed that so much could fit into such a small space.

A tall, thin woman in a bright green sweater smiled at her while she stacked tins of tomatoes on a shelf. 'Hello there,' she said. 'Just arrived?'

'I got here on Friday,' Kate replied. She walked closer and held out her hand. 'I'm Kate O'Rourke, the new doctor.'

'Good Lord in heaven, the new doctor,' the woman exclaimed and wiped her hand on the back of her skirt. She grabbed Kate's hand, pumping it up and down. 'Hello and welcome. Lovely to have a woman doctor at last. I think the women around here will be very happy to meet you. Dr Pat is lovely, but it can be a bit awkward to talk about, er, personal things with a man, if you know what I mean. My name's Sorcha, by the way.' She drew breath.

'Hi, Sorcha,' Kate said smiling. 'Nice to meet you. I like your shop.'

'It's a bit of a mishmash,' Sorcha remarked. 'Not one of your Dublin emporiums. That's where you're from, isn't it?'

'That's right. I suppose my accent gives me away.'

'You don't have much of an accent,' Sorcha replied. 'But you talk a bit posh for here, so I assumed you had to be from the big smoke.'

'Posh?' Kate asked laughing.

'Yes, you know, like a convent-educated woman. From south county Dublin or somewhere similar.'

'You have a very good ear.'

'I like to listen to people's accents and guess where they're from,' Sorcha said. 'We get people from all over Europe here, so it's a bit of a sport for me. I've got quite good at it,' she added proudly.

'I'm sure you have,' Kate agreed.

'But why aren't you in the surgery this morning?' Sorcha asked after a moment's pause.

'Pat's doing the morning shift,' Kate explained. 'I'll take over after lunch. So I thought I'd go a for a walk and look around and get to know the village.'

'You've come to the right place,' Sorcha remarked. 'If you wait a little while, the Monday-morning crowd will be in and start gossiping. You'll get everyone's latest news in a flash. Not all of it the gospel truth as some people go in for a bit of embroidery.'

Kate laughed. 'I see. But I think I'll go for that walk, though. It wouldn't do for me to start gossiping on my first day. Or any day, really,' she added.

Sorcha nodded. 'Quite right. A doctor must always remain above all such things.' She paused. 'But you won't mind if I tell them you're here? And that you're from Dublin and very pretty?'

'Of course not,' Kate replied, her face turning pink at the compliment. She picked an apple from a basket. 'I'll have this to eat on my walk,' she said and groped in her pocket for change.

'It's on the house,' Sorcha said.

'Oh, that's very kind. Thank you.'

'You're welcome, Dr Kate. Say hello to Tom in the pharmacy. He'll be delighted to meet you. And don't forget to call in to say hello to the new hairdresser. She just reopened in what used to be the old barber's. Now it's unisex, if you don't mind. Very flash place, too. We're beginning to get very modern around here.'

'Not too modern, I hope,' Kate said, and put the apple in the pocket of her jacket.

'Not at all,' Sorcha assured her. 'We're very fond of the old ways, if you know what I mean.'

'That's reassuring.' Kate walked to the door. 'I'll be off now. Nice to meet you, Sorcha.'

'Lovely to meet you,' Sorcha said. 'See you around.'

Kate left the shop and continued down the main street towards the sea. She popped into the chemist shop and introduced herself to the pharmacist, a nice man in his fifties who was busy serving a line of customers but shook her hand and wished her a hearty welcome. Then she walked on, passing the hairdresser's that wasn't open yet, and a few little cottages. She stopped in front of a long, low building with a sign that said 'Sandy Cove Wellness Centre' and glanced into the shop window with its array of jars and bottles with various creams and lotions. *Must be Cormac's products*, she thought and jumped as his face appeared in the window. They stared at each other for a second, before he smiled and gestured for her to come in.

Intrigued, Kate opened the door to chimes of tiny bells and stepped into a large bright room with white walls and a light blue carpet. A reception counter stood at the far end beside a door that led to something called 'Body and Soul Space' according to a sign on the door. A light smell of lavender wafted around in the warm, welcoming room.

'What's the Body and Soul Space?' Kate asked.

'The yoga and meditation area,' Cormac said from behind the counter that ran the length of the room with its stacked shelves. The counter was littered with baskets of dried herbs, booklets on well-being and how to treat various ailments in the natural way, bunches of dried flowers and polished stones of numerous shapes and colours. The whole space exuded calm and tranquillity.

'What a lovely place,' Kate said, looking around.

'Yes, it is,' Cormac agreed. 'Kamal and Sally did a great job.'

'Are they the owners?'

Cormac nodded. 'Yes. Kamal is from India and Sally is an O'Rourke, like you. Some distant cousin, I suspect.'

'Must be,' Kate agreed. 'And they did a perfect job. This is a little different from one of those hotel spas. But still…'

'A haven for stressed souls?' Cormac suggested. 'Very close to nature. There's a massage room as well, and a treatment room for facials and things like that and a small gym.'

'Something for everyone, then. Somewhere to come to look after your whole being – body and mind. So healing and soothing.' Kate stopped. 'Could you tell me the class schedule? I used to do Pilates but I'd love to try yoga.'

'Of course.' Cormac handed her a brochure. 'Everything you need to know is in here. The schedule is slightly slimmed down for the low season, but I'm sure you'll find something that'll suit you.'

Kate folded the brochure and put it in her pocket. 'I'll look at that later. I want to go for a walk on the beach and get some sea air before afternoon surgery.'

'Good idea.' Cormac beamed. 'Your first day, is it?'

'Yes.' Kate picked up a smooth pink stone and turned it in her hands. 'This one feels like silk to touch.'

'It's a piece of granite polished by the ocean.'

'It's lovely to hold. How much is it?'

'For you, nothing. Call it a welcome gift.'

'Oh, thank you,' Kate replied, heart beating faster as their eyes met. 'That's my second gift today. Sorcha in the grocery shop gave me an apple.'

'Sorcha is a great woman.'

'Very nice,' Kate said, beginning to feel restless. Cormac's small talk seemed a little forced somehow, as if he wanted her to leave. There had been a tiny spark between them a moment ago, but maybe she had imagined it. 'Perhaps I'm disturbing you,' she said after a while. 'I'm sure you have more important things to do than chat to me.'

'Not really. My usual routine. Mondays are generally quiet around here, but I have to get an order ready for a health shop in Waterville. Dried herbs and lavender for their tea selection.'

'You grow the herbs here?'

Cormac nodded. 'In my greenhouse. And I have a little lab there where I make up a few things for my clients.'

Kate played with the smooth piece of granite in her hand. 'Clients? You mean your patients?'

His eyes were suddenly wary. 'I don't have patients. I'm not a doctor.'

'But people come to you for your healing powers, don't they?'

Cormac shrugged and looked away. 'It happens.'

'And do you manage to heal them?'

'Sometimes.' Cormac looked at Kate with a serious expression. 'Look, I know what you're thinking – claiming healing powers and saying that my remedies can cure serious illnesses is a risky business and could even lead to lawsuits, but I would never do that. I use old recipes handed down through generations that have been known to cure certain ailments. Like carrageen moss, which is known to have antibacterial properties that is great for congestion and coughs and also for dry skin, if applied topically. But I only say it could help, not that it can cure.' He held out his hands. 'And these are just like anyone's hands. Do they have healing powers? I don't know. Maybe it's the belief that cures, not the actual hands. I only know that there is more to healing than conventional medicine, but that could be in the human body's own ability to heal itself, like when you break a bone.'

'Of course,' Kate replied. 'But…'

'And whatever the healing properties of my hands,' he continued, 'the people who come to me believe in them and that makes them feel better. Perhaps that belief in itself is part of their recovery – maybe it makes them feel calm.' He drew breath and let his hands fall by his sides, looking at Kate as if to challenge her to contradict him.

She looked back at him and felt herself shiver. There was such passion in his green eyes and she felt that he was being honest, even if he wasn't telling her everything. 'Doctors don't know everything either,' she concluded. 'Healing is sometimes mysterious, that's true. And they might have known more about it in ancient times than we think.'

'The dark ages were perhaps not so dark, after all,' Cormac said with a glimmer of a smile.

'Maybe not.' Kate put the stone in her pocket, knowing it would be something she'd have with her always. 'I have an hour now before I have to go back and face my first day in the surgery.'

'The beach is just around the corner,' Cormac said.

'I'll be off, so,' Kate said.

'Enjoy your walk and good luck on your first day.' He walked to the door and held it open.

'Thank you,' he said as she walked out.

Kate stopped in the doorway. 'For what?'

'For not asking me too much about my remedies. Or telling me not to hand them out.'

'Why should I?'

Cormac shrugged, still holding the door. 'You might feel they're not quite right. Not really safe, or something. But I haven't killed anyone yet.'

Kate laughed. 'I have to say, though,' she continued in a serious tone, 'that conventional medicine is safer. It's been tried and tested by scientists over the years. It's all very well to talk about healing hands, and so on, but doctors have studied for many years and know best how to cure a person who's ill. As you say, it can be dangerous to dabble in things you don't fully understand.'

'Even if I manage to cure what you could not?' Cormac asked.

'Is this about the new ointment?' Kate couldn't help asking. 'I know Pat tried to ask you about that. It seems to work very well. What little I've seen of its effect, anyway.'

Cormac's expression was suddenly bland. 'Just a bit of luck, that's all. Goodbye, Dr Kate,' he said abruptly. 'Enjoy your walk.' He started to close the door, and Kate felt like she should leave.

She stood outside, wondering about his odd behaviour. Had she had stepped on a sore spot, asking about his healing and that new ointment? Was he hiding something? She ran her finger over the smooth stone in her pocket and remembered the look in Cormac's eyes when he had given it to her. There was a lot more to him than met the eye, she felt. An awful lot.

# Chapter Eight

When Kate got back from her walk, Pat was in the kitchen having a sandwich. He smiled as she came in and gestured at a plate piled with more sandwiches. 'Bridget made us a bite to eat,' he said.

'More than a bite,' Kate said and sat down at the table. She picked up a sandwich. 'The classic egg and spring onion sandwich. My favourite.' She glanced at Pat as she took a bite. 'How was morning surgery?'

'Not too bad. Mostly coughs and colds, a blood sample, a baby with a rash and one of my older patients with high blood pressure who needed his medication adjusted and a stern lecture about smoking. The usual mix, really.' Pat poured water into his glass from a blue jug on the table. 'How was your morning?'

Kate swallowed her bite of sandwich. 'Very nice. I walked around the village for a bit and met Sorcha in the grocery shop and said hello to Tom in the pharmacy. Then I went down to the Wellness Centre and had a little chat with Cormac.'

'Oh?' Pat wiped his mouth. 'And what did you think? Of the Wellness Centre, I mean.'

'It's really great. So calming, somehow. There is a really relaxing atmosphere in there, it's so close to nature, and the sky and water. I'm thinking of trying a yoga class.'

Pat nodded. 'Good idea.' He rose slowly, looking suddenly pale and drawn. 'Must go for my rest. Good luck with the afternoon surgery. Let me know how you get on.'

'Of course.' Kate looked at him, alarmed by his sudden pallor. 'Are you all right, Pat? Maybe I should check your pulse?'

'No. I know what's wrong with me, and a rest is all I need. I'll be fine, don't worry.' He smiled wanly at her and left, while Kate suddenly lost her appetite as a lot of questions shot through her mind.

'Howerya, Kate,' Bridget's voice boomed as she walked into the kitchen.

'Hello, Bridget,' Kate replied absent-mindedly. 'Lovely sandwiches.'

'Thought you'd need something solid before the afternoon surgery.'

'What's wrong with Pat?' Kate asked. 'He looked so pale just now.'

Bridget picked up a sandwich and sat down at the table. 'High blood pressure and a bit of arrhythmia. But it's under control as long as he takes it easy.'

'Oh.' Heart arrhythmia wasn't serious once it was controlled with medication, Kate knew. But was the work as GP at a busy practice the ideal lifestyle? 'I see now why he has to retire.'

Bridget shrugged. 'He could carry on if he had a bit more help, but his wife has other ideas. I think she wants them to live together at last and spend more time as a couple. She's winding down at the family firm and will be handing it all over to her niece eventually. Then she and Pat will live happily ever after in Killarney, playing golf and going to dinners with her posh friends in those fancy country clubs over there. Blissful, right?' Bridget's smile didn't reach her eyes.

'Not really for Pat, though?' Kate said, surprised at the touch of venom in Bridget's voice.

'A nightmare for him, I think. He'll have to get out of the old cardies and corduroys and dress in designer golf gear and a suit for the evening. Country doctor becomes man about town. Can't you see it?'

Kate laughed. 'No.'

'But he'll do it to make her happy.' Bridget put her sandwich on her plate. 'It's a very sad situation. Sad for us here in Sandy Cove, and sad for him and for Mick, too. But Pat adores Helen and will do anything for her. I just wish someone could tell her it might not be what he wants. But she seems to think it'll be good for him and the slower pace of life will suit him better.'

'But maybe it will be good for his health?' Kate suggested, feeling a little awkward talking about Pat behind his back. It wasn't really any of her business. She had just arrived, and it seemed strange to be discussing the personal life of someone she hardly knew, even if it was quite obvious that Pat was not well and needed to slow down.

Bridget shrugged. 'Maybe.' She checked her watch. 'Oops, it's nearly two o'clock. Time to get back to work. And you need to wash your hands and put on that white coat.'

'White coat?' Kate asked. 'I thought it wasn't worn by doctors any more.'

'Not usually, and probably not in city practices,' Bridget replied as she put the leftover sandwiches in the fridge. 'But Pat still puts it on and the patients like it. Gives a doctor more authority, if you see what I mean. And I think it's better for hygiene, too.'

'Probably,' Kate agreed and got up from the table. She was quite happy to put on a white coat. Anything to make her look like a 'real' doctor to those who might think her too young and inexperienced. 'I'll just run upstairs and get my stethoscope.'

'Great. I'll go and see if the first patient has arrived.'

Minutes later, Kate was sitting at the desk in the surgery wearing a slightly too big white coat, the stethoscope around her neck, waiting for her very first patient. She ran her finger over her father's watch and sat up straighter as the door opened. She rose and extended her hand to the older man. 'Hello. Seamus Lonergan, is it? I'm Kate O'Rourke, the new doctor.'

The man stopped. 'Oh. I thought I would see Dr Pat,' he said, sounding annoyed. 'I heard you'd arrived, but I didn't think you'd be starting so soon. Where's Dr Pat? I wanted to see *him*,' he said as he started to cough.

'Dr O'Dwyer isn't here right now,' Kate replied. 'But I'll be happy to help you. That cough doesn't sound so good. How long have you had it?'

'Long enough,' the man said and started to back out the door. 'I'll come back when Dr Pat's here. I don't want to be examined by a woman.'

'Don't be such a wimp, Seamus,' Bridget said behind him. 'Go back inside and let Dr Kate look at you. You need something for that cough and I know your wife will give out if it doesn't stop.'

'I'm not going to undress in front of a woman,' Seamus argued.

'Who's asking you to undress?' Bridget retorted.

'I'm just going to listen to your lungs and your heart,' Kate cut in.

'I'm not taking off my vest,' Seamus said, crossing his arms protectively across his chest.

'Of course not,' Bridget replied. 'We can work around it, can't we, Dr Kate?'

'We can indeed,' Kate replied, trying desperately not to laugh. 'Just take off your pullover and open your shirt so I can get the stethoscope inside.'

'Sit down on the chair,' Bridget ordered.

'Okay.' Seamus sat down and with a bit of a struggle managed to get his sweater off and unbutton his shirt.

Kate slipped the stethoscope inside and listened to a rather wheezy chest and a rattling cough. But despite it sounding quite alarming it wasn't as serious as she had first thought. 'I think you have a touch of bronchitis,' she said when she had finished her examination. 'I'll give you a prescription for some steroids and a cough medicine with codeine to take at night. That should help you sleep. The cough should get better soon, but come back if it doesn't.'

Seamus nodded and buttoned his shirt. 'I will.'

Bridget patted his shoulder. 'There you go, Seamus, it wasn't that bad now, was it?'

'No,' Seamus admitted. 'She's not bad at all. For a woman,' he added.

When Seamus left, Bridget clicked her tongue. 'Men! Such babies, aren't they? You don't get women complaining about seeing a male doctor, do you?'

'Never,' Kate agreed. 'He seemed very attached to his vest.'

'Vests are important to men of that age,' Bridget remarked. 'Their mammies told them they'd catch pneumonia if they didn't wear them, even in the summer. It's like a security blanket.'

Kate laughed. 'Great to know. I'll be careful with vests from now on.'

'Good plan,' Bridget agreed and left to usher in the next patient.

Kate tossed her head and laughed. Bridget was such a tonic and a huge help; Kate was thankful she was here, ready to help at all times. Otherwise Kate would find herself struggling, trying to cope with patients like old Seamus, still stuck in the past. Were they all like that around here?

'How did your first day go?' Pat asked over the dinner that Kate still had to remind herself to call 'tea'.

'Not bad. Once I realised that a man's vest is a no-go area for a female doctor. And a few other little things that require training in diplomacy. Like asking patients about their family history and their diets. Country people sure like to keep their personal details to themselves. Or is it just me they don't want to tell things to?'

'You're new and young and from Dublin,' Pat remarked.

'And I'm a woman,' Kate filled in. 'Some of the older people seem to think I should have been a nurse and left the doctoring to men. Some of them even said so.'

'They'll get used to you. Just stick to your guns and let them know you're just as good as any man – even better.'

'That would take years.' Kate cut into the steak on her plate. 'Sorry about the steak. It's a little overdone. I'm not very good at cooking, I'm afraid.'

'It's fine,' Pat reassured her. 'Nice flavour and the spuds are really good. You shouldn't have to cook really.'

'Oh, I don't mind.' Kate looked at Pat while she cut another piece of steak. 'How are you feeling? Bridget told me about your… the problem with your heart.'

Pat drank some water. 'I'm fine. I just get tired sometimes. It's the medication rather than the actual condition that makes me tired. It slows my heartbeat and that makes me feel faint. But I'm being sensible, don't worry. My father had the same condition and lived to ninety-five. And he worked here as a GP until he was nearly eighty. I assisted him as soon as I was out of medical school. We were a good team.' Pat smiled wistfully. 'Great times, and a wonderful way to get experience.'

'Did Mick never want to be a doctor?'

'Sadly, no, never. He knew he wanted to be an actor when he was in his teens. Don't know where that came from, but it was as if he was born to it.'

'He's a wonderful actor.'

'So he is,' Pat said and pushed away his plate. 'Tell me about Cormac. What did you two talk about?'

'Nothing much.' Kate put her napkin beside her plate. 'Just small talk, really. I tried to warn him of the dangers of handing out cures to people who might be seriously ill. But he skated around it and then he practically threw me out of the place when I asked about that ointment.'

'Hmm.' Pat looked thoughtful. 'Helen said he clammed up when she asked about it. Apart from saying that it's a new recipe and he's just testing it, he refused to give her the ingredients. There must be something special in it apart from the usual herbs.'

'It smells of something strong, you said?'

'Yes. That's what I've heard. Could be coal tar. They used that for eczema in the old days. Still do.'

Kate nodded. 'Keratoplastics. Yes, it's used for certain skin conditions. But I doubt that's what's in it. It makes the skin peel. Old Jim's wound wasn't peeling. It was healing nicely and won't even leave a scar.'

'That's true.' Pat mused over the subject for a moment. 'I have a feeling there is something up in the mountains, like a plant or a root, he has found by accident and then started using it on animals just to see if it worked.'

'And it cured a nasty wound on someone's Labrador,' Kate filled in, remembering the conversation with the old couple in the hills.

Pat brightened. 'That's right. Thank you for reminding me. Pity they threw away the jar. But maybe we should go and look at that dog? Mrs O'Meara's, wasn't that what they said?'

'I think that was the name.'

'I know who they mean. A woman who lives on her own near Jim and his wife. She's an artist. Maybe we could call on her? See if she still has some of the ointment? I'd like to have a look at it.'

'So Helen could get it analysed?' Kate filled in.

Pat nodded. 'Exactly. It could be something new that would work where other things haven't.'

'I can think of a lot uses,' Kate said, feeling excited. 'Like acne scars that can be difficult to get rid of, and maybe even scars from burns. But it does need to be administered properly, and maybe analysed in a lab before we recommend it. Not that I don't trust Cormac. But I would prefer it if people in town didn't see him as some kind of doctor.'

'I agree,' Pat said, nodding. 'Could you go and have a chat with Mrs O'Meara and take a look at her old Labrador, do you think? Tomorrow morning, perhaps, while I'm in the surgery.'

'Of course,' Kate said. 'Just tell me where she lives and I'll be on my way first thing.'

Pat nodded. 'Excellent. I hope you'll be able to find out more. But be careful.'

'Of the dog?' Kate asked. 'Is it aggressive?'

'No, but Mrs O'Meara can be a little… tricky.'

'I'll use my best manners and diplomacy.' Kate winked. 'At least it won't involve a vest.'

Pat laughed. 'That's true.' He collected his plate and got up. 'Let's tidy up. It's time for the evening news. And then I want to watch that healthcare special they're doing on *Prime Time*. I want to see if the government has managed to find a solution to the current crisis.'

'That'd be the day,' Kate said, carrying her own plate and putting it in the dishwasher. 'I'll say goodnight when we've tidied up. I want to talk to my sister on Skype.'

'Where is she?' Pat asked.

Kate turned on the dishwasher. 'In New York. She's a fashion photographer.'

'Sounds exciting.'

'She loves it.'

Pat looked around the kitchen. 'All done and tidied away. Sheila, our cleaning lady, will be here in the morning. And when Bridget moves in, you won't have to cook any more.'

'That's a relief. For you,' Kate added with a laugh. 'I don't exactly do French cuisine.'

'I'm sorry you even felt you had to cook at all.' Pat smiled at her. 'But if you're a not so great cook, I'm completely useless.'

'A typical doctor, in other words,' Kate grinned. 'My dad was just like that. Brilliant with sick people, awful in the kitchen.'

'You miss him, don't you?' Pat asked as he wiped the kitchen counter.

'Terribly,' Kate replied as she hovered in the doorway. 'But working here has been helping me a lot already. My father often talked about this village and how he would one day come here and find out more about our family's history. He never got the chance to do that. But now I can, and that makes me feel closer to him. And working at the practice is so comforting. I feel that I'm continuing his work, somehow.'

'Of course you are,' Pat agreed. 'Just like me having taken over my father's practice. It helped me a lot just after he passed away.'

Kate nodded. 'Exactly.'

He patted her on the shoulder. 'I'll say goodnight now. You go off and chat with your sister.'

'Goodnight, Pat,' Kate said, cheered by the thought of talking to Tara. She had so much to tell her about the day. She'd laugh when she heard the story about the vest. And maybe, she thought, Tara might be more willing to talk about their dad this time. It would feel good to start accepting what had happened instead of trying to push it away.

But Tara was too full of her own news to listen to Kate. 'I've got the most amazing thing to tell you,' she chortled as soon as Kate turned on the Skype connection. 'I've landed a job as assistant to Joe Mancini.'

'Who?' Kate asked, staring at the image of Tara sitting cross-legged on the sofa in her New York living room.

'Joe Mancini,' Tara repeated. 'Only the most famous photographer in New York. He's the one who takes those shots of celebrities against the most incredible backdrops. He did the one with Brad Pitt balancing on a boulder over the edge of the Grand Canyon. It was an ad for Louis Vuitton.'

'Oh,' Kate said, not having seen the ad or ever heard of Joe Mancini.

'Is that all you can say?' Tara asked, sounding disappointed. 'This is the most wonderful break for me ever. And we're going on a shoot in South America for *National Geographic*. I'm packing for the jungle. We're going up the Amazon River in a canoe and sleeping in tents and then we'll do a feature on these tribes that live in the rainforests there. It's going to be a huge adventure.'

'The Amazon?' Kate exclaimed. 'In a canoe? Are you mad? What about your glam life in New York? This will mean a whole month of bad hair days.'

Tara rolled her eyes. 'Oh, please. I'm a professional photographer. You have to cope with things like that for amazing jobs. And in any case, after nearly two years here, I'm a little sick of the glamour and the rat race. I need to get away from it all and this is the best break ever.'

'How incredible,' Kate said, realising that her stories of her new life in Sandy Cove paled to insignificance. What was Seamus Lonergan's vest compared to a trip up the Amazon River?

'Isn't it? I can't believe it's happening,' Tara said, looking starry-eyed. 'But we're leaving in a few days and then I won't be able to reach you for a long time. We'll have a satellite phone, but only for emergencies. I might be able to send you a text when we're in range, but up in the jungle, we'll be cut off from everything.'

'Oh, God,' Kate said, realising there would be no more chats like this for a good while. 'I'll miss talking to you.'

'Me too,' Tara said with a sad little sigh. 'But I'll be back in a few weeks, and just imagine all the things I'll be able to tell you.'

'Be careful in the jungle,' Kate said, suddenly worried. 'Bring plenty of mosquito repellent and sunblock. And don't swim in the river, it's probably full of crocodiles, piranhas and parasites. Boil every single drop of water you'll be drinking and don't eat raw fruit and salads, and—'

'I knooowww,' Tara groaned. 'I've read up on all of that. I knew you'd worry. But please don't. Joe has been up the Amazon several times and there is a fully trained nurse in the crew who grew up in Brazil. And there are doctors there, you know. We'll be hot and sweaty, but fine.'

'Have you gone to get the shots you need?' Kate interrupted. 'Dysentery, dengue fever…'

'Not yet. But we've been advised to get vaccinated against hepatitis, cholera and yellow fever. I'll do them all before we leave. They'll probably make me sicker than the actual diseases.'

'Rabies, too,' Kate said. 'There are snakes and monkeys and leopards in the jungle.'

'Isn't it exciting?' Tara said, beaming. 'I can't wait.'

Kate saw Tara on the screen trying to take it all in. Tara going on some kind of camping trip in the Amazonian jungle was so far removed from her glamorous lifestyle and fashionable image. 'I can't believe you're really doing this,' she said. 'You can't live without your hair straighteners and scream if you break a nail. How on earth are you going to cope in the jungle?'

Tara laughed. 'I know what you mean. But this is going to be such a huge challenge. It'll be hard, but I really want to give it a go. Photographers who go out on a limb like this are the ones who get to the top of their profession. I want to learn how to do photo shoots in harsh environments and produce pictures like the kind of award-winning photos you see in books and magazines, and even get bought up by art galleries. I want to make a name in photography, and this is the best way to do it. Don't worry, sis. I'll come back with fantastic material. Joe has even given me one of his cameras. A Leica, no less. It's like being given the crown jewels.'

'Oh, God,' Kate said in a near whisper, slowly realising that Tara was truly committed. 'I won't be able to sleep until you get back.'

'Watch my Instagram photos. I'm going to post some shots whenever I can.'

'I will,' Kate promised, feeling a dart of loneliness. Tara was taking off in a new direction and she was doing it on her own. It felt as if part of her was being ripped away. And she would now not have any opportunity to tell Tara about the O'Rourke family history she was beginning to discover through Cormac.

'Bye, darling,' Tara said, blowing her a kiss. 'Good luck with the doctoring. Take care, and don't worry. I'm flying solo for a while, but we'll soon hook up again through the airwaves. Love you.'

'Bye,' Kate whispered.

The screen went blank and Kate sat on her bed in the little room, staring at it, her eyes full of tears. Tara was going far away, too far for chatting on Skype. Who knew what would happen to her or how she would feel when she came back? It felt like the beginning of a new phase in both their lives. A phase where from now on, she was on her own.

# Chapter Nine

Early next morning, Kate headed once again up the hillside, this time in her own trusty little Renault. She loved her car. It might not have been flashy, but it took her where she wanted to go and when she was driving, she felt safe and relaxed, looking forward to arriving at her destination. She had read somewhere that a lot of people were happiest when they were driving. It was true, she mused, as she trundled up the winding country roads, glancing at the green fields dotted with sheep and the clouds scudding across the sky, this was the best moment of the day. An Irish ballad wafted from the speaker, the engine purred, the heating was turned to the ideal temperature and she could go wherever she wanted; this time to meet the enigmatic Mrs O'Meara, who Bridget had later told her was 'fierce'. Perhaps she was just eccentric, Kate supposed, like a lot of artists.

Mrs O'Meara was a textile designer and created wonderful cloths and tapestries with her loom, Pat had told her. When Kate had googled her name she had found that Mrs O'Meara was very well known. Some of her work was hanging in official buildings, including the hospital where Kate had worked. She had often glanced at the enormous tapestry depicting an Irish landscape and marvelled at its vivid colours and beautiful shapes. At that time she had only known the artist as COM from the embroidered signature at the bottom. But now she knew that it was Clodagh O'Meara and that she had a Labrador that had been cured by Cormac's mysterious ointment. Not only that, Bridget had told her. Clodagh O'Meara was Cormac's aunt, which might make Kate's mission difficult, if not impossible. But no matter, Kate thought; here she was, driving through the beautiful countryside to meet an artist whose work she had admired. Even if she came back none the wiser, it would still be an interesting morning.

Clodagh's little bungalow was perched on an incline overlooking the bay on the Waterville side. The picket fence, the small garden and the blue door with seashells stuck to the wall around it told Kate that this was the house of someone artistic who loved nature.

Kate parked the car and sat there looking at the view for a moment. Gone was her sadness and worry about Tara and her earlier feelings of being all alone. Had she been in Dublin, she would have felt sad and lonely, but not here, in this beautiful, gentle place, full of friendly people. Although she had just arrived, she already felt at home and there was a wonderful feeling of peace and tranquillity despite the wild winds and unpredictable weather. It would be hard to leave when her contract was up, but she would have learned so much and would take a lot of that feeling with her wherever she went. She'd be stronger and more independent, she felt. But she wasn't there yet. There was still a long way to go.

Kate got out of the car at nearly the same time as the blue door opened and a tall woman dressed in a long red wool skirt and a black polo neck appeared, a black dog at her side barking loudly. Kate froze. She hadn't expected the dog to be so big.

The woman gave a sharp command to the dog, who stopped barking. 'Hello,' she said. 'Are you Kate, the doctor?'

'I am,' Kate said, opening the gate in the fence. 'How did you know?'

'Bridget called just now. Said she didn't want your visit to be a surprise if I was working. But I'm not at the moment. I'm just sketching. If I were working, I wouldn't let you in.'

'Oh.' Kate stayed by the gate looking at the dog, who looked back at her with suspicion, growling softly.

The woman tapped the dog on the nose with her finger. 'Behave yourself.' She smiled at Kate. 'Don't worry about Brian. His bark is worse than his bite. Just like my late husband. My two daughters laughed when I named the dog after him. But it makes me feel he's still here.'

Kate laughed and walked up to the woman and held out her hand. 'Hello, Mrs O'Meara. I'm very happy to meet you.'

Clodagh grasped Kate's hand tightly. 'Hello, Kate. Please call me Clodagh. I know I'm a hundred years old to you, but I prefer to be called by my first name.'

'A hundred?' Kate exclaimed. 'Gosh, no. You're like one of those ageless women who will never be old.' It was true, she thought. Clodagh's red hair had grey streaks and her face was lined, but apart from that she looked sprightly with blue eyes that sparkled with intelligence and humour.

'That's a lovely thought. But I'm nearly eighty, you know. Not that I worry about it, but I feel it sometimes, especially in the morning when the old bones creak and refuse to move the way I want.' She pulled the dog away and stepped aside. 'But enough standing here in the cold. Come in and have a cup of tea. I'll put the kettle on. Brian, go and lie down in your bed.'

Kate laughed as the dog slunk off and she stepped inside into a bright living room with white walls covered in an array of artwork. The room smelled faintly of wool, paint and turpentine. Big and small tapestries on the walls glowed in vivid colours, interspersed with watercolours of Irish landscapes and even a few little oil paintings depicting the beaches, the ocean and the night sky dotted with stars. They were all beautiful and Kate was in awe. Then she discovered a loom by the picture window holding an unfinished piece of cloth. A table littered with small squares of fabric stood by the loom and the rest of the room was taken up by a large red sofa piled with cushions in every colour of the rainbow. There was no fire in the fireplace but the sun streaming in through the picture window provided enough warmth.

'What an amazing room,' Kate exclaimed, staring at all the wonderful artwork and then looking out at the view of the coastline and the Atlantic. 'It's like an Aladdin's cave of colours and textures.'

'A bit of a mess,' Clodagh said and took a pile of magazines and newspapers off the sofa. 'But sit down and I'll get you a mug of tea.'

'Oh please, don't go to any trouble,' Kate said. 'I only popped in to say hello and ask you about that ointment Cormac gave you.'

Clodagh stopped in her tracks. 'Oh? You mean that stuff Cormac made up for Brian's injury?'

'Yes. I heard it cured the wound very quickly.'

Clodagh nodded. 'It did. Incredible, really. Poor old Brian had ripped his side on some rusty barbed wire up the mountain. It made a nasty gash that got infected. I tried everything and even the antibiotic cream the vet gave me didn't work. Then Cormac, who happened to pop in for a visit, said he had some new stuff he wanted to try. Something he had found near the castle, he said.'

'O'Rourke's castle?' Kate asked.

Clodagh nodded, still holding the pile of magazines. 'Yes. That's the only castle around here. And it's not even a real castle. But anyhow, that's where he got whatever it was. He had no idea if it would work, it was just a hunch, he said. Some black-looking gunk he had in one of his jars. I put it on twice a day and the wound healed. That's it, really.'

'Could I take a look at the injury?' Kate asked.

'Of course. Brian, come here,' Clodagh called. There was a clicking of claws on the wooden floor and the dog trotted in from another room.

Kate eyed him nervously but Brian wagged his tail and sniffed at her leg.

'He's accepted you,' Clodagh said. 'Have a seat and make friends. I'll go and get that tea.'

Kate sat down on the sofa and Brian sat on the floor beside her, still wagging his tail. Kate noticed his fur had been shaved off his left side and bent to look. All she could see was a thin pink line among the stubble where the wound must have been. It seemed to have healed completely with not much scarring. 'When was he injured?' she asked Clodagh who had just appeared with two mugs of tea.

'About three weeks ago. It was truly nasty and went septic very quickly. Poor Brian was really sick with it. The antibiotic cream from the vet cleared up the infection, but it was still inflamed and itchy. And then Cormac came with his magic mixture and it was like a miracle. It calmed the inflammation and stopped him scratching at it.' Clodagh put the mugs on a small table by the sofa and sat down beside Kate, ruffling Brian's fur. 'But now you're as fit as a fiddle, aren't you?'

'You have no idea what was in the cream?' Kate asked.

Clodagh handed her one of the mugs. 'No. Not a clue. It smelled funny, but Cormac's stuff always does. He never adds perfume to anything.'

'And…' Kate hesitated, taking a sip of tea. 'Do you still have the jar it came in?'

'The jar?' Clodagh looked up from cuddling Brian. 'Oh yes, I think I still have it. I'll go and have a look in the kitchen where I keep Brian's worm tablets and flea spray. Hold on a second.' Clodagh got up and went out the half-open door to the kitchen, where Kate could hear her rummaging around. Then she could hear a mobile phone ring and Clodagh answered it. After a short conversation that Kate couldn't hear, Clodagh came back into the living room. 'Can't find that jar, I'm afraid. I think Cormac took it back with him. He recycles all his containers, so he must have reused it for something else.'

'I see,' Kate said with a feeling she had just been lied to. 'That phone call… Could it have been Cormac?'

'Sorry about that. But maybe you could ask Cormac himself?' Clodagh suggested, her expression impassive.

'Yes, maybe,' Kate said and got up. 'But I think we both know that's a dead end. Anyway, thanks for the tea. It was lovely to meet you and to see your beautiful work. What are you working on right now?'

Clodagh turned to the table. 'I'm doing something new. Quilting. This will eventually be a kind of collage that could either be hung on the wall or used on a bed. It's all recycled material, just as my tapestries are. I love reusing things that people have worn. I get textiles from charity shops and cloth recycling centres, even some end bits from fashion houses. Silk, cotton, wool, cashmere, whatever I can get my hands on.' Clodagh rifled through the colourful squares on the table. 'All this will be used and hopefully turned into something that will last for years.'

'It'll be beautiful,' Kate said, admiring the squares of material. 'I'd love something like that for my bed.'

'Well, I could make one for you. It'll take time, of course.'

'I don't mind waiting,' Kate declared, excited at the idea of having her very own bespoke quilt.

Clodagh smiled. 'I like the idea of making a quilt for the new doctor.' She studied Kate for a while. 'I'll have to get to know you a little better while I work, so I can design a quilt that would be personal. I'd love you to call in now and again while I make it. Would you have time to do that?'

'Of course,' Kate said. 'I'd love to come back to see you and watch the quilt grow.' It was true; she had liked Clodagh instantly, and despite suspecting she had been told a lie, she was ready to forgive. It wasn't Clodagh's fault Cormac was so protective about his ointment, and she was probably very fond of her nephew. In any case, getting to know Clodagh better might bring her closer to the mystery of whatever herb Cormac had found at the castle. Was it some plant that only grew there? Or moss from the walls of the tower? Or…

She stopped herself. There was only one way to find out. She would have to go and look there herself.

The afternoon surgery passed without too much trouble. Apart from a few complaints about not getting antibiotics for a bad cold, nobody seemed to mind being examined by a young woman doctor, and some of the female patients even expressed their delight. The only hitch was a middle-aged woman who peered at Kate, asking how old she was and demanding to see proof of her qualifications.

'You should perhaps put your diplomas on the wall here in the surgery,' Bridget suggested when the woman had left. 'Not that I think anyone else will complain. That Mrs O'Dea is a bit of a nosy biddy and the worst gossip in the village. I think you might have been a little more diplomatic, but that was my fault. I should have warned you.'

'Warned me about what?' Kate asked with a dart of irritation. 'I just used my usual approach. Don't know why she didn't like it.'

'Telling her she was a little pale and showed signs of constipation?' Bridget laughed. 'Yeah, that would have come as a bit of a blow.'

Kate smirked. 'I was just guessing by the way she looked and the slight stomach ache she complained about. That was all that was wrong with her. You didn't hear this, Bridget, but I suggested she eat more fibre and told her to get a laxative at the chemist's. I don't think she suffers from the more interesting anaemia she had diagnosed herself. I told her to come back for a blood test tomorrow morning and to be fasting. She didn't really want to do that, but I told her she was at the age where her cholesterol levels might be high. She didn't seem to like that much either.'

'I bet she didn't.' Bridget handed Kate a bunch of papers. 'We're nearly finished for today. You just need to file this and send a few emails to the hospital for the specialists' referrals.'

Kate took the papers and turned to the computer on the desk. 'I'll have them done straight away.'

'Great.' Bridget glanced out the window. 'Here's John now to collect me. We're going to the builder's to see about all the renovations we're doing on our house. I hope you don't mind about us moving in here?'

'Of course not,' Kate replied. 'It'll be nice to have the company.'

'It'll be a little crowded with us and Mick here when he comes back. He wants to stay here while he writes that play.'

'Oh?' Kate turned from the computer screen. 'He's still going to live here too?'

'Yes. And Pat, of course. But your bedroom is separated from the other four, so you'll still have your privacy. And your own bathroom.'

'Oh, I don't mind at all,' Kate declared. 'Much better than rattling around by myself in this big house. I hope we'll all get on with each other.'

'Of course we will. It'll be a motley crew. But we'll be like one big family,' Bridget said with a reassuring smile. 'And you won't have to cook for yourself at all.'

'That's a relief,' Kate said. 'Whatever I produce doesn't even deserve to be called cooking.'

'I could teach you a few basic recipes,' Bridget offered.

'Thanks,' Kate said, not really listening. Her mind was on Mick and the fact that he'd be in the house all day long, writing a play. He would be here every night and they'd be thrown together at all times.

Kate knew that if Tara heard about this, she'd never stop nagging about hair and make-up. And she was right, Kate thought, looking down at the old blue shirt she wore under her white coat. Maybe it was time to smarten up. A visit to the hairdresser's might not be a bad idea, for a start. A new look would give her confidence as well and might make more of an impact on the patients. Smart and professional would be a better image than her careless, thrown-together look that was easy but maybe a tad messy. It wasn't so much about impressing Mick, but the fact that he'd be here was a wake-up call.

*Next stop the hairdressing salon*, Kate thought, even if it meant cutting all her hair off.

Kate sat in the hairdresser's the next morning and stared at herself in the mirror, amazed. She hadn't had all her hair cut off, but nearly. Gerry, a young man with platinum-blond hair and multiple earrings beamed at her as he took off the cape. But Kate didn't return his smile while she tried to take in the fact that the woman in the mirror was really her. The difference in her appearance was startling. She wouldn't normally be ready to make such a drastic change, but it felt right. 'I look different,' she mumbled, still slightly shocked.

'You look so cool,' Gerry exclaimed. 'I knew the minute you came in that it had to be super-short. And I was right. Just look at the way it makes your eyes enormous. Just like Audrey Hepburn. Gorgeous.'

Kate reflected, slowly realising what he meant. The short hair was startling, but it did make her eyes look huge and also exposed her cheekbones. The shock was slowly replaced by delight. It was a great cut, something she hadn't expected in such a small rural salon. She turned her head this way and that, marvelling at how the new hairdo changed her appearance. 'It's really fabulous,' she said. 'Where did you learn to cut hair like this?'

'I trained in Dublin,' Gerry replied as he ran his fingers through her hair. 'Robert Chambers in Grafton Street. Ever heard of them?'

'Of course,' Kate replied. 'But I could never afford to go there. I knew they had a hairdressing school there, too. Well, you must have been at the top of your class.'

'I was, actually,' Gerry admitted. 'Not bad for a lad from the wild west of Ireland, eh?'

'Not bad at all,' Kate agreed.

Gerry brushed the loose hair off her neck with a soft brush. 'And that's where I met Susie. My business partner,' he explained. 'She's from Galway. We decided to come here to my home town and set up a little business. We only just opened.'

Kate looked around the bright little salon that was fitted out with the latest dryers and heating lamps. 'You did a great job. I'm sure everyone's delighted to have a hairdresser so close to home.'

'Yes, they are. Except some of the older men are a little iffy about having their hair cut in a unisex salon. They'd prefer a real old barber's with only men, but the barber's closed down last year so they have no choice.' Gerry laughed as he took a broom from a cupboard and started to sweep up the hair on the floor.

'Look at all that hair,' Kate said, still amazed at her transformation. 'You must have cut off most of it.'

'Ah sure, but what's left is totally fabulous. I wish Susie was here to see you. But she's gone to Waterville to do a big shop.'

'I'll pop in later to say hello,' Kate promised as she paid the bill.

'She'd love to meet you.'

Kate said goodbye and left, feeling a cold draught on her neck when she got outside. This new hairdo would take a while to get used to. But she loved the way she looked and couldn't help admiring herself in every shop window she passed. Then she laughed and told herself to stop acting like a teenager. Time to get real and get back to work. It was lunchtime, and then she had to do afternoon surgery. No time to admire herself in shop windows or mirrors.

She looked forward to the afternoon and all the different patients she would meet. Her first day had gone well apart from a few minor hiccups. Today would be even better, even if she hadn't quite worked out what Cormac was up to. He was a hard nut to crack, and she wondered if she'd ever be able to understand his attitude to healing. The thought that people around here would go to Cormac with serious complaints was worrying. She had nothing against natural remedies for certain conditions, but how could she convince Cormac that people should seek medical advice too? His methods were helpful but they needed to be used as well as, and not instead of, conventional medicine. There had to be a way for them to work together, and in this way provide an even better health service for sick people. That would be ideal.

Kate sighed as she realised that this perfect scenario was next to impossible. Cormac would probably balk at any suggestions from her and then the tension between them would be even worse. How strange to feel so drawn to him and at the same time disagree with nearly everything he said. She didn't think she could cope with that kind of stress on top of everything else. It would be better to avoid him altogether. But how? *Impossible in this small village*, Kate thought.

# Chapter Ten

Still wrestling with the problem, Kate walked into the kitchen where Pat and Bridget were having a discussion in muted tones, neither of them looking very happy.

'What's up?' Kate asked, startled by the glum faces.

'A bit of trouble,' Pat explained. 'Bridget says half the patients have cancelled their afternoon appointments, including that little boy with a bad rash and the man with high blood pressure. I wanted you to have a look at that one specially as you have experience in that area. We even got an electrocardiogram monitor sent to us by the HSE. It arrived this morning. I wanted you to be the first to use it.'

'That's terrific,' Kate said. 'I didn't think they'd ever give those to GP practices.'

'They do now because they're trying to unburden the A&E wards in the hospitals,' Pat explained. 'I was really excited for you to use it. But now he cancelled his appointment.'

'Cancelled?' Kate repeated. 'Why?'

'He didn't say,' Bridget replied, glancing at Kate. 'Love your hair, Kate. It really suits you.'

'Thanks,' Kate said, absent-mindedly touching her hair. 'But… what on earth made those patients cancel?'

Pat shrugged down at the plate of salad in front of him. 'No idea.' He looked back at Kate with regret in his eyes. 'I have a feeling… I'm afraid…'

'That it's my fault?' Kate sank down on a chair.

Pat shrugged. 'I don't really know. But maybe your approach is too… honest?'

'It's that Mrs O'Dea woman,' Bridget cut in, handing Kate a plate with salad and ham. 'I bet she's the one who's been saying things about the new doctor behind your back. She didn't like to hear the truth about her health.'

'What truth?' Pat asked.

'That all she suffered from was constipation, and that she's getting older and needs to keep an eye on her blood pressure and cholesterol,' Kate told him. 'I suppose I didn't handle that with a lot of diplomacy.'

Pat laughed. 'I suspect you're right.'

'What would you have told her?'

Pat thought for a moment, pushing his glasses onto the top of his head. 'I might have called it something fancy like constricted gut and handed her a prescription to give to the chemist, who'd know what I was up to.'

'And then Mrs O'Dea would feel like an interesting case and get a lot of sympathy all over the place,' Bridget filled in.

'Oh dear,' Kate lamented.

Pat shrugged. 'I would have told you, but I had no idea she was coming in.'

'It was a last-minute appointment yesterday afternoon,' Bridget told him. 'And I was too busy to warn Kate about her.'

'Even if you had, I still might have done the same thing,' Kate said glumly. 'I'm not used to wrapping things up in cotton wool. I prefer the direct approach, calling a spade a spade. I always feel a patient should be told the whole truth about their health. Is this going to be a problem round here?'

'Only with Mrs O'Dea and some of her friends,' Bridget said.

'But the damage is already done,' Pat added. 'Mrs O'Dea has a big mouth and gossip spreads fast. I'm sorry, Kate, it's really not your fault.'

'But what can we do about it?' Kate asked.

'Nothing, really,' Bridget replied. 'Just carry on as before and hope nobody with a serious illness goes to Cormac for those natural remedies and gets even worse.'

'Could we talk to Cormac?' Kate asked. 'Get him to tell people who need a real doctor to come here?' Kate had hoped to avoid him, but it seemed she'd have to face this problem head-on.

'Maybe.' Pat looked doubtful.

'Be my guest,' Bridget muttered as she sat down with her own salad. 'He can be very stubborn, you know.'

'Oh really?' Kate said, sticking out her chin. 'But so can I.'


That stubborn feeling stayed with her through the day. As some of the patients had cancelled their appointments, they finished early and Kate found herself turning off the computer just after four o'clock. She told Bridget to call her if anyone should want a late appointment, and headed down to the Wellness Centre to have a little 'chat' with Cormac.

It seemed a bit insane to her that traditional healing from plants and berries still went on when proper healthcare was available to everyone. But maybe old superstitions were more alive here in rural Ireland. These people were still walking in the footsteps of their ancestors, and traditions that had been handed down for centuries were still respected and treasured. So unique and eerie, Kate thought, but also something doctors like Pat had had to cope with on a daily basis, especially with the older patients. He seemed to have handled it all very well, blending the old with the new, telling his patients what they wanted to hear while slyly treating them with conventional methods they wouldn't have agreed to had he not fooled them. That way everyone was happy and all was well. Until Kate arrived.

And suddenly all the fears Kate had that she wasn't good enough in Dublin came back to her.

It had happened after a hectic weekend in the A&E. There had been a horrific traffic accident on the motorway with many dead and badly injured. Kate had worked with the other doctors, trying to save lives, treat bad injuries and talk to family members of the victims. After more than eighteen hours on duty, Kate was near to collapse in the staff room, unable to stop crying. She felt she hadn't done enough, not talked to each individual patient who was facing surgery, not managed to say anything soothing to their families and not really given the comfort she felt they needed. 'I don't have what it takes,' she'd said to her colleagues, 'I couldn't pull myself together to give those people any hope or comfort.' But nobody listened as they were all exhausted, and Kate was left on her own with a horrible feeling that she had failed her father, instead of continuing his legacy.

Was she failing him again? She'd thought coming here might be the break she needed to remind herself how passionate she was. But all the stuff with Cormac was making her feel like she wasn't quite right for the job.

She should probably have done some kind of course in rural patient care, she thought. But how would she have managed that? This way she had been thrown in at the deep end and put her foot in it immediately. Not her fault really, but she should have realised. And Pat and Bridget should have warned her, she thought with a dart of irritation at how they had just let it happen. Of course, if Cormac wasn't around, things would not be so difficult. But then there would have been someone else, some wise old woman with 'healing powers' or 'knowledge' handed down through generations, which might be even worse.

She arrived at the Wellness Centre and pulled at the door. But it wouldn't budge, and no little bells chimed like they had when she was there the last time. A sign on the door said 'Closed'. Kate pulled at the door again, despite knowing it was no use.

She was frustrated to think that the things she had rehearsed in her head might be wasted. What if more patients cancelled tomorrow? It was only just after four and still daylight. Where was Cormac? She was determined to talk to him, but she didn't know where he lived or where he went when he wasn't at the Wellness Centre. Then an idea popped into her head. The greenhouse. It must be at the back of the house…

Kate walked around the back of the long, low building and discovered a greenhouse that was bigger than she had imagined. It faced down towards the south coast and she saw little lights on here and there over beds of plants and flowers. She also saw a figure moving around at the far end. Cormac. He was alone, so here was her chance for that honest chat she had planned. Kate swallowed nervously and pushed the door open.

As she entered, Kate felt she was in a different world. It had been breezy and cold outside, but here the air was nearly tropical. At the other end of the greenhouse, the colours of flowers in full bloom glowed in the dim light. Kate nearly expected to hear birdsong, but the only sounds that broke the silence were her own footsteps on the packed earth.

'Hello.' Cormac's lilting voice made Kate turn around. They stared at each other for a moment before Kate cleared her throat.

'Hello, Cormac,' she said. 'I was looking for you at the Wellness Centre.'

'Why?' he asked, coming closer, a watering can in his hand. He was dressed in a moss-green cotton T-shirt the colour of which made his eyes even greener.

Kate took off her jacket, immediately feeling hot. 'Why did you close up so early? I thought you might be having hordes of clients by now, all wanting you to lay your healing hands on them.'

'Uh, no,' Cormac said, looking confused. 'I don't know what you mean.'

'Yes, you do,' Kate snapped, angry at the thought that he might be lying. Had he solicited patients and lured them away from the surgery? 'You know very well that a lot of patients have cancelled their doctor's appointments,' she said hotly. 'And that many of them feel that I, being a woman and from Dublin, am not qualified to treat their ills. So then I assumed that they now come to you for your old remedies. And that is a very dangerous thing,' she ended lamely, so incensed she didn't know how to go on.

'Do you always jump to conclusions like this?' Cormac asked with a bland expression. 'Isn't that also a little risky?'

'What do you mean? Conclusions? What conclusions? It's all very clear what's going on. And for the record, I'm actually very competent.'

'But of course you are,' Cormac said and put the watering can on a shelf beside him. 'Whoever said anything to the contrary?'

'Nobody. Yet,' Kate replied. 'But they will. Please don't pretend people haven't been here already asking for herbal cures.'

'Nobody's been here today asking for anything at all.'

'Oh yeah?' Kate glared at him.

'Yes.' Cormac paused. 'There's a good reason for that, you see.'

'And what would that be?' Kate asked, unnerved by his calm.

'Today is Tuesday.'

'So?'

'The Wellness Centre is closed on Tuesdays.'

'Oh,' Kate said, feeling stupid. 'I see.'

'You do?' Cormac lifted one eyebrow and his normally angelic face took on a hint of irony. 'Must be the only thing you see today, then.'

'Well, yeah...' Kate muttered. 'Full marks to you for that little victory.'

'Victory? I wasn't aware there's a war, or even a conflict.'

Kate folded her arms across her chest. 'There won't be one if you behave responsibly.'

'In what way?' Cormac asked.

'You know exactly what I'm talking about. Allowing people in town to rely on your cures instead of coming to see me. Not today, obviously, but generally.'

'Oh. That's what you mean.'

'Yes.'

They regarded each other for a while. Then Cormac took a deep breath. 'Healing is a complicated issue, you know. Maybe there are ways of getting a person to recover that you don't understand? There are healers who can trigger the body's healing powers by simple methods handed down through the generations. If you read Irish ancient history and folklore, you will find plenty of examples of healers who have cured what was thought to be incurable.'

'And you're one of them?' Kate enquired.

Cormac looked back at her with an expression that made her feel very strange. 'I might be. Some of my ancestors were, in any case. My lineage goes back to before the fifteenth century, when the liaigs were revered and respected.'

'Liaigs?' Kate asked.

'A liaig was a herbalist and physician and had a high legal status in society in those days,' Cormac explained. 'They were granted lands by the Celtic chieftains they had treated.'

'Really?' Kate asked, forgetting her anger. 'I've never heard of them.'

'I have a book about that subject,' Cormac said. 'If you're interested. Tells the whole story about healing in the old days. Written by a professor of Celtic studies.'

'Sounds interesting.'

'I'll lend it to you if you want.'

'Thank you.'

'It might help you understand the people around here.'

Kate knew what he meant and she was seriously intrigued. But she was determined not to let him know. 'I don't think they're that hard to understand.'

Cormac's eyes were serious. 'You might be a trained doctor but you have a lot to learn, Kate.'

'From you?' Kate asked with just a hint of irony.

'Not necessarily,' Cormac replied. 'Just by being a bit more open-minded. Not so stuck in your groove.'

'My groove?'

He nodded. 'Yeah. That groove of being the hotshot Dublin doctor who knows everything about the latest research and treatments.'

'What do you mean?' she asked angrily.

'Don't be so clinical, is all I'm saying.'

'Clinical?' His words suddenly made her furious. 'Who's jumping to conclusions now?' she asked. 'You seem to assume a lot about me without actually knowing what I'm like as a doctor.' She turned away from him. 'I see that nothing I've said has made the slightest impression on you.'

'Not really, no,' he shot back. 'Simply because you got it all wrong. But I'm willing to forgive you for that as you don't know any better.'

'How very noble of you,' Kate snapped. 'You know, I thought I would come here to suggest that we might work together, that we might…' She stopped. 'But I can see that it would be impossible. You will always stick to your own ideas and not even listen to mine. You think you know better than me, don't you?'

'I might consider what you just said.' Cormac's eyes were suddenly amused. 'And I'm also going to lend you that book. I know you'll find it very interesting. I'll drop it off later this evening.'

'I suppose I can't stop you,' Kate said, moving towards the door. 'I'm leaving now.'

'So you are. Goodnight to you, Kate. See you later, then. Have a nice evening.'

'I certainly will.' Kate went to the door and opened it.

'Bye for now.' Cormac's voice echoed eerily down the length of the greenhouse.

'Goodbye,' Kate replied. She banged the door shut and stepped out into the cold air.

Despite her fury, she felt a frisson of excitement as she went over their heated argument. *What was that?* she wondered. *That little spark I felt as we argued? No, stop it*, she told herself sternly. *Don't imagine things that aren't there.* She hadn't got anywhere with him. Nothing could persuade him that a trained doctor was the only person who should be allowed to treat illnesses. He wouldn't even admit patients were seeking him out. Like a solid piece of rock hewn out of the mountains, he stood firm against reason.

He was impossible to break, and Kate couldn't stop thinking about the fire in his eyes. They were at opposite ends of the spectrum of healing and medicine, but what he had said to her about the healers of ancient times had sparked her interest. Maybe he was right about that, at least. She couldn't help but look forward to reading the book he mentioned, but she would never let him know that. Something he said had made her want to go back in time and learn some of that ancient craft, the sorts of things that her own ancestors might have known. Perhaps it might help her.

And then there was something else about him that made her heart beat faster. The way he had looked at her just before she left. She should hate him for what he represented. But hate was far from her mind as she walked away.

# Chapter Eleven

The wind howled around the mountainside and whipped at Kate's jacket, tearing at her woolly hat and bringing tears to her eyes. The muscles in her legs ached and her heart beat like a hammer in her chest. She feared that if she didn't stop walking soon, she'd definitively have a heart attack. Then, mercifully, the group of people above her stopped to drink from their water bottles and she managed to catch up, taking her bottle out of her backpack and drinking the cold water as if her life depended on it, which, she thought, it probably did. She wondered if it had been a good idea to agree to come with Mick and his friends on this tough hike. But it had been such a glorious morning she couldn't resist the challenge.

'You okay?' Mick asked her.

'I'm fine,' she gasped, trying to meet his grin with a smile. But it probably looked more like a grimace.

'We're nearly there,' he said and put a reassuring hand on her shoulder. 'It's been a tough climb, but so worth it, don't you think?'

She looked at the sweeping views of the snow-capped mountains and the blue ocean below, at the coastline and the islands, and nodded. 'Oh yes. It's stunning up here.'

'You've done very well,' Mick said approvingly. 'It's hard going at the best of times. But if you're not super-fit, then it's a bit harder.'

'I'm really not that fit,' Kate confessed. 'I haven't been on a hike for months. But I'll start doing a bit more from now on. Maybe I shouldn't have agreed to join you, but it sounded so tempting.'

'You're very brave,' Mick said. 'Hope you're feeling okay.'

'Grand but exhausted,' Kate assured him, cheered by his words.

'Only a few hundred metres and we'll be at the top,' Mick said, smiling.

'Can't wait.' Kate put her water bottle back into her rucksack. 'I never thought I'd do Carrauntoohill.'

'But now you have. I'll take a photo of you when we're there so you can show your sister. I bet she's not doing much hiking in Manhattan.'

'She's not there right now, she's in the Amazon jungle,' Kate said glumly, thinking she hadn't heard from Tara for over two weeks. She'd been at the start of the journey then, all gung-ho and excited, sending selfies of her in a canoe and a couple of other ones of the wildlife, including a scary-looking crocodile which had sent shivers up Kate's spine.

'Oh?' Mick said, sounding impressed. 'Some kind of photo assignment?'

'Yes. A feature for *National Geographic*. She's there with her boss and a whole crew. I don't even want to think about what dangers she might be facing.'

'I'm sure she'll be fine,' Mick soothed. 'Didn't you say she's your twin? In that case I wouldn't worry. She must have the same spirit as you, and the same guts and determination. Can't imagine she'd be in much danger if she's travelling in a group, anyway.'

'I suppose,' Kate said, feeling only slightly reassured. 'Hey, why don't we do a selfie together?' she suggested. 'Tara is one of your biggest fans, you know.'

'Really? In that case, we'll do a little video, if you like. Just to say hi and good luck in the jungle,' Mick replied. He held out his hand. 'Okay, here we go. Last climb and then we'll be up there. The views are even better than here.'

The rest of the climb was easier than Kate had feared. Fired up by the promise of something spectacular, she followed Mick up the rest of the steep slope, feeling happy and carefree and finally enjoying this amazing day.

It was early December, and she had been in Sandy Cove a whole month now, during which life had finally settled down into quite a pleasant routine. Some people still avoided coming to Kate for medical help, but on the whole, the practice was busy and there was a good atmosphere of working together.

Pat seemed happy with her and the fact that he could now take a break whenever he needed, and Bridget was a true star, keeping everything together and making sure the practice was running like clockwork. After the Mrs O'Dea debacle, she had started making a list of the patients of the day, adding little comments beside each name, so Kate would know what to expect and how to treat them. It was a huge help, especially as she now had Tom, the pharmacist, on her side, who dispensed vitamins pills and food supplements to the patients who demanded antibiotics when none were needed or should even be taken. Kate would then recommend they take an 'immune booster', which seemed to placate the patients looking for some kind of medicine.

'I've put capsules of omega 3 and multivitamins in little bottles I get for dispensing generic drugs,' Tom said. 'And then I print a label with their names and how much they should take and stick that on. Looks very medical and serious. Of course I tell them what's in it and that it's only food supplements, but as you recommended it, they're happy.'

'Brilliant,' Kate said, feeling like giving him a hug. 'You're a genius, Tom.'

Tom grinned. 'Ah sure, we have to keep their paws off the antibiotics. You can tell them about the dangers of taking antibiotics against viruses till the cows come home and they still won't listen. Humouring them like this works better.'

'A good solution, I think,' Kate said.

Tom's scheme was perfect and nobody seemed to guess that they were being manipulated in the name of medical security. This way, there were no more complaints and the patients were happy.

Bridget and her husband John, a schoolteacher in his late fifties, had moved in two weeks ago, and the house felt a lot more like home as a result. Mick had also returned and seamlessly melted into the group, adding a little extra excitement to Kate's daily life.

She hadn't spoken to Cormac since their clash in the greenhouse, only bumped into him now and then in the village and at the Wellness Centre when she went there for her yoga class. He was polite but seemed a little distant and had not stopped to talk. The book he had promised to lend her had not materialised, but Kate had decided to try to find it online when she had a moment to look.

What he had said about the subject had piqued her interest and now she really wanted to find out more.

And then, this morning, just as the church bells rang for Sunday mass, Bridget had handed Kate a thick book, telling her Cormac had delivered it on his way to church, saying it was for Kate. She'd left it on her bed and she couldn't wait to read it. There was something about the ancient healing skills that resonated with her. Cormac said it might help her understand people in this area, but she knew that it would also teach her a lot about him. Despite their clashes, she was drawn to him in an odd way, and whenever they met, she felt vibes she couldn't explain.

Mick had stopped above her. 'Just a few more steps and then you'll be up here and you'll see the best view in Ireland,' he shouted against the sound of the wind. 'Especially on a frosty day like today.'

Kate climbed slowly to join him and finally stood there, at the top, beside a giant steel cross, where the others were taking photos and slapping each other on the back. They shouted their congratulations, barely audible as the wind roared around them. The cold air brought tears to Kate's eyes and she wiped them away so she could see the view clearly. She blinked and gasped as her vision cleared. The view from the top was truly amazing. The mountain overlooked three U-shaped valleys, each with a lake, their blue waters glinting in the early winter sunshine. The frost had kissed the tips of the heather that grew down the slopes, making them look like they were covered in a million tiny stars.

'That's Com Cailli,' Mick said in her ear, pointing to the east. 'Otherwise known as Hag's Glen. Then you have Coomlaughra, or "hollow of the rushes", and to the south is Curraghmore, "the great marsh".'

Kate nodded, rendered speechless by the cold, crisp air, the immense blue sky and the landscape below. 'Thank you,' she said to Mick. 'For bringing me up here. It was hard, but so worth it. I can't find the right words to describe it. It's… it's majestic.'

'I know,' Mick said, and put his arm around her in a friendly hug. 'I felt the same the first time I came here. It's breathtaking.'

'So immensely beautiful,' Kate murmured.

'Exactly.' Mick took out his phone and backed away. 'How about that video, then? You look so cute in your blue hat and your cheeks so red. Say hi to Tara.'

'Hi, Tara,' Kate shouted. 'I'm at the top of the highest mountain in Ireland, how about that?'

Mick laughed. Then he moved closer, put his arm around Kate again and held the phone aloft. 'Hi from me as well,' he shouted. 'Your sister was very brave to come up here to Carrauntoohill and climb up with some very experienced hikers.'

'And now we have to get down, which might be even trickier,' Kate added. She blew a kiss at the phone. 'Lots of love from me.'

'And me,' Mick said and turned off the phone. 'Phew. That was a bit of an effort in this wind. I hope the sound worked. We'll check it when we get down.'

'She'll love it,' Kate said, thinking it wouldn't compete with crocodiles and snakes in the Amazon jungle, but at least she could show Tara she was doing something exciting.

The climb down was less exhausting but quite hairy at times as they descended the steep slopes and gullies. But they arrived down in one piece just as dusk was falling. Stiff and sore, her legs like jelly, Kate fell asleep in Mick's car as he drove them home and only woke up as he pulled up outside the front gate.

'Here we are,' he said. 'Home safe and sound. A glass of wine and some of Bridget's food seems lovely right now.'

'Oh yes,' Kate said, sitting up and rubbing her eyes. 'Sorry for conking out like that. But I was exhausted.'

He turned to her and smiled. 'Of course you were. Not that you weren't great company, but I understand. It was a very hard day for you.'

'I'm glad I did it,' Kate replied, stretching her arms over her head. 'I think I'll have a bath before dinner, though. I'm as stiff as a board.'

'Good idea.' He put his hand on her arm. 'Before you go in, I'd just like to say thank you… for keeping an eye on Dad. It feels reassuring that you're here and that you have eased his burden of the practice. But I also know that you help out in other ways and that you make sure he gets plenty of rest. And,' he added, 'I know that you go with him on his house calls every Saturday, even though you don't have to. I really appreciate that you go with him on these mad drives up the hills. He's not as strong as he pretends. And if something should happen to him…' Mick stopped. 'Well, you know.'

'Of course I know,' Kate said gently. 'But I like going with him. It's great experience for me. I've learned so much already. Not about medicine, but about people.' She looked at him and wondered if he knew that she wasn't doing it for him, or for Pat, but for herself. She had become so fond of Pat and she knew he felt the same about her. It was a little like the father–daughter relationship she had lost. Meeting Pat was like finding her father again. 'We get on so well,' she said, trying to play down the emotions that welled up inside.

'That's great.' Mick opened the door. 'Let's go inside before we both fall asleep,' he continued in a cheerier voice. 'I don't think Bridget and John would appreciate having to carry us in.'

Kate laughed and got out of the car. As they walked to the front door, she looked up at the old house, the ivy-covered walls and the lights in the windows. It was such a welcoming house, and each time she stepped inside, she felt as if the house put its arms around her. *Home is where the heart is*, she thought, *even if it has been broken*. But this house was only a temporary home for her. Would she ever find one of her own?

After an enjoyable dinner in the kitchen with everyone, including Pat, who had just arrived from Killarney, Kate went to bed early in order to read Cormac's book. It was an old leather-bound volume translated from Irish with the title *Irish Herbalists in the Early Middle Ages*. It smelled faintly musty, just the kind of book she might have found in her father's library.

She opened the book, intending to skim through the chapters and just concentrate on the most important parts, but soon found herself absorbed in the history of ancient Celtic medicine. It was truly fascinating, and as Kate read on, she was amazed to learn that herbs growing in Irish bogs, fields and meadows were unique to the west of Ireland and that the herbalists of the day, called 'liaigs' as Cormac had said, were granted lands by the Irish chieftains in order to keep these plants protected. She also learned that these herbal physicians were trained in highly regulated medical schools, run by generations of physician families. They made sure that medical knowledge from all over Europe was studied and applied, and in this way a kind of sophisticated medical practice was used all over Ireland.

*How amazing*, Kate thought, resting the book on her chest. *Maybe Cormac's ancestors were such herbal physicians.* That would explain a lot.

She read on and learned that the 'liaigs' had a high social status in the Middle Ages, being one of the Gaelic learned orders. And the lands that had been granted to them always had herb gardens, or 'luibh gort', which had to supply the locals with medicinal remedies. They also had a book with remedies that was passed on to the next generation. That was truly fascinating. Kate had never read about this part of Irish history – her Irish lessons had been mainly about learning the language and a bit about Irish folklore, not about the ancient art of healing or anything, in fact, about life in ancient times. Incredible.

She closed the book and stared into space, still mesmerised by what she had read. It made her feel differently about Cormac's attitude to healing. It also told her that these ancient healers were not quacks or snake oil merchants, but learned men who studied anatomy and travelled far and wide to find new cures, some of which were still used in modern medicine.

*It's all connected*, she thought. *And we should come to an agreement – talk about how we can work together.*

But Kate already knew it would be an uphill struggle to get Cormac to listen. He was too stubborn, too proud and set in his ways. He couldn't even be honest with her. And then... There was this *feeling* when they were together. What was it that made her feel so strange? He was stubborn and so mysterious, as if he had come here from some other world. Maybe a throwback to his ancestors in medieval Ireland. In those days, the healers were a kind of nobility, and Cormac had an aristocratic air about him. It was like a fairy tale, and as Kate fell asleep, she dreamed of those ancient times and men and women with healing powers, one of them looking faintly like Cormac in medieval garb.

# Chapter Twelve

Having stayed awake until the early hours reading the book about ancient healing, Kate arrived at yoga bleary-eyed. She saw Cormac coming in through the back door and went to meet him, holding out the book.

'Hi,' she said, feeling a little shy, as she remembered how he had featured in her dreams the night before. 'Thanks for the book. I read it all in one go. It was so amazing.'

He took the book, smiling at her. 'You read it all? You must have stayed up all night.'

Kate laughed. 'Nearly. But I just couldn't stop. It was all the stories that fascinated me, and the different remedies mentioned at the end. Unbelievable.'

'I hope it opened your mind a little. About natural remedies, I mean.'

'Yes, it did. It made me feel that…' Kate stopped. 'I was going to talk to you about how reading that book gave me an idea about us. But this is not a good time for such a discussion. I'll be late for my class, and then I have to go back for afternoon surgery. Could we meet for tea or coffee later today? Around five?'

'I promised to look in on my aunt this evening. How about tomorrow morning?' Cormac suggested. 'I'll be in the greenhouse.'

'Great,' Kate replied. 'I'm going for a run on the beach anyway, so I could swing by here on the way back. Around ten or so?'

Cormac nodded. 'That's fine. See you then, Kate. Enjoy yoga.'

'Thanks, I will. I need it after yesterday. I foolishly agreed to climb Carrauntoohill with Mick and his gang of hikers. And now I'm so stiff and sore I can hardly walk. But I made it to the top,' she added proudly.

'That was brave,' Cormac said, looking impressed. 'Yoga should help loosen you up.'

'I hope so.' Kate walked to the door to the studio. 'See you tomorrow, Cormac.' He cheerfully waved and disappeared, the door swinging shut behind him.

Kate went into the yoga studio and relaxed on her mat, looking forward to her meeting with Cormac and a long talk about what she had read in that old book and how it was connected to modern medicine – and him. She wondered fleetingly what she'd wear, but then stopped herself. How silly to think like that. They were only meeting to discuss the book, it wasn't a date.

Sitting cross-legged on her yoga mat, Kate smiled at the women who trickled into the studio. It was a haven of peace and tranquillity with its white walls, large windows overlooking the ocean and lavender-scented candles in front of the little bronze buddha statue on a shelf against the opposite wall. Kate had initially thought yoga was merely a series of stretches that might be good for stiff muscles, but once she started she found out how wrong she was. The twice-weekly yoga classes gave her much more than that. It was physically challenging but so soothing for the soul, she discovered.

As the class progressed, she found her mind drifting, and all the stressful thoughts that had whirled around floated away and disappeared. Even her problems with Cormac and her feelings for him seemed far away, and as she concentrated on her breathing and posture, the niggling thoughts and frustrations didn't seem so hard to face any more. At the end of the class, she closed her eyes and lay in the final corpse pose, her whole body soft and relaxed. The only thing coming into her mind was the beautiful Wild Rose Bay she had glimpsed during her walks, and the tower standing above it for so many centuries. That was a place she longed to go and discover. While the near-hypnotic sounds of the Eastern music wafted through the room and she breathed in the light scent of lavender, she made a promise to herself to go there, to find out more about her father's roots which, after all, was part of her heritage. Hers and Tara's.

It rained heavily all night, but as Kate pulled back the curtains in the morning, she saw it had stopped and the sun rising above the mountains in the east cast a rosy glow on the garden below. Raindrops glimmered on the grass and shrubs and as she opened the window, she breathed in the fresh, cold air and felt a surge of energy. She pulled on a pair of leggings, a cotton T-shirt and a thin fleece, pulled her fingers through her short hair and padded downstairs to the kitchen, where she found Mick making himself a mug of tea.

He turned as she entered. 'Morning, Kate. You're up early.'

She checked the time on the clock over the cupboard. 'It's just past eight. Not that early, really.'

'But you're going for a run?'

She nodded. 'Yup. I'm trying to get fit so I'll survive the next killer hike.'

'Good idea,' he said. 'But hey, don't overdo it. You wouldn't want to burn yourself out.'

'No danger of that,' Kate reassured him. 'I'm the hyperactive type. I love running and here, in this beautiful landscape, it's not even a chore.'

'I know what you mean,' Mick replied. 'Do you want some tea?'

'Thanks. I'd love some,' she replied, opening the breadbin. 'I'll have a slice of Bridget's soda bread with that.'

He held out his hand. 'I'll pop it in the toaster for you. Sit down and I'll get it all ready.'

'Thanks.' Kate sat down and was soon sipping tea and eating a slice of toasted soda bread covered in honey, while she wondered why Mick was being so nice to her. Was he naturally this gentlemanly, or was it because he wanted to ask her more questions about being a doctor? Whatever it was, she decided to sit back and enjoy it.

'So,' Mick said, folding his arms, looking at Kate. 'What about this healer lad, then? Cormac, I mean. Have you had a chance to talk to him at all?'

Kate sipped her tea and took a bite of toast. 'Not really. But I'll be meeting him after my run. He gave me this fascinating book about healers in Ireland in the Middle Ages. I never knew these people even existed.'

Mick looked thoughtful. 'Oh yes, my teacher in primary school used to talk about that a lot. These healers were revered around here in ancient times. In fact, now that I think about it, he said that there is a small bog near O'Rourke's castle where some of the plants used to grow. I think that land belonged to the family of herbalists. Maybe they were even O'Rourkes?'

'You think they might have been?' Kate asked, forgetting to eat.

'It's possible. But your man, Cormac, probably knows more. He could even be taking plants from there himself for his remedies. You should ask him.'

'I will,' Kate said.

'It would be interesting to explore the difference between modern medicine and the natural approach,' Mick continued. 'And to what extent a guy like Cormac actually believes in his own powers and how much he pretends.'

'I don't think he pretends,' Kate said hotly. 'He seems very honest and genuine. I think the more important question would be if medicine is something one would choose as a great career, or a path you're born to follow?'

'That's a very tricky question,' Mick said after a moment's silence. 'I think we touched on this before. No voice from above, you said yourself.'

'I did,' Kate agreed. 'But still, now that I think about it, I feel there is something in my heritage that pointed me in this direction. Maybe just my interest in medicine. Don't forget that both my father and grandfather were also doctors.'

'There could be something in your genes all right,' Mick said, looking interested. 'And it could come from the O'Rourkes around here in ancient times.'

'What about you?' Kate asked as she finished her tea. 'Your father is a doctor. I think he's one of those people who have the calling. But you don't.'

'No. Never did. Must be that I don't have the genes. I have no idea where the acting thing comes from. Is that in my genes? There are no actors in my family as far as I know.'

'You just wanted attention,' Kate teased.

Mick smirked, not rising to the bait. 'Yeah, I suppose it's the narcissistic streak I was born with.'

'You do modesty so well,' Kate said, enjoying their repartee. 'Did you have to practise that a lot in your acting classes?'

'No, it came naturally,' Mick retorted. 'Nice try, my dear. But you'll be waiting a long time for me to get annoyed.' He shot her a cheeky smile. 'In fact, I doubt you'll ever be able to annoy me. Water off a duck's back, ya' know.'

Kate laughed. 'I should have known better. You're as tough as nails.'

'Tough on the outside but incredibly soft on the inside, that's me. And you…' He paused.

'Yes?'

He looked at her intently for a second. 'You're hard to figure out. You're a bit of a softie but there is a hard core of determination and strength inside. Good combo, I think.'

'I take that as a compliment, so thank you.'

'It was, and you're welcome.' He glanced at the clock on the wall. 'Is it that time already? I'd better get some writing done.'

Kate got up and put her mug on the draining board. 'And it's time for my run. Thanks for the tea and the chat. See you later, Mick.'

'Have a good run,' Mick replied. 'Say hi to Cormac. And be careful.'

Kate stopped on her way to the door. 'Careful? Why?'

Mick winked. 'He might have powers you won't be able to resist.'

Kate felt her face turn pink. 'Oh, please. Enough of the pop psychology. You're making things up just for fun.'

Mick grinned. 'Ah, but there might be a grain of truth in it.'

'Bye, Mick,' Kate said and closed the door behind her.

Once outside, she went through the front gate and broke into a slow run down the street, jumping up on the bank and down onto the flat sand. Then she put her earphones in, turned on her playlist and settled into a steady rhythm along the deserted beach.

It was truly a glorious day now that the clouds had scattered and the sun shone from a nearly clear blue sky. The blue-green water of the ocean, the dark green slopes of the mountainsides and the grey and black rocks all blended into a beautiful mix of sights and colours. Kate ran for another half hour, until she approached the Wellness Centre and the greenhouse outside before which she saw a figure sitting on a rough wooden bench. It was Cormac, she saw as she approached. He waved and smiled. She slowed her speed, wiped her forehead with her sleeve and stopped, panting and smiling as she reached him.

'Hi,' she said, trying to catch her breath. 'Lovely day, isn't it?'

'A grand day,' he replied, squinting against the bright light as he looked up at the sky. 'There's even a bit of heat in that sun today.' He looked at her approvingly, his teeth white against his freckly face. 'You're glowing.'

'Sweaty, you mean?' she asked, wiping her face again.

'That's healthy though,' he replied. He got up and took a towel from the back of the bench. 'Here. I thought you might need it.'

She took the towel and gave her face a good rub. 'Thanks. Should have thought of bringing one.' She took the bottle of water from her belt and drank deeply.

'You're fit,' he remarked, eyeing her body. 'Not a pick on you.'

'Not fit but skinny,' she said with a laugh.

'I wouldn't say that.'

'Oh, thank you. That's very kind,' she said, not sure what he really meant. The way he looked at her made her feel a little self-conscious all of a sudden.

He sat down again. 'Sit beside me,' he said.

She joined him on the bench, draping the towel around her neck. 'I'm trying to get fitter so I can survive the hikes with Mick.' She turned to him. 'What do you do to keep fit?'

'Pilates here at the centre,' he said. 'A workout in the gym a few times a week, and then I walk a lot. I don't have a car and that forces me to move.'

'Where do you live?' Kate asked.

He pointed up the hill. 'Up there, in that cottage on the edge of the cliffs.'

Kate looked in the direction he was pointing and noticed a white cottage with a thatched roof overlooking the small beach on the other side. 'Lovely place to live.'

'It is. I rent it from a nice woman called Cordelia. She and her husband used to live there but it became too small when they had two children close together. They live in a bigger house on the Ballinskelligs side.'

'Oh.' Kate kept looking at the cottage and at the big pink house further on. 'That's Willow House, isn't it? I heard someone talk about it.'

'It is,' he replied. 'It's owned by a family called the McKennas. Has been there a long time.'

'So I see.' She turned her gaze back to him. 'I suppose you live close enough to walk to work, but how do you manage to get around without a car?'

'I have a bike if I need to get somewhere far. Like over to Dingle to see my family. And my aunt Clodagh does the shopping for me if I need to stock up. She has a car that she drives to the shops in Waterville once a week. It's an old Golf and she loves it like her own child.'

Kate laughed. 'She's a gas woman. But very nice,' she added.

'She is. She liked you, too.'

They were silent for a while, looking out over the ocean. Then Cormac cleared his throat. 'So,' he started. 'The book. Tell me. What did you take away from it?'

'Lots of things,' Kate replied. 'I suppose mainly that the healers of ancient times knew so much about the human body. And they knew everything about herbs and plants and their healing qualities. And that they studied it for a long time and went away to Europe to learn from other healers. It was quite humbling to read about them, really.'

'It makes nonsense out of the notion that modern doctors invented healing.'

Kate looked at him and nodded, at the same time appreciating his thick black eyelashes and the deep green of his eyes that looked at her so earnestly. 'I suppose it does if I had such notions, which I don't.'

'Oh, I meant generally.'

'Of course.'

'Did reading it make you think differently about me?' he asked.

Kate looked away from his probing eyes. 'Yes, it did,' she said. 'I realised that studying medicine isn't everything, and that there is a lot more to it than just science you learn from books. I think you have a great understanding of people, and that must be your strength. I, on the other hand, rely a lot on my training and I need to work on my people skills. Your healing and mine could be combined instead of clashing with each other. If we worked together and shared our knowledge, we could give people who come to us even better care.'

'How do you mean?' Cormac asked, looking doubtful. 'How can we work together when we have such opposing ideas?'

'Well,' Kate started, 'I see your way as mainly preventive because it can boost people's general health with food supplements and herbal infusions. And I could recommend some of it to my patients once we agreed on how to do it.'

'I'm not sure that would work,' Cormac cut in. 'I think it could cause a lot of conflict and confuse people.'

'You don't want to share your ideas with me, then?'

He looked at her for a moment. 'Not in the way you describe. I was hoping that reading that book would open your eyes to healing in a different way.'

'Your way, you mean?' She looked back at him. 'It did, but we could learn from each other, and to do so I would need to work out what actually does work for certain ills and what's merely superstition.'

'You don't trust me?'

Kate sighed. 'It's not about trust, it's about facts and science.'

'And about a gift for healing,' he cut in.

'Your gift, you mean?' she asked. 'I'm beginning to believe it's real in a way. I know you're the seventh son of a seventh son, but were there healers among your ancestors?'

'There were,' he replied. 'A long time ago. I think it must be in my blood, apart from the peculiarity of my place in the family. I have always wanted to learn about natural remedies, about things that come from the earth that can help with certain health problems and even cure them.'

'Why didn't you study medicine?' Kate asked.

Cormac shrugged. 'I never really wanted to learn like that. But my family wouldn't have had the means to pay for such training. I did a chemistry course at Cork University but dropped out after two years. I felt I had learned enough. In any case, my knowledge doesn't come from books. It comes from learning handed down through the generations, from living here and from knowing about nature, the bogs, the fields and what grows there. And you know what? It's in your blood, too.'

'How do you mean?'

'Some of the O'Rourkes were physicians and herbalists in the fourteenth century. The land just below O'Rourke's castle was once a herb garden that belonged to them.'

Kate felt her pulse quicken. 'Really? I had no idea. That's fascinating.'

'But of course to you that's just like an old fairy tale, isn't it?' Cormac said with a hint of scorn in his voice. His eyes suddenly flashed. 'I know natural healing seems like crazy witchcraft to most doctors.'

Kate eased herself away from him. He seemed a little defensive about his lack of qualifications. 'I don't think that at all,' she said hotly. 'Especially now that I've read that amazing book. Please don't jump to conclusions, Cormac. Didn't you hear what I just said? My take on this is that modern, conventional medicines are often based on old remedies, but they have been scientifically tried and tested. That makes them safe and maybe also more effective. But I have huge respect for natural remedies and what they can achieve, and even more so now. It's just that you have to be careful with the things that haven't been tested. You can't claim to cure things and stop serious illnesses from being treated correctly by trained doctors.'

'I never claim anything,' Cormac interjected.

'Maybe *you* don't,' Kate replied. 'But you know very well that people in town are coming to you more and more, believing you have some kind of magic.' She paused. 'Can I ask you something?'

'Of course,' Cormac said, a guarded look in his eyes.

'If you, or someone close to you, was seriously ill, would you go to a doctor?'

'I would,' he said without hesitation. 'If it were a matter of life or death. I do know my limitations. I might be able to help someone with health problems better than a doctor, but I'm not in any way qualified to save a life or cure something truly serious. And I would never try. That would be irresponsible.'

'That's a relief.' Kate smiled at him. 'And I do believe you're helping people. Like with the ointment you use.'

'The new one? I've only just begun to use it.'

'It seems to work very well, especially to reduce scarring.'

'Could be.'

'Wouldn't it be great if it could be developed and sold in pharmacies?' Kate said, feeling excited at the thought of a new cream that might erase scars. That was often a problem after wounds had healed but left scars that could be disfiguring.

'I think you're being a little too optimistic. I haven't used it on that many people yet, so I have no idea if it works on everyone.'

'What's in it?' Kate asked, dying to know exactly what the active ingredient in this ointment was.

'Oh, this and that. Not something I'd like to talk about just now. It's nothing strange, I can assure you. Just a combination of things.'

'What things?' Kate asked, a feeling of frustration creeping in.

'That's my business,' he said curtly.

Kate bristled. 'You're not going to tell me?'

'No.'

'But maybe you should. And maybe it would be a good idea to have it analysed and patented. If it does what I think it does, wouldn't it be a good idea to try it generally? To have it available to more people?'

'I'm not so sure it would,' Cormac replied, looking stubborn.

'Isn't that a little negative? You could…' She stopped, knowing it was useless to try to persuade him. His eyes had a hard, unwavering expression that told her he wasn't going to budge. They were so different in many ways. Kate with her academic background had a confidence that Cormac lacked. He relied on his deep knowledge of plants and roots, and also an amazing understanding of people. The way he worked was hard to grasp but now that she had read about the old ways, she had begun to see where he was coming from. She had wanted to make him see how the two could be combined, but his pride stood in the way. It would take a long time to break down his defences, some of which could be due to a chip on his shoulder about his lack of qualifications. She didn't think any less of him because of that, but he probably thought she did. 'I don't want to get into an argument with you, Cormac,' she said, her voice softening.

'Neither do I.' He looked at her and smiled. 'I like you, Kate. I know we're in disagreement and I know we'll have arguments about all of this, but I feel that maybe you're beginning to see my point of view.'

'I'm not sure,' Kate said, feeling confused. 'There's so much I still don't understand. But this place, this whole area, is so different to what I'm used to. There's a spiritual feeling here, a connection to nature that I didn't have growing up in Dublin. I need to learn more.'

'You do,' Cormac agreed. 'You need to become more integrated, more like a local. Get in touch with your roots.'

'How do I do that?'

He shrugged. 'It's up to you. I can't tell you how to live.'

'I suppose.' Kate got up and handed the towel to Cormac. 'I have to go. Thanks for the towel and the chat.'

He took the towel. 'It was a pleasure. I like your hair, by the way. It suits you.'

'Thanks.' She stood in front of him, hesitating. There was so much more she wanted to say to him, so much she wanted to ask. But she felt he was clamming up and wouldn't be in the mood to answer. His defences were up, and there was suddenly something about him that was strangely forbidding. It made her shiver. Sitting there, on the edge of the beach on that bench made out of driftwood, the wind ruffling his dark red hair, he looked as much a part of the

Irish landscape as if he had grown out of the soil. There was an eerie beauty about him, and something beguiling and deeply moving in his voice. Or was that idea simply because of the strong attraction she felt whenever they met? She didn't know, and it made her feel confused and nearly dizzy. She shook herself slightly and moved away. 'Got to go. Bye for now, Cormac.'

His eyes softened as he looked back at her with a little smile hovering on his lips. 'See you very soon,' he said, as if he knew exactly when and where they would meet next time.

She waved and broke into a run, heading back the way she had come, the wind cooling her hot cheeks. The conversation had cheered her up despite their argument. At least he had admitted he'd tell his clients to see a doctor if they were seriously ill. That was something positive she could tell Pat.

And she felt like she had got to know him a little better. He was more self-taught than she had realised. As he talked, she had been moved by the passion in his eyes, and it had dawned on her how much natural healing and ancient remedies meant to him. It would be difficult to get him to agree to cooperate with her and Pat and make him trust them. His own heritage was in his bones, and it would take a lot of persuading to get him to see her point of view. But she was more than willing to try.

He hadn't asked much about her, though. Did that mean he wasn't interested and saw her as an intruder? He had said she needed to become more integrated, be more like a local. As she ran, she realised it was true. She was an O'Rourke, after all, and her ances-tors had been important here once. It was the country her father had longed to return to and often spoken about. He had told Kate and Tara stories about the village and how he would one day come back and find the place his family had left over a hundred years ago. She slowed to a walk as she left the beach, her mind drifting to those ancient healers. Were they connected to her family? And did that mean certain memories had been passed on to her? One thing was for certain, she wasn't getting Cormac's help and would need to focus if she was going to convince everyone to stop cancelling their appointments.

All these thoughts troubled her as she arrived back at the house, and she felt more confused than ever. But one thing was clear: she couldn't keep the image of those luminous green eyes out of her mind.

# Chapter Thirteen

'Hey, bookworm, how about a night off?' Mick asked, sticking his head through the door of the living room on Friday evening the following week. 'It's nearly Christmas and we've done nothing but work for over a week. Let's go and have dinner at The Wild Atlantic Gourmet and then go to the pub afterwards. They're doing a traditional evening tonight. Music, dancing, loads of craic.'

Kate put the book about heart disease on her lap and looked at Mick, feeling slightly dazed. She had picked up the book at random after a hectic day in the surgery, feeling she needed to brush up on the early signs of heart disease. It was a subject that had always fascinated her. 'Craic?' she said. 'I'd forgotten what that was.'

He came in and took the book from her. 'We're young, cute and single, we need to mingle.'

Kate laughed. 'Yeah, you're right. Especially you, who must be used to going to glam events all the time.'

Mick winked. 'I know. I'm suffering from withdrawal symptoms. It's a shocking waste for a good-looking man to stay at home night after night.'

'That sweet modesty again,' she teased. 'You do it so well.' He had been in the house several weeks now, and his cheerful attitude never failed to make her smile.

He patted his hair, glancing into the mirror over the fireplace. 'Modest is my middle name. Ah, come on, Kate, let's go out and have a bit of fun. Drink, dance, flirt, what do you say?'

'Sounds too good to resist. But do you really need me to tag along if you're hoping to find someone to flirt with?'

'You're my security net. If I don't have any luck, I won't look desperate.'

Kate threw a cushion at him. 'Mick O'Dwyer's security net? How can I resist?'

Mick caught the cushion. 'There you go. I knew you'd be flattered.'

Kate laughed and jumped to her feet, suddenly full of energy. Mick's enthusiasm was so contagious, and she found herself looking forward to the evening. They had fallen into an easy, fun relationship, without any undertones, and had become firm friends during the time they had been together in the house. No longer in awe of his celebrity status, she felt perfectly comfortable in his company. Mick introduced a light-hearted atmosphere and made the evenings at dinner fun and interesting. The two of them would discuss everything from politics to music, books, even fashion, and had different views about nearly everything. They argued hotly at times. Mick would tease Kate mercilessly and she would respond in kind. Pat, Bridget and her husband John would watch and laugh as they sparred across the kitchen table.

'You've persuaded me,' Kate told him. 'I'll just go and put on something glamorous and go and tell Bridget we won't be here for dinner. I hope she hasn't started cooking yet.'

'No, she's in their bedroom and John is at a parent-teacher meeting, so dinner will be late. Dad's having a bath. I'll let him know when he comes out.'

'Okay.' Kate checked her watch. 'It's only six thirty. I'll see you in the hall at seven.'

'Perfect. Looking forward to the glam. I might go and put some glitter in my hair.'

'That'd make you look fab,' Kate said and left to go upstairs to get ready. Not that she had anything glamorous in her wardrobe, but she'd do her best to look good. She hadn't had a night out since she left Dublin, and she was looking forward to the evening. She'd meet some more of the locals in the pub and have fun. She ran up the stairs, feeling excited. She had been too stuck in a routine lately, working more hours in order to ease Pat's burden, even taking on the morning practice some days so he could go for walks or just read. This meant several full days a week, which gave her an idea of what it would be like once she was on her own. Pretty exhausting, she found, but it was only for six months anyway.

All this extra work helped turn her mind away from Cormac, who she hadn't seen since their talk on the beach about two weeks earlier. She hadn't even seen him in reception at the Wellness Centre – a new girl had been there to look after things as Cormac had taken some time off, she explained. Kate didn't want to ask where he had gone, and she kept looking around for him at the beach and in the village, but there was no sign.

Once in her room, she opened her wardrobe and scanned the row of clothes. What would be the right thing to wear for an evening out in Sandy Cove? Then she spotted a red cashmere sweater Tara had sent her from New York. 'Just the right shade of red for the Christmas parties,' she had said in a Skype conversation shortly before she left for that mad trip to the Amazon jungle. 'I've bought one for me, too.' *Where is she now?* Kate wondered, feeling a dart of worry. She had sent a brief email a week ago to say she was fine and would be heading back to New York for Christmas, and that was only two weeks away. Two weeks of worry for Kate, but she was determined not to imagine the worst.

She pulled on the red sweater and a pair of black jeans. She put in gold hoop earrings and a touch of mascara and was good to go. Kate looked at herself in the mirror and agreed that Tara had been right. The warm red of the sweater looked gorgeous with her short brown hair, and her eyes sparkled with anticipation of the night ahead. Dinner, music and Irish dancing – what a treat, especially with Mick.

She was about to go to Bridget's room when her phone pinged. She picked it up from the small table by the bed and looked at the caller ID. It was from Tara and it said, *Skype?*

Her heart beating, Kate turned on her laptop, and sitting on the bed, switched on the Skype connection. A flickering image of Tara's face came into view. 'Hi, Kate,' she shouted. 'How's tricks?'

'Tricks? Bloody hell, Tara,' Kate nearly sobbed. 'I haven't heard from you for weeks and all you can say is "how's tricks?" How are you? Where are you? Are you okay?'

The image became sharper and Kate could see that Tara was deeply tanned and, despite her hair hanging in messy strands around her face, she looked fine, if very thin. 'I'm grand, darling,' Tara shouted. 'And I'm on my way home. I'm in this small town I don't even know the name of. This trip has been amazing. I've seen things you wouldn't believe. The wildlife in the Amazon is out of this world. I haven't been able to message you, sorry. And I couldn't post anything on Instagram either. The connections kept breaking, so we gave up. In any case, we can't post much before the article is published because of copyright, so you'll have to wait. We're taking a small plane to Mexico City and then we get on an American Airlines flight to New York. We'll be there tomorrow, I think.'

'Thank God for that!' Kate said with relief.

'Yeah, I'm looking forward to getting back. Camping is all very well for a while but it gets tiring very quickly.' Tara's eyes focused on Kate. 'But what about you? You look – oh my God, your hair. You cut it all off! It looks fab! I must do that too. And you're wearing our sweater. Hot date, is it?'

'Not really. Just going out to dinner with Mick.'

'Are you mad? You don't "just" go out to dinner with Mick O'Dwyer!' Tara exclaimed. 'So… you've been dating him behind my back? Are you two an item now? In love?'

'Nooo,' Kate groaned. 'Just friends. Please don't turn it into the love affair of the century. It's totally not. Absolutely, definitively, and that's final!' Kate almost shouted the last words, in her frustration of trying to explain that she wasn't looking for romance. She was growing very fond of Mick, but it had to be on friendly terms and nothing more. The feelings she had for Cormac were all mixed up with their different takes on healing. It was too confusing to even try to understand.

'Stop shouting,' Tara complained. 'I hear you, even if it's hard to believe.'

'He's a nice guy, though,' Kate said, calming down. 'And we're friends. And now we're going to have dinner and then we'll go to a pub for some trad music and Irish dancing.'

'Oh, that sounds divine.' Tara sounded envious. 'I hope you have fun. You can show off your Irish dancing skills. Remember when we won all those medals when we were kids?'

'That was a long time ago,' Kate said, smiling at the memories.

'It'll all come back to you, I'm sure. The signal is getting wonky again, so we'd better stop. I'll be in touch in a couple of days when we've landed in New York. Then I'll tell you all about the trip. And about Joe. We're…' Then the connection broke and Kate was confronted by a blank screen. She closed her laptop, happy that Tara was okay and that she was on her way back. The 'Joe' she had mentioned had to be her boss, and Kate hoped there weren't complications of the kind Tara usually got herself into. But she'd find out in due course. It was a relief that Tara had finally understood that Mick and Kate were not involved in any way. But the fact that there was someone else occupying Kate's secret thoughts was something she didn't want to reveal to her sister. Or to anyone.

After a delicious dinner at the little restaurant, they walked the short distance to the pub on the main street of the village. They could hear the music echoing down the street, which made Kate quicken her step in time with the lively tune.

'I see you're a fan of Irish dancing,' Mick remarked.

'I used to love it. Tara and I were junior champions when we were nine.'

'You should have joined Riverdance.'

Kate laughed. 'Yeah, that would have been a fun, short career. Those dancers have to retire when they're in their forties. It's a tough life, too.'

'I know. Better to dance just for fun. Looking forward to seeing you stepping it out.'

'I haven't danced for years,' Kate protested. 'I'm sure I'll be hopeless. But I'll give it a go if you promise not to laugh.'

'I swear.'

They walked into the crowded pub where a space by the bar had been cleared for dancing. The band consisted of four musicians playing the banjo, the fiddle, the bodhrán, which looked like a small handheld frame drum, and the tin whistle, and they were excellent. Mick got Kate a glass of lager and a pint for himself, and they stood at the bar, listening to the music while they drank. Then someone jostled Kate's elbow, making her spill some of her beer. Annoyed, she turned to glare at the culprit, and looked straight into Cormac's smiling eyes.

'Kate,' he said, touching her arm. 'I'm really sorry. Did it do much damage to your lovely jumper?' He looked unusually tidy in a denim shirt and beige chinos and his hair was neatly brushed.

He stood so close she could feel his warm breath and see the deep green of his eyes. Confused, Kate stepped away and dabbed at the drops on the front of the red sweater. 'No. All gone. Most of it went on the floor.'

'Should have looked where I was going. Shall I get you another?'

'No thanks, I'll have one later.' She put the nearly empty glass on the counter.

'In that case,' he said, holding out his hand. 'Will you dance with me? It's quite an easy dance if you let me show you the steps.'

She looked at him in surprise. Then she glanced at Mick, but he had started a conversation with someone beside them and didn't seem to notice. She smiled and nodded at Cormac. 'I'll dance with you. But I know the steps already.'

'You do?' He beamed. 'In that case, let's go.'

She took his hand and off they went. Kate was a little unsure at first but once she got into the swing of it she found it all came back to her and she fell into step with Cormac, letting the rhythm carry her away to another place, another time. Dancing with Cormac brought a new dimension to their friendship, and as their hands touched, their shoulders connected and he grabbed her and whirled her around, Kate's pulse quickened and she felt a spark that hadn't been there before. They danced together as if they had practised for months, their feet tapping the floorboards in time with the nearly hypnotic music. There was a connection between them born of the music, and Kate felt as if she was floating, flying with Cormac into some kind of trance. Other couples had joined them, but Kate and Cormac danced in the middle, the rest of the crowd clapping in time with the rhythm. Then the music suddenly ended and they stopped, breathing hard, eyes locked. There were roars and whistles from the onlookers and shouts of 'More!' Kate, her head spinning, smiled but called, 'No more. I'm exhausted.'

Cormac had fixed on her with a strange expression as they went back to the bar. 'You're a surprising woman, Kate O'Rourke. Where did you learn to dance like that?'

'Miss Hannigan's School of Dance in Dublin,' she replied. 'I was junior champion when I was nine. Haven't danced since then, but it seems to have come back to me in a flash.'

'It certainly did,' Cormac said, his eyes full of admiration.

'Like riding a bike,' Mick said. He held out his hand to Cormac. 'Hi, I'm Mick. I don't think we've actually met, even though I've heard so much about you it feels like I know you already.'

Cormac shook his hand. 'Howerya, Mick. I feel the same. Dr Pat and Helen talk about you all the time. Nice to finally meet.'

'Yes,' Mick replied. 'Finally. And hey, there are a lot of things I'd like to talk to you about, but tonight is not the right moment. I'll pop into the wellness place next week, perhaps.'

'Great,' Cormac replied. 'Any time at all.'

'Thanks.' Mick handed Kate a glass of beer. 'Here. Let's not spill this one, eh?'

'I should have bought that,' Cormac protested, still holding Kate's hand after the dance. 'As I made you spill most of the first one.'

'That's okay.' Kate eased her hand out of Cormac's grip. She took the glass from Mick and sipped it. 'Thanks, Mick.'

'Thank you for the dance,' Cormac said politely.

'Thanks for asking me.' Kate looked at him awkwardly, tongue-tied. His sudden appearance had given her a jolt and the incredible dancing had been a further shock to her system. Being this close to him made her heart beat faster and she looked at his mouth and wondered for a second what it would feel like to kiss him. 'You're an amazing dancer,' she said, trying not to show her feelings.

Cormac shrugged. 'Not really. You inspired me. We dance well together.'

'We do… did,' Kate said, stumbling over the words. Why did he suddenly make her feel so strange?

Mick moved at Kate's side and cleared his throat. 'I, uh, see someone over there I want to talk to. You okay for the moment?'

'Of course,' Kate said, feeling it was fine as they were not on a date, just there as friends. The band started again, this time playing a slow ballad. 'You go ahead.' When Mick had walked away, she listened to the lovely music for a while, enjoying the cold beer. She met Cormac's eyes and they looked at each other as the music played on. The moment felt too loaded with emotion for Kate and she stepped sideways, but he took her hand and pulled her closer.

'Would you be free to come for a walk with me on Sunday?' he asked her.

Kate nodded, breathing in the scent of him. 'Yes. Where do you want to walk?'

'I want to show you my favourite place in the whole world,' he said.

'Is it far?'

'Not by distance. But the way there is a bit rough. You have good walking boots, I imagine. And sticks for hiking?'

'Yes, I do,' Kate replied.

'Good. I'll see you on the main beach at ten.' He let go of her hand and disappeared.

'Where did Cormac go?' Mick asked, having reappeared with a pretty blonde woman at his side.

'I don't know,' Kate said. 'I think he left to go home.' She looked at the woman and held out her hand. 'Hi. I'm Kate.'

The woman shook Kate's hand warmly. 'I'm Susie.'

'Susie owns the hairdressing salon,' Mick cut in. 'I thought you two might have met.'

'No,' Kate said. 'It was Gerry who cut my hair.'

'He did a good job,' Susie said, glancing at Kate's hair. 'Great cut. It suits you.'

'Thank you.' Kate finished her beer. The band was taking a break and it was easier to talk. She noticed how Mick looked at Susie and how they both seemed to be enjoying each other's company.

'You know what?' she said. 'I'm tired. I think I'll head home.'

'I'll walk with you,' Mick offered, giving Susie an apologetic glance.

'No, don't be silly,' Kate protested. 'It's five minutes away. I'm perfectly capable of walking back by myself. You stay and have fun.'

'Are you sure?' Mick asked.

'Of course.' Kate nodded. 'Nice to meet you, Susie. I'll pop into the salon for a trim soon.'

'Yes, please do,' Susie replied. 'So great to meet you, Kate. I've heard so much about you.'

'You have?' Kate said, surprised. 'From whom?'

'Mostly people in the village who've been to see you. But also from Cormac. I get my herbal teas from him. He says you're a gifted doctor. But I think he's a little sweet on you, actually. I haven't seen him dance like that with anyone before. There are great vibes between you, aren't there?'

'Oh… uh,' Kate stammered, not knowing how to handle this. Susie seemed nice and not a bit nosy, but that comment felt far too personal coming from someone she had just met.

'I'm sorry,' Susie apologised, looking contrite. 'I didn't mean to pry. Please forget I said that.'

'It's forgotten,' Kate promised. 'I'll be off now. Have a great evening.'

Kate pushed through the throng to the door but Mick caught up with her before she left. 'Thanks, Kate. Very decent of you to leave me with Susie. She's cute, don't you think?'

'Lovely,' Kate agreed, smiling at him. 'I'm glad you found someone to flirt with.' She pulled the door open. 'I wasn't pretending. I'm really very tired.'

'I know. You've had a long day. Goodnight, Kate. See you tomorrow.'

'Night-night, Mick.' Kate waved at him and stepped out into the dark, chilly night. She pulled up the collar of her jacket against the cold wind and set off home. But she hadn't taken more than a few steps when someone called her name behind her. Kate turned around and saw a woman approach. 'Yes?'

'Hi,' the woman panted as she drew nearer. 'I saw you leave. I wanted to catch up with you in the pub but didn't get a chance.' She held out her hand. 'I'm Sally O'Rourke.'

'Oh,' Kate exclaimed and shook the woman's hand. 'You're the owner of the Wellness Centre. How nice to meet you.' She had heard so much about this woman and had been dying to meet her. And she was an O'Rourke, who might know a lot about her family and its history.

'Same here.' Sally paused. 'Are you on your way home? I was going to try to find you in there, but perhaps you're tired of all the noise? Would you like to come back to my place for a glass of wine or a cup of tea? Please say no if you're too tired.'

'No, that's fine. It sounds very nice.' Kate felt revived by the fresh air, and in any case, she wanted to meet Sally. She knew she'd be busy on Saturdays with Pat on his rounds, so tonight would be the perfect opportunity to get to know another Sandy Cove resident.

'Okay, great.' Sally pointed in the opposite direction. 'My house is this way. The one on the hill up there. Not far at all.'

They walked the short distance to the house, while Sally told Kate about herself. 'I grew up in this village,' she said. 'And then I went to France and met my husband and I lived there until a few years ago, when I wanted to come back to my roots. My husband and I split up early in our marriage and then found each other again quite recently. We were both a little mad and too stupid to realise we should have tried to sort out our differences, but there you are. No use crying over what could have been. In any case, we're together again, and he loves living here. Our daughter Jasmine is married to a lovely boy from Dublin and they live and work in Paris but they have a little cottage outside the village that they're doing up and they're here as often as they can be. You'll meet them at Christmas.'

'I'm looking forward to that,' Kate said. They walked up the incline to a white house with a green door and window frames painted the same colour. There were lights on in all the windows and the house looked warm and inviting.

'Here we are,' Sally said and opened the front door to reveal a small hall and a large, bright living room beyond. 'Take off your jacket and hang it over there on the hallstand. Matthieu,' she called,

'I met Kate O'Rourke in the pub and brought her home for a cup of tea. Come and say hello.'

A tall, grey-haired man walked towards Kate as she entered the living room. His brown eyes twinkled as he shook Kate's hand warmly. 'Good evening, Dr Kate,' he said. 'Welcome to our house.' His voice was deep and his French accent charming.

Kate returned his smile. 'Thank you. Lovely to meet you, Matthieu.'

Sally stood on tiptoe and kissed his cheek. 'Hello, mon chéri. The music was lovely. You should come next time.'

He nodded. 'I think I will. But tonight I was too busy with accounts and emails. I run the business side of the Wellness Centre,' he explained to Kate. 'But I also talk to my daughter regularly. She is in charge of the financial consultancy in Paris that I started. Doing it wonderfully, too. But she wanted some advice this evening, so I stayed behind. I'm still doing a few analyses online, so if you'll excuse me…'

'Of course,' Kate said.

'You go ahead,' Sally urged him. 'Kate and I will have a bit of a natter while you work.' She turned to Kate. 'Tea, or wine? Or both?'

'Tea would be lovely,' Kate replied.

'Herbal or real? I have a fabulously relaxing brew Cormac makes up. Very tasty.'

Kate nodded. 'Perfect.'

'Would you bring me in a cup, please,' Matthieu cut in as he walked to a door on the opposite side of the room. 'Goodnight, Kate. Come for dinner sometime.'

'Thanks. I'd love to,' Kate replied, smiling at him.

When her husband had left, Sally tidied her shoulder-length light brown hair with her hands. 'Please, sit down on the sofa and put a log on the fire while I go and make that tea. Won't be a moment.'

Kate did as she was told and once she had put a log on the glowing embers, it flared up and there was soon a blazing fire that warmed her instantly.

'Here we are,' Sally chanted, carrying a tray that she put on the coffee table. 'Tea for two and a good old chat, just the thing for a cold evening like this.'

'Lovely,' Kate said, smiling at her. Sally was so charming, and there was a twinkle in her hazel eyes that made Kate feel at home. This woman's happiness was contagious.

Sally sat down and handed Kate a mug. 'Just smell this. It's divine. Cormac won't say what's in it but it makes me sleep like a princess after drinking it.'

Kate sniffed at the fragrant tea in her mug. It had a light purple colour and smelled like a garden full of flowers in spring. 'Lavender?' she asked. 'And roses, or something.'

'There must be some lavender in there,' Sally agreed, sipping from her mug. 'But the rest… I have no idea. A great mixture anyway.'

'It's lovely,' Kate said, having drunk nearly half of it.

'Yes.' Sally put her mug on the table. 'So how are you enjoying Sandy Cove?'

'I love it.' Kate smiled at Sally. 'It's such a wonderful place, like something from a book. I didn't know a village like this still existed.'

'And Cormac?' Sally asked. 'How are you getting on with him?'

'I'm not sure, really,' Kate replied.

'How do you mean?' Sally asked.

'It's a little complicated as we're so different, and he… Oh, I don't know,' Kate ended, feeling embarrassed. 'I've never met anyone like Cormac before. I don't quite know how to deal with him.'

'I saw you dancing. You both looked so amazingly in tune.'

Kate nodded. 'Yes, I think we were. When we were dancing. But…' She stopped, not knowing quite how to go on.

'I think he feels just as confused,' Sally said, putting her hand on Kate's arm. 'I think he feels a little inferior and nervous around you. Cormac is passionate about helping people and making them feel better. He's trying to live up to his family's reputation and the beliefs about his own healing powers. And he might be a little sensitive about his lack of education when it comes to conventional medicine and science. He relies a lot on old remedies and his own instincts. Maybe you're shaking his confidence a little.'

'Yes, but I don't think any less of him because of that. In fact, I'm a little in awe of him because he seems to have such empathy and connection with people, which I'm trying so hard to find myself. And he gave me this amazing book to read about ancient Celtic medicine, which was fascinating. It really opened my eyes to how sophisticated medicine was in the Middle Ages.'

'Did you tell him that?'

Kate sighed. 'I tried, but I don't think he really listened.'

Sally smiled. 'I know. He can be a bit stubborn. But when you get to know him better, you'll discover how gentle and kind he is. He loves nature. Plants and flowers, birds and insects. He has an amazing knowledge about all of that.'

'That doesn't surprise me,' Kate said, remembering Cormac tending to his plants in the greenhouse.

'There's a lot to Cormac you have yet to discover, I feel.' Sally lifted the teapot. 'More tea?'

Kate put her mug on the tray. 'No thanks. I think I'd better be off. That tea's made me sleepy.'

'Me too,' Sally said, and stifled a yawn.

Kate got up. 'Thanks for the tea. It was lovely to meet you.'

'At last,' Sally said, and scrambled to her feet. 'Us O'Rourkes should stick together.'

Kate laughed. 'We should. Not that I have any idea how we're related,' she added.

'I'd say we're twelfth cousins or something,' Sally suggested. 'But whatever, it's the same blood. We were wild in the old days. But we have acquired a more polite veneer since then.'

'I suppose,' Kate said. 'But I wouldn't know what happens if we're scratched.'

'We turn into wild hussies.' Sally laughed. 'You know that some of our ancestors were healers?'

'Yes, Cormac told me.'

'And that they lived just above that beautiful hidden little bay called Wild Rose Bay?'

Kate nodded. 'Yes, he told me that too, and that the tower above it is called O'Rourke's castle.'

'No idea why, but I'm guessing they hung out there a lot in the old days. Those O'Rourke rebels.' Sally laughed and kissed Kate's cheek. 'Goodnight, dear distant cousin. Sleep tight.'

'I'm sure I will.' Kate went into the hall and put on her jacket, Sally in tow.

Just before she left, Sally put her hand on Kate's shoulder and looked deep into her eyes. 'Cormac is special, don't forget that.'

Kate nodded. 'I know,' she said. 'I won't forget.'

'Good.' Sally let go and stood back while Kate opened the door. 'Sweet dreams,' she said behind Kate as she walked down to the front gate.

Kate turned and waved, before she started her walk home, her mind full of questions. Sally had told her a lot about Cormac, but she still didn't know what to make of him – or her own feelings. She didn't want to dwell too much on those vibes between them. It was something she shied away from. Romance had been far from her mind when she came to Sandy Cove. She didn't want to fall in love with anyone right now, not until she had faced the grief that was gnawing deep inside.

She walked slowly through the quiet streets on her way home, looking up at the stars, wondering if she'd ever find the piece of her heart that was missing.

# Chapter Fourteen

Kate woke from her slumber with a start, shooting out of bed to the sound of a crash and a string of swear words, wondering what on earth had happened. The sound had come from the bottom of the stairs. She raced out of her room to the top of the landing and peered down, holding onto the handrail. In the dim light she could see a figure lying at the foot of the stairs, moaning and complaining. 'Mick?' she shouted. 'Is that you?'

'Yes,' he grunted.

'Oh my God, did you fall?'

'Yeah,' he groaned.

'Are you okay?' Kate asked as she ran down the stairs, her heart beating, praying he wasn't badly hurt.

'No,' Mick said through clenched teeth. 'My ankle's gone.'

'Don't move,' Kate ordered as she put on the light and went to his side, discovering that his ankle was at an awkward angle, his foot sticking out. He looked back at her and she saw to her relief that he didn't seem too groggy, just in pain. 'Ugh, that looks bad,' she said with a grimace. 'But maybe it's not broken, just sprained? Let me have a look.' Kate felt his foot and ran her hand gently to his ankle.

'Jesus, that hurts,' Mick grunted between his teeth.

'I think you've torn your Achilles tendon,' Kate announced. 'That's worse than a break. You need to go to hospital and get that looked after. And whatever you do, don't move your head.'

Mick grunted in reply, his face white and his breathing laboured.

'You're in awful pain,' Kate said, taking his pulse, which was strong but rapid.

'I know,' Mick mumbled.

'We must call an ambulance,' Kate said, relieved that he was able to talk. She couldn't be absolutely sure but she didn't think he had damaged his neck or his back. But he needed to get to hospital as soon as possible. She tried not to panic or even think about what could have happened – his neck broken and… No, it was too horrible.

'Bridget,' she called up the stairs, her throat so dry she could hardly get the words out. 'Are you awake?'

Bridget's face came into view upstairs. 'What's all the racket on a Sunday morning?'

'Mick fell down the stairs and I think he's snapped his Achilles tendon,' Kate told her, regaining some of her composure. 'If you call an ambulance, I'll go and get him some morphine.'

'I will,' Bridget said. 'I'll call from Pat's landline in his bedroom.'

'Morphine?' Mick asked, momentarily more alert. 'Is it that bad?'

'You tell me,' Kate replied.

Mick screwed his eyes shut. 'It's that bad,' he said between his teeth.

'The ride in the ambulance will be very painful without it. I have some in my bag in the surgery for emergencies.'

Kate quickly located the morphine and gave Mick a shot while Bridget called an ambulance and John came down with some pillows and a blanket. 'Just to make him more comfortable,' he said.

Kate nodded. 'Just don't move his foot or his head. Don't bother with the pillow, just cover him up to get him warm. The paramedics will have a cast to put it in to keep it stable. And they'll put him in a neck brace.'

Bridget's face appeared again upstairs. 'Ambulance on its way. We were lucky. There was one available in Killarney. But they'll take him to Tralee hospital. I phoned them and they're on standby. An orthopaedic surgeon has been called. I'll just call Pat and tell him what happened so he knows.'

'No,' Mick exclaimed, his eyes fluttering open. 'Don't bother Dad. He has a day off. Let him enjoy it.'

'Okay. Don't worry, we won't tell him,' Kate soothed, praying the ambulance would be there soon. He needed that neck brace even more than the cast for his leg. 'How do you feel?'

Mick smiled sleepily. 'Much, much better. That was a great shot you gave me. Have you got some more?'

'Don't push it,' Kate replied, happy that the morphine had had a good effect.

John covered Mick with a blanket.

'What do you want me to do?' Bridget asked as she came back down the stairs.

'How about a cup of tea?' Kate suggested.

'Great idea,' Mick mumbled.

'Not for you. For me,' Kate said. 'You can't eat or drink. I'm sure they'll want to perform surgery.'

'You're so cruel.' Mick glanced at her without moving his head. 'You're cute in those pyjamas.'

'Thank you.' Kate looked up at John. 'Could you go and get a couple of rolls of stretch bandages from the surgery? They're in the cupboard by the desk. I'm going to see if I can secure that foot so it doesn't move too much. Then the paramedics will put it in a plastic cast.' She looked at Mick. 'It might hurt a little bit.'

Mick nodded. 'It's okay. I think the stuff you gave me is kicking in big time.'

'Thank God for morphine,' Kate said. 'What on earth were you doing running around in the dark like that?'

'I left my phone downstairs,' Mick mumbled sleepily. 'I heard it ring. Call from LA.'

'LA?' Kate asked.

'Yeah. About my play. Could be big. So I ran to get it.' Mick closed his eyes and drew breath. 'But I missed it.'

'They'll call you back,' Kate reassured him.

John came back with the bandages and Kate gently eased Mick's foot into a better position and carefully secured it with some of the bandages while Mick grunted in pain a few times. 'There,' she said. 'That should help to make the trip to hospital less painful.'

The sound of steps on the gravel outside followed by the doorbell made Kate sag with relief. 'They're here.'

John went to admit two paramedics carrying a stretcher. Mick was soon expertly dealt with and brought outside to the waiting ambulance.

'Here.' Kate handed him his wallet and phone, knowing that he'd be desperate to be back in touch with whoever had been ringing him.

'I'm sure they'll call back very soon.' Her heart ached for him, as she knew how much this meant. He had worked so hard to write this play and he had been waiting to hear from his agent for days. He had been checking his phone and his emails every half hour lately, hoping and wishing that his play would be produced somewhere. His agent had told him to expect a call from LA in the next few days. And when they'd finally contacted him, this had happened. She shuddered, thinking it could have been much, much worse, realising in that moment just how much he had come to mean to her. They had become so close, and shared so many things about themselves during the past few weeks.

'Thanks, Kate,' he said as the stretcher was carried out. 'For everything.'

'You're welcome,' she said and patted his shoulder, feeling at that moment enormous gratitude not only that Mick was going to be all right, but that she had been there to help him. *That's what being a doctor is all about, really*, Kate thought. A brilliant medical career in Dublin suddenly didn't seem so important any more.

When the ambulance had driven off, Kate went inside, closed the front door and leaned against it, her knees weak. 'Oh my God, that was some morning,' she said, her thoughts still on Mick and that sudden feeling of contentment to have been in the right place at the right time. She looked down at her wrinkly pyjamas. 'And I'm not even dressed yet. I'd better go and have a shower and then call the hospital.'

'Tea and toast in the kitchen first,' Bridget ordered, holding Kate's dressing gown. 'I have it all ready for you.'

'Sounds good.' Kate took the proffered dressing gown, put it on and went into the kitchen, where tea and a basket of toast and fresh rolls had been put on the table. She sank down on a chair and helped herself, soon enjoying a cup of freshly brewed tea and toast with marmalade. 'Heaven,' she breathed, the stress of the past hour slowly easing. 'Thanks, Bridget.'

'You're welcome. You looked after the poor lad so well. I hope he won't be in too much pain.'

'He will for a while, but they'll keep him on the morphine until the pain eases.' Kate swallowed the last piece of toast.

'He'll be fine, even if it's going to be difficult for a while,' Bridget said and joined Kate at the table, pouring herself a mug of tea. 'You can relax now that you know he's in good hands. The paramedics will phone through to the hospital with all the details of his condition and then they'll take it from there.'

'I know. I shouldn't worry.'

'Not at all,' Bridget agreed. Then she sighed. 'I'm so fond of that boy, you know.'

'Me too,' Kate said, knowing it was true. Who would not be fond of Mick with his twinkly eyes, sense of humour and cheeky grin? 'He's lovely.'

'He thinks the world of you, too,' Bridget said with affection. She suddenly sat up and listened as the faint sound of bells could be heard. 'Holy saints, that's the bell for mass.'

'What?' Kate asked, alarmed, staring at the kitchen clock. 'It's nearly eleven!' she exclaimed and shot up from her chair, splashing tea on the table. 'I was supposed to meet Cormac at the beach at ten.'

'Oh?' Bridget said, looking curiously at Kate. 'You were?'

'Yes. We were going for a walk. He was going to show me…' Kate stopped. 'What must he have thought when I didn't show up?' she groaned. 'What will I do? I don't have his phone number.'

'I don't think he even has a phone,' Bridget suggested.

'He doesn't?' Kate stared at her. 'How on earth does he manage?'

'Who knows. Telepathy?' Bridget suggested. 'Go down to the beach and see if he's still there. It's a lovely day, so he might just be walking on his own.'

'I hope he might. I'll see you later, Bridget,' Kate said and ran upstairs.


A quick shower was all Kate could manage before jumping into her jeans, shirt and sweater, and then she ran down the stairs again, laced on her walking boots and grabbed her jacket in the hall. She raced out the door and down the street to the dunes and the beach, barely noticing the balmy sunshine and the soft breezes. The beach was quiet with only a couple walking with a toddler, the woman with a baby in a pouch on her chest, and a man walking a dog. Kate looked wildly around, but there was no sign of Cormac. Breathing hard, she jogged up the steep incline at the far end, thinking she'd have a better view from there. Once at the top, she climbed up on a boulder and scanned the beach below, without success. Then she turned and looked in the other direction, towards the coastline to Ballinskelligs. The bright sunlight was blinding, but she found her sunglasses in the pocket of her jacket and slipped them on, shading her eyes with her hand. Then she saw him: a tall figure wearing a rucksack outlined against the horizon, standing about fifty metres away, staring out to sea.

Kate took a deep breath. 'Cormac!' she shouted, waving her arms, nearly toppling from the boulder.

He turned his head and looked at her. In the strong light behind him, she couldn't see his face and it was impossible to tell if he was annoyed or happy to see her. Kate jumped down from the boulder at the same time as he started to walk towards her.

'You came,' he said when he was closer. 'I thought you weren't coming, so I started walking.'

Kate stopped as she reached him. 'I'm sorry I'm late. It was… there was an accident.'

'I thought so,' he said. 'I saw the ambulance. It's not Dr Pat, is it? His heart—'

'No, it was Mick. He fell down the stairs and snapped his Achilles tendon.'

Cormac made a face. 'Ugh, that must have been painful.'

'Very. And it took a while to sort everything out. But he's on his way to hospital and will be operated on later today. I'll know more when he's in recovery.'

'How awful for him. But lucky he had you to help him.'

Kate shrugged. 'I didn't do more than any other doctor would have done.'

'I'm sure you did more than that.' Cormac started to walk away. 'But come, we have a lot of walking to do. Did you bring your sticks?'

'Oh, God,' Kate said, alarmed. 'I forgot them.'

'That's okay. I have two, so you can take one of mine should we need them.' He handed her a walking stick. 'Here you are. You won't need it until we begin going uphill.' He started to walk down the path. 'Come on, it's this way. The path is good because it hasn't rained much lately. The slope might be okay, too. But it's a bit of a challenge all the same. You'll see when we get there.'

'Where are you taking me?' Kate asked as she followed him, amused by his mysterious tone.

Cormac glanced at her over his shoulder. 'To O'Rourke's castle in Wild Rose Bay. Isn't that where you wanted to go?'

# Chapter Fifteen

*O'Rourke's Castle*, she thought as they walked on at a swift pace, Cormac charging ahead, Kate half running behind him. *At last I get to go there.* She knew it wasn't a real castle, and that it mightn't even have belonged to an O'Rourke, but it was something that had been part of her family history since the turbulent times in the early Middle Ages. She wasn't sure why Cormac was bringing here there, but she sensed that he had considered what she'd said about traditional healing and perhaps realised she was more open to it than he had thought. Or did he feel she needed to see the place where the ancient healers had harvested the plants and roots for their remedies?

She felt a dart of excitement at the thought of seeing the tower up close. Ever since she had seen it from afar and heard the name, she had wanted to explore it, but it seemed inaccessible to anyone but sheep. She had a sketchy idea of the place from what Cormac had told her. Some of those physicians from ancient times had grown their herbs and remedies there, and the land had been granted to them by the chieftains of the times. Would she sense the vibes from the past as she touched the old stones and looked across the bog and fields where the herbalists had grown the plants for their medicines? A feeling of having been there before? Would she feel closer to her father as she stood there? He had wanted to research the family history but never got a chance to come here. But she felt he was there with her in spirit all the same.

On they walked, along the old path that wound its way at the edge of the cliffs and inlets and down a steep incline to a group of ruined houses.

'These are from the eighteenth century,' Cormac said as they took a break. 'But where we're going, the remains are older still.'

'I can't wait,' Kate said, feeling excited.

Cormac pointed. 'We have to get down there first.' At the bottom of the hill Kate glimpsed the tiny bay she had seen before, where the waves lapped its white sand.

'What a lovely little beach,' she exclaimed. 'It's Wild Rose Bay, isn't it? I've seen it from afar but never been there.'

'That's right,' Cormac said. 'Not very well known, as it's hard to get to.'

'I can see that,' Kate remarked, gazing down the steep incline. 'How on earth are we going to get down there?'

Cormac looked back at her and smiled. 'Use the stick I gave you. It's only half of the walk. We have to get up to the tower from there. But there's a path a little further up once you've climbed for a bit.'

They stepped sideways down the hill and then carefully descended further to the steps that had been cut into the cliff face. Finally down, Kate jumped onto the sand with a sigh of relief at Cormac, who had arrived ahead of her. 'Phew. I'm glad I'm down finally. That's a bit hairy, just before the steps.'

'I know. But I'm used to it.'

'You're like a mountain goat,' Kate teased.

'You're not that bad yourself, girl.' Cormac took two bottles of water from his rucksack and handed one to Kate. 'Here. I'm sure you're thirsty. I brought some lunch for us both as well, just in case we don't make it back in time.'

'Oh.' Kate took the bottle. 'Thank you. That was very thoughtful. I didn't know how long we'd be out, so…'

'And then you were busy with Mick's accident,' Cormac filled in.

Kate drank from her bottle. 'Yes. It was a dramatic morning, I have to say.'

'You're fond of Mick, I take it.'

Kate nodded. 'Of course. He's very nice.'

'Yes, he is. There's no side to him at all, I've heard,' Cormac agreed. 'And you're very suited to each other.'

'What?' Kate nearly choked on the water. 'We're not… I mean, Mick's just a friend, that's all.'

Cormac looked at her for a moment. 'You're sure about that?'

'Very sure,' Kate replied sternly. 'Why did you think there was something between us?'

Cormac shrugged and looked away. 'Oh, well… Maybe I was just a little worried.' He put away his bottle and began walking. 'But let's get going. We have to get up that slope and along the cliff to get to the tower.'

Kate put her bottle in her pocket and followed his tall figure as he continued across the beach at a swift pace. She watched his auburn hair blowing in the wind and wondered what he had meant. Worried about what? That she and Mick had fallen in love? But that wasn't likely to happen. Her feelings were heading in another direction altogether. Was that not obvious to him? Did Cormac not also feel this connection when they were together? And what did it all mean? Were they falling for each other, or did they simply share an interest in medicine and healing? He was so difficult to read, but he had been in her thoughts and in some of her dreams ever since they'd had that argument on the beach outside the Wellness Centre. She felt more confused and troubled than ever before, but she fought to stop herself thinking about it as she tried to concentrate on the walk and the tough slope they were about to climb.

Cormac stopped just above the foot of the slope and looked down at her. 'You okay?'

'Grand,' Kate said, panting. 'But could we slow down, please? I'm a bit winded already.'

'Sorry.' Cormac laughed and held out his hand. 'Here. I'll give you a little lift.'

'Thanks.' Kate took his hand and he pulled her up to stand beside him.

Their eyes locked for a moment. Cormac touched Kate's cheek. 'Let's take it slowly, and we'll be grand,' he said softly.

They were so close Kate could feel his warm breath on her face and smell the herbs and flowers from his clothes. 'Okay,' she whispered, still looking into those beautiful green eyes.

'You can trust me, you know.'

'I do trust you,' she replied without thinking.

His eyes softened even more as he looked at her. 'I'm glad to hear that.' Then he stepped away. 'We have to continue. Grab your stick and come this way. The path is steep but then there are steps. It's not that hard, really.'

Kate grasped her stick and followed him, climbing slowly and carefully upwards, her mind and heart full of what had just happened between them. It didn't seem that important, but his words and that look in his eyes had said more than if he had spelled it out. She looked down at the beach and the headland beyond and suddenly felt a dart of pure joy to be here with this handsome, intriguing man for whom she was beginning to have feelings she had never experienced. She had been in what she thought was love before, but it had never felt like this. Or was it some kind of spell Cormac had put her under to lure her into something she wouldn't be able to resist?

They reached the tower after nearly an hour of hard climbing that seemed tougher to Kate than the hike she had been on with Mick. But they were finally there, and as she rounded the tower and saw what was on the side that hadn't been visible from below, she gasped with pleasure. On the sheltered side of the ruined tower was a beautiful meadow covered in purple heather. An Arbutus tree stood nearby, full of white flowers and red berries. The pale winter sunshine gave the meadow a golden hue. As Kate looked up at the majestic mountains towering above her, she felt as if she had stepped back a thousand years in time and entered an enchanted realm.

'This place is heavenly,' she exclaimed and looked around her in delight. 'Thank you for bringing me here, Cormac.'

He smiled at her. 'I knew you'd like it.'

'Like it? I absolutely adore it.' She looked up at the jagged walls of the tower. 'Not much left of it, is there?'

'No. And I wouldn't go inside. It's crumbling and you might get hit by a stone.' Cormac gestured at the steps leading to the opening in the tower. 'Come, sit down here and we'll have the sandwiches. You can see everything from here.'

Kate joined him on one of the steps, and sitting on her jacket, she enjoyed the mellow warmth of the sun while she bit into the cheese sandwich he had given her. She looked out across the heather to the view of the mountains, still stunned by the beautiful sights. There was a faint smell of woodsmoke and she could see a hawk gliding high above her, looking for its prey.

'How's the sandwich?' Cormac asked her.

'Delicious,' Kate replied, looking around her. 'So this is where those physicians used to grow their herbs and flowers?'

Cormac nodded. 'That's right. And those plants, or something like them, still grow here. And this is where I often come to look for things to use.'

'Like that new ointment?' Kate asked.

'Yes.'

'Are you finally going to tell me what's in it?'

Cormac left his seat on the step and bent down to take something from the ground. Then he straightened up and held out his fist to Kate. 'Hold out your hand.'

Kate stretched out her hand. 'Yes?'

Cormac put a handful of damp earth in her hand. 'There. That's the magic ingredient.'

Kate looked at the lump of what looked like clay. 'This? Are you having me on?' She squeezed the clay in her hand. 'It's just like the clay used for pottery. Kind of rubbery.'

'That's right.'

'What's magic about it?'

Cormac sat down again and looked at her. 'Have you ever heard about the earth in a place in Fermanagh?'

'Fermanagh in Northern Ireland?' Kate asked. 'Yes… Hold on, let me think. I did read about that a few years ago. Earth from a churchyard was found to contain some microorganism that can kill bacteria, as far as I remember.'

'That's right,' Cormac said. 'It was just folklore, they thought, but then a microbiologist analysed a sample and found a strain of a microorganism that could be used as an antibiotic. It's limestone clay, which has antibiotic properties. And when I read about that, I thought the clay here might have the same properties. It has an even higher amount of limestone than in Fermanagh. And the legend says that there was healing in the earth here.'

'Oh.' Kate looked at the lump of clay in her hand. 'So this is what's in your ointment?'

'Yes. I mix it with coconut and oregano oil. It's been amazing for wounds that are difficult to heal.'

'Yes, I saw that wound on old Jim up the mountain.'

Cormac nodded. 'Yes. I've given it to a few more people since then with the same result.'

'Amazing,' Kate mumbled, rubbing the clay between her fingers. She looked at Cormac. 'But, like I said before, if it's that efficient, shouldn't you patent it or something, so it could be distributed more widely?'

Cormac shook his head. 'No. That's not possible.'

'Why not?'

Cormac pointed at the field in front of them. 'Can you see what's at the end of this little field?'

Kate squinted against the sunlight and spotted a tall, thin boulder where Cormac was pointing. 'It's a standing stone.'

'That's right. And you know what that means, don't you?'

Kate thought back to what her father had told her about standing stones. 'Eh, uh, that the fairies or spirits will get you if you mess with it? But that's just superstition, isn't it? We read about these standing stones in school. They're from Neolithic times, and nobody really knows why they were put up.'

'Would you mess with it, though? Or the land around it?'

'Hmm,' Kate said, 'maybe not. Just in case. And as it's been there for thousands of years, it would feel wrong to disturb the peace in a place like this.' She looked at the standing stone, solid and so, so old, and felt a little shiver going up her spine. 'It's kind of sacred, isn't it?'

Cormac laughed. 'Exactly. Nobody in Ireland would touch it. Not even a modern medicine woman like you.'

'That's true.' Kate stared at the lump of clay in her hand. 'This could be a great product for scars and problem skin, you know. But I'd like to have it tested to see what's in it all the same, just to find out exactly what beneficial properties it has. Even if you don't want to patent it.'

'What do you mean?' Cormac asked.

'I mean, untreated things like this on wounds could cause problems.'

'It's safe enough,' Cormac stated.

'How do you know?' Kate asked, suddenly concerned.

'It's cured quite a few wounds by now. And I have no means of getting it tested anyway,' Cormac said, his eyes wary.

'I'm sure there is a way.' Kate felt a sudden chill as the atmosphere between them changed. She had felt so close to him as they climbed the slope and arrived at this beautiful place. But now that she had started to question the use of his ointment, they were suddenly on opposite sides again. 'Helen said she wanted it tested, but I could see if I can get someone at Cork University Hospital to analyse it instead.'

Cormac frowned. 'You said you trusted me.'

'That wasn't about this.'

'I thought it was about everything. You don't believe what I just told you, then?' Cormac asked, his eyes cold.

'About the healing properties of the earth in Fermanagh? Yes, I do. And this could be the same. Have it tested, and then we'll take it from there.'

'So you need proof before you trust my instincts?' Cormac turned away from her and got up.

'Yes,' Kate said in a near whisper. 'I'm sorry, Cormac.' She looked at him helplessly, trying to analyse her feelings for him. Was it just the spirits, or fairies playing tricks? she wondered. It didn't seem possible to have a relationship of any kind with someone who disagreed with everything she believed in. There was no way out of that dilemma, and she realised that even though the attraction between them was obvious, it could never lead anywhere. She looked away and tried to pull herself together. 'I feel a little weird,' she said with a nervous laugh. 'This place has a strange atmosphere.'

'Yes, it does.' Cormac looked out across the field to the standing stone. 'The earth and the old stones hold memories we will never know. Maybe I shouldn't have brought you here.' He laughed bitterly. 'For a moment there I thought we were in some historical romance. Before your doctor brain kicked in.'

'I can't help thinking the way I do.'

'No,' Cormac said, 'you can't. And I can't, and we'll never agree.'

'No, we won't,' she said, feeling a little sad.

His expression as he looked at her echoed her thoughts. 'We should go,' he said, his voice dull. 'It'll take an hour or so to get back, and then the walk across the cliffs will be another hour. It gets dark so early right now, and we wouldn't want to get stuck in bad light. Could be dangerous. We have to make sure we can see where we're going.'

'I know,' Kate said, feeling that he wasn't referring only to the return journey. She slowly got off the step and put on her jacket.

Cormac put on his rucksack and zipped up his jacket. 'Ready?'

'Yes,' Kate replied, her spirits sinking. Before they set off, she took a last look around. 'I'll never forget this place. I'm sorry if I upset you, but…'

Cormac shrugged. 'I should have known better, I suppose.'

'I'm at the opposite side of healing from you.'

Cormac nodded. 'It's a case of modern medicine against the ancient art of healing. The heart versus the head,' Cormac said, a sad look in his eyes.

'Something like that,' Kate replied.

'But let's get going,' Cormac urged, as a dark cloud passed across the sun, plunging the tower and the land around it into near darkness. He started down the slope, walking sideways, using his stick to avoid falling. Kate followed his lead, his words echoing through her mind. *My heart or my head*, she thought. *Which of the two will win?*

# Chapter Sixteen

After saying a curt goodbye to Cormac at the beach, Kate walked in a daze through the village. She had felt such strong vibes between them as they sat talking on the steps of the tower, and she couldn't quite understand why. They shared a passion for healing, but in different ways. What had happened between them seemed trivial but she knew that they were disagreeing about much more than just the ointment. When she had voiced her doubts they seemed to have hurt him to the core, and the spell was broken. They came from completely different backgrounds and upbringings, didn't share any kind of common interests apart from healing and medicine, but still, she felt she had met a kindred spirit. How was that possible? Or was she just dreaming, pretending she was the heroine in one of those historical romances, just like Cormac had said? That was her guilty secret. She had read soppy romantic stories as a teenager and dreamed about finding that kind of love in real life.

As she went into the house, Kate tried to clear her mind of all those romantic notions. She didn't need such distractions right now, not when Mick was in hospital. Pat and Helen would be so worried when they found out. And in any case, she only had around five months left here, and it would be foolish to get into a relationship with someone in these circumstances. She was still dealing with the grief of losing her father and she wasn't ready to fall in love with anyone, she told herself.

Kate felt in her pocket for the keys but her fingers found the little lump of clay Cormac had given her. She looked at it and squeezed it in her hand before putting it back in her pocket, finding her keys in the other one.

The house was quiet and empty; Bridget and John were off on a walk and Pat wasn't back from Killarney. Kate wondered if Mick or the hospital had phoned him, or if she should tell him herself. She checked her watch. Four o'clock. Dusk was falling and Pat would have packed up his golf clubs and headed back to Sandy Cove. Maybe better to phone the hospital to find out how Mick was before she spoke to Pat.

Kate picked up the phone in the hall and dialled the number to the hospital. She was told Mick had been operated on a few hours earlier and was already out of the recovery room and in a ward. She was put through to the ward and asked the nurse on duty how he was.

'Sore but fine,' the nurse said. 'He has snapped his Achilles tendon and has his leg in plaster, which will stay on for around two months. The surgeon wants him to stay in for a week in order to assess his recovery and for him to practise walking with crutches.'

'Oh, good,' Kate said, relieved. 'Is he awake?'

'Yes. Do you want to speak to him?'

'Yes, please.'

'He's still a little out of it from the morphine,' the nurse warned. 'But here he is.'

There was a short silence, during which Kate could hear an exchange that ended with: 'Put her on. I wanna say thanks.' Then Mick came on the line. 'Kate? Howerya?' he asked, his voice hoarse.

'I should ask you how *you* are,' Kate protested.

'Yeah, sure,' Mick slurred. 'I'm very fine, thank you very much, girl. A bit of pain in the old leg and feeling really stupid, but apart from that, everything's grand.'

'Oh, good. I hear they want you to stay in for a while.'

'Yeah. One of the nurses is a real auld battleaxe. Her name's Flora, would you believe. Anyway, it all went well, and they didn't have to chop off my leg or anything.'

'That's lucky,' Kate said, trying her best not to laugh. 'I take it you're still feeling the effects of the morphine?'

'Yeah,' Mick rambled on. 'Great stuff, that.'

'Did you call Pat?' Kate asked.

'Not yet. I wanted him to be home when he hears.'

'He should be home soon,' Kate replied. 'I'll tell him.'

'Good. Thanks, Kate. You're a real brick. I think you saved my life, so I have to say thanks for that.'

'I didn't, but you're welcome. You should try to sleep now.'

'I will,' Mick promised. 'Very tired. Bye, Kate.' He hung up before she had a chance to say goodbye.

Kate smiled and put down the phone. He was still a little drunk on morphine but otherwise seemed fine. She would be able to tell Pat he was on the way to recovery. Mick would be in plaster for a long time, but he'd be here with plenty of people to help him. And he'd be able to do some final editing on the screenplay. It wasn't too bad, and she would play it down even more when she told Pat what had happened.

The phone ringing made her jump. She picked it up thinking it was the hospital. But it wasn't.

'Hello,' Cormac said, his voice a little hesitant. 'I just wanted to say… to hear your voice, really.'

'Hi, Cormac,' Kate whispered. 'I thought you didn't have a phone.'

'Says who? Of course I do. I just don't want anyone to call me so I pretend not to have one. I don't have your mobile number, though, but I was hoping you'd answer the landline.'

'Here I am,' she said.

'Yes.'

'I'm sorry about today,' she started. 'I didn't mean to be snarky.'

'I know you didn't.'

'I just felt a little cornered.'

'I understand. Let's not talk about that for the moment.'

'No.'

He cleared his throat. 'How is Mick?'

'Fine. I spoke to the hospital just now and he's already had surgery, which was a success. He's resting.'

'Good.' Cormac paused. 'I just got a text message from Helen. She says she wants to speak to me.'

'Oh, really? About what?' Kate said, intrigued.

'No idea. I felt obliged to give her my number when I was there that night for dinner. I had forgotten about it, actually. I wondered if you'd spoken to her? You haven't told her about the soil, have you?'

'No, Cormac. And I won't, if you don't want me to,' Kate replied. They may have argued but she would never betray someone's trust, and it hurt her that Cormac thought she would.

'She's going to call me later tonight. I think she wants to talk about the ointment. She said she was interested in finding out more about it when we had dinner.'

'I see. Well…' Kate stopped, not knowing what to say. 'I won't take any sides in this.'

'You still think I should give in? Have the earth tested?' Cormac asked hotly. 'If I tell Helen that's where the ointment comes from, that sacred place will be trampled on by a whole herd of people from a pharmaceutical company.'

'Well…' Kate knew it was pointless to explain how she felt, even though she understood his point of view. It would be awful if the tranquillity and ancient beauty of that place were ruined and exploited. 'Whatever my opinion, it would be terrible for the peace to be disturbed. But even if Helen finds out where the soil is from, she won't have the power to do that.'

'She might, actually,' Cormac said, his voice bitter. 'I don't own the land around the tower.'

'Who does?'

'I think her family does.'

Later that evening, after having been told what happened to Mick, Pat joined Kate and Bridget in the kitchen for their meal. The more Kate had been thinking about Cormac, the more she was sympathising with his situation, and she wanted to help him.

'All's well with Mick,' Pat said. 'I just got off the phone with the sister in charge and she told me he's doing as well as can be expected. He's pretty shocked, and I'm not sure how he'll feel about being laid up here for two months.'

'We'll look after him,' Bridget announced as she ladled soup into bowls. 'Potato and leek followed by pork chops and mash,' she said as she handed Pat a bowl. 'Hope that's all right.'

'Wonderful,' Pat replied, smiling at John, who had just come in. 'We'll have an invalid on our hands, it appears.'

'What else did they say at the hospital?' Kate asked, sitting down.

'I spoke to the ward sister,' Pat replied. 'She said he was recovering well and that they had already stopped the morphine. Then Mick came on the line and assured me he was fine, apart from feeling really stupid for having stumbled down the stairs like that. But he was trying to answer a call from some producer in LA, he said. They're going to call him back tomorrow. I hope that'll be good news.'

'I'm sure it will,' Kate said. 'They'd hardly call him to say no, would they? Isn't this exciting for him? He hasn't even finished the play and he already has interest from Hollywood.'

'It is if it comes through,' Pat said as he finished his soup. 'But let's not count any chickens yet.'

'We'll just be very excited and support him whatever the news,' Bridget said as she sat down. 'But I'm more worried about how to keep him amused during his convalescence. He'll be so bored, poor lad. He'll be working on the play, but he won't be able to move around the way he's used to.'

'We'll think of something,' Kate said. 'He could always help with the filing on the computer. I find that such a chore at the end of the day.' She finished her soup. 'That was delicious, Bridget.' She turned to Pat. 'Can I ask you something about Helen?'

Pat smiled. 'Yes? What about her?'

'It's more about her family, I think,' Kate continued. 'And the land they own around here. The land around O'Rourke's castle, actually. It appears they own that. How come?'

'Oh.' Pat looked startled. 'That land. It's just a few acres, really. But they don't own it as far as I know. I think it's been O'Rourke land since the old days.'

'Helen's mother's family were O'Briens,' Bridget filled in as she collected the soup bowls.

'That family has nearly died out around here,' John added. 'They were chieftains in the old days. But the old legend says they bequeathed that bit of land to the herbalists of the day. And they were O'Rourkes.'

'Oh,' Kate said, her heart beating faster. 'But who owns it now?'

'Must be the O'Rourkes on the other side of the headland,' John replied. 'There's an old farm there. Used to be owned by someone called Liam O'Rourke as far as I know. Another branch of your family, Kate.'

Kate shrugged. 'I've never heard of them.'

'Oh yes,' Bridget said. 'I know who you mean. He used to graze his sheep up the mountain around there. A bit of a hermit, I think. Doesn't socialise much.'

'So he owns that land, then, and not Helen's family?' Kate asked.

'I think so. It's not worth much,' Pat said. 'Why do you ask?'

'No reason,' Kate said non-committally. 'It's just that I was there today. With Cormac.'

'Really?' Bridget looked at Kate curiously. 'You were there with Cormac?'

'Yes,' Kate said, trying not to blush. 'We went on a walk together to Wild Rose Bay and then up to the tower. It's so beautiful there.'

'That's a tough walk,' Pat remarked. 'But it must have been lovely there today. It's a gorgeous spot. I went there with Helen when we were engaged. And we were young and fit,' he added with a little laugh.

'It's truly heavenly,' Kate said. She took the plate Bridget handed her. 'Thanks, Bridget, this looks amazing.'

'Try it with my apple sauce,' Bridget said, and put a jar on the table.

'Nobody cooks a pork chop like Bridget,' Pat declared as he took his own plate. 'And the meat around here is the best.'

'Our village butcher has won several prizes,' John announced as he dug into his helping. 'That's because he uses only local produce.'

'I haven't met him yet,' Kate interjected, happy that the conversation had turned away from her outing with Cormac.

'You should call in,' Bridget suggested. 'His shop is the one with the striped awning. Very old-fashioned, with the original floor tiles.'

The conversation turned to other matters and Bridget, John and Pat chatted on while Kate's thoughts turned to what she had found out and to Cormac's concerns. While she understood how he felt, she was still anxious to have the soil analysed, if only to find out what was in it. It was her medical curiosity that made her want to know, but Cormac was suspicious about her intentions. How could she get through to him that she meant well? It seemed to her that it might not be a bad thing for the clay to be made into some kind of cream or ointment to use on scar tissue. Helen wouldn't trample all over the land; she was probably just looking to take a sample and then see what could be done with it. What was wrong with that? But maybe there was a problem with access to the land around the tower?

'Did you know there's a standing stone in the field by the tower?' Kate asked, interrupting the conversation. 'The one near the tower, I mean.'

'Uh, yes,' Pat replied, looking startled. 'What of it?'

'Nothing,' Kate mumbled as she finished her pork chop. 'I just thought it was interesting to see it.'

'Standing stones are sacred,' Bridget declared. 'I have never been up there, so I didn't know about it. But they're quite common around here. Nobody wants to disturb them, though. It could bring very bad luck.'

Pat nodded. 'That's the belief. But I'm not sure it's true. And Helen thinks it's nonsense. There's so much superstition around things like that, even in this day and age.'

'The fairies are all around us,' Bridget said darkly. 'I'd never disturb a standing stone.'

# Chapter Seventeen

Cormac called Kate the following evening with the news that a team from Helen's company was going to the tower to take samples that week.

'Have you been talking to her about the soil?' he asked.

'No, of course not,' Kate exclaimed. 'Why would I?'

'Because you were so anxious to have it analysed,' he said with a touch of anger in his voice. 'Well, now you'll get what you wanted.'

'Well, yeah, but that's not the way I wanted it done.'

'Does it matter?' he asked bitterly. 'I can't go there any more, in any case. Helen told me I was trespassing. So that's the end of my remedies. That field is unique, and I don't know where else I'll find anything as powerful.'

'Ha,' Kate said. 'That's not going to be a problem. She doesn't own the land, you see.'

'What do you mean? Who owns it?' Cormac asked.

'Some farmer called Liam O'Rourke. Another distant relation to me, I suppose.'

'Are you sure?'

'Absolutely. I heard it from Bridget's husband. He knows everyone around here.'

'I see. But Helen might have asked for permission to excavate.'

Kate laughed. 'Excavate? Aren't you being a little dramatic? She's just going to take a sample or something. I'm sure she has permission to do that. You could find that out very easily by asking this Liam O'Rourke himself,' she said. 'How did she know about the earth and its possible magic ingredients anyway? You've been so secretive about the ointment up to now.'

'I think she guessed it. Could be part of the family history. And then someone saw me up there a few days ago and she must have realised what I was doing. She was very pleasant and charming, of course, but I could sense the hard core of her determination.'

'I know what you mean.' Kate sat down on the sofa in the living room. 'But I'm sure you're worrying about nothing. She'll just want to take a small sample or something.' She could feel Cormac's panic. 'Why is this such a huge threat to you?' she asked.

'I have a feeling this could be the start of something bad.' Cormac paused. 'Please try to understand, Kate. I feel the peace will be disturbed up there, and that I won't be able to go back there to collect plants and roots. Maybe it's the end of something very precious and unique.'

'I understand that you're concerned and that—' Kate stopped. She wasn't sure if she was the right person to try to calm him down, and he was still suspicious of her motives. 'It might not be as bad as you think,' she ended in a comforting tone.

'I don't think you understand how bad it could be,' Cormac said. 'But I don't expect you to. Thanks for trying to help, in any case. Bye for now, Kate.'

'Bye, Cormac,' Kate whispered, even though he had hung up.

She and Cormac were very different, but she felt deeply sad for him. That little field up there meant more than any other place on earth to him. But maybe she could help in some way… She thought for a while, then looked up a number on her contact list and dialled.

The call was answered straight away. 'Hi, Kate, Jane here. How the hell are you? Country life agreeing with you?'

'Yes, I'm beginning to really enjoy it,' Kate replied, smiling as she listened to the voice of her friend and colleague. 'How's life in the fast lane?'

'Ah sure, the A&E department isn't the same without you. Things aren't too bad, though. Quite calm today as the flu season hasn't kicked in yet.'

'Oh, good. Listen, I'm calling to ask if you know any micro-biologists at Cork University Hospital. I have a feeling you said something about that once.'

'I might have. Why?'

'I need something analysed privately.'

'Like what?' Jane enquired.

'Oh, it's a bit complicated. I'll tell you about it when I see you next time.'

'Oh, okay. Hang on, let me have a look in my notebook…'

Kate waited while Jane searched, muttering to herself.

'Here we are,' Jane finally said. 'Liz Watson. Works in the main lab, but she does private analyses as well. I'll text you her details.'

'Terrific. Thanks a million, Jane.'

'No problem. Lovely you hear from you. Oops, there goes my beeper. Ambulance coming in. Talk soon. Will send that text as soon as I can. Bye for now, darling.' Jane hung up while Kate felt a dart of nostalgia, missing that adrenaline kick of coping with an emergency situation in a big city hospital. It had been hard work, but so exciting all the same to be part of a medical team that had to deal with with all kinds of medical emergencies, even if had been exhausting. But she'd be back there one day, stronger and more able to cope. She had learned so much by working in this little surgery, and she felt she looked at patients in a different way now.

The text message came through half an hour later with the contact details of the microbiologist in Cork. Feeling excited, Kate dialled the number and got Liz Watson straight away. 'Hi, Liz. My name is Dr Kate O'Rourke. My friend Jane O'Grady gave me your number.'

'Really?' Liz said in her pleasant Cork accent. 'How's Jane these days? Still working up there in Dublin?'

'Yes, she is. I used to work there, too, but now I'm doing a stint as a GP in Sandy Cove in Kerry.'

'Lovely part of the world,' Liz said. 'I'm sure you're enjoying it.'

'Oh yes, I love it,' Kate replied. 'A whole new experience. But the reason I'm calling you is that I need something analysed.'

'Don't you normally send your blood samples to Tralee?' Liz asked.

'Yes, we do. But this isn't a blood sample. This is a lump of earth. It's something that is said to have healing properties and has been known to heal difficult wounds. Like the soil in Fermanagh, actually.'

'I see,' Liz said, sounding less enthusiastic. 'Send it over and I'll take a look.'

'I really appreciate it, Liz,' Kate said.

'No problem. Jane's a close friend, so any friend of hers is a friend of mine. I'll do it as soon as I get it so you don't have to wait.'

'Thank you so much. That's very kind. And let me know if you're coming this way. I'll treat you to dinner at The Wild Atlantic Gourmet.'

'Brilliant,' Liz replied. 'I've heard it's excellent. I'll be in touch again as soon as I have the results. Bye for now.'

'Bye, and thanks again,' Kate said and hung up with a feeling of satisfaction. If she got the soil tested quickly enough, she hoped that Helen wouldn't need to excavate. Then the beautiful field was saved. Next step – a call to that farmer. Or maybe not call him at all? Nobody had objected to Cormac going to the tower all this time, so why would that happen now, all of a sudden? *Leave things alone*, she said to herself. *Asking questions would only stir things up.* She felt relieved as the thought hit her. Doing nothing was absolutely the best policy here.

But she still wondered what Helen was up to. Maybe she would start a big digging project if the earth was found to have some magic ingredient. Not only might it reduce scarring, it could also be used as an anti-ageing product and make huge profits for her company with some clever marketing. The possibilities were endless – and frightening. Kate simply had to find out what was in that soil. There would be no stopping Helen if it was something she could use, but now Kate's curiosity was working overtime. Whatever happened, she had to know as soon as possible – if only to help Cormac cope should the news not be in his favour. She got up to get that little lump from the pocket of her jacket. It had to be sent off straight away. There was no time to lose if she was to be a step ahead of Helen.

*

The following day was hectic, as many older people with coughs and colds demanded attention. Pat and Kate worked together, splitting up patients between them. At the end of the day, both exhausted, they had a welcome cup of tea in the living room. They went through the day and which patients they had seen and what had been prescribed, Pat making sure Kate had all the correct data. They both gave a start when there was a commotion in the hall. Kate rushed out and was startled to see Mick arriving at the door on crutches, being helped by a paramedic.

'Mick!' Kate exclaimed. 'Home already?'

Mick laughed as he hobbled in. 'You don't sound delighted to see me, Kate.'

'Well, I'm…' Kate stammered. 'I didn't expect them to release you so early.'

'Ah well, they needed the bed. There were twenty people on trolleys yesterday. I just couldn't bear to stay when I was feeling okay. And I'm such a whiz on these.' Mick waved one of the crutches in the air. 'I said I had plenty of help at home and two doctors to look after me, so they let me go. Thanks, mate,' he said over his shoulder to the paramedic, who put a bag on the floor.

'Take care,' the paramedic said, touching Mick's shoulder as he left. 'Don't waltz around on those crutches too much.'

'I won't,' Mick promised. Then he beamed at Kate and Pat. 'So what's for tea? I'm starving.'

Kate laughed. 'You're priceless. You should still be in a hospital bed feeling the effect of the anaesthetic.'

Mick sagged against the crutches. 'Well, I do actually. I was dying to get home, but now I feel a little wobbly.'

'Of course you do,' Kate said, rushing to his side. 'Enough of the bravado and get into bed. We'll get you something to eat on a tray.' She put her arm around his waist. 'Do you think you can get upstairs to your room, or should we rig up a bed down here?'

'I can manage the stairs,' Mick replied, breaking away and hobbling down the hall. 'I think I can even manage to get into my PJs all by myself.'

'Okay,' Pat said. 'If you're sure. I'll let Bridget know you're back.'

'No, let me tell her,' Mick protested. 'Bridget?' he shouted. 'Look who's home.'

Bridget rushed out of the kitchen, wiping her hands on her apron. 'Holy saints in heaven,' she exclaimed when she saw Mick. 'Did they let you out already? What were they thinking? How are you feeling?'

'I'm fine, darlin',' Mick said, hanging on his crutches. 'I'll just need a lot of TLC for about two months.'

'Two months?' Bridget asked, looking shocked. 'That's a very long time. You could get so spoiled you're ruined for life. But we're not going to let that happen, are we, Kate?'

'No,' Kate declared. 'I was just thinking that we need help with filing patient reports and things like that. It'll be brilliant to have more time for patients.'

'Exactly,' Bridget said. 'But right now, I think we do need do to spoil him a little. If you can get up to your bedroom, I'll bring you your tea in bed. We'll have roast chicken tonight, your favourite.'

'Oh, Bridget, I love you,' Mick said with a sigh. 'I'll get into bed straight away, so.' He started up the stairs and managed to get to the top with impressive speed.

Kate looked up at him in awe. 'You're amazing on those things,' she shouted up the stairs. 'You'd think you've been at it all your life.'

'I'm just multitalented, darlin',' Mick called back. 'Hey, come up and see me after tea,' he added before he disappeared from view.

Kate laughed. 'Talk about making an entrance.'

'He seems okay,' Pat said, looking relieved. 'I'll go and call Helen and tell her. She'll want to come over to see him. She might even want to stay for a few days.'

'Terrific,' Kate said. She knew that Mick's convalescence wasn't going to be easy. He might be all gung-ho and happy right now, but it wouldn't take long for such a gregarious, lively man to get seriously bored. He was already a little moody, and Helen fussing around him might make him feel even more irritated. She also couldn't help but think that Helen's arrival might cause extra tension in the house. How would Cormac feel about her returning to town? Would he want to confront her? Suddenly Kate was even more desperate to have her own sample of that clay tested. She hoped it would sort everything out.

# Chapter Eighteen

Kate's misgivings proved to be right. Helen arrived the next day and started to fuss around Mick and run the house like a sergeant major. Looking after him had to be done to a strict routine, and she drew up schedules and rules on a large sheet of paper that she pinned up on the noticeboard in the kitchen. Everything centred around Mick. The fact that a busy GP practice was in the same house seemed of no importance. Kate found herself either escaping into the office or going out for long walks or runs on the beach just to get away from the house and Helen's incessant orders and rules. Pat didn't seem to mind at all, and just let it all wash over him as he stuck to his own little routine. But he was used to her, Bridget said in private to Kate early one morning.

'The only reason their marriage works is that he lets her have her way about things that don't matter, but he still decides the things that do,' Bridget added in a conspiratorial whisper just before Helen sailed in, asking for breakfast on a tray for Mick.

Kate suppressed a giggle as Bridget handed Helen the perfectly laid tray with everything Mick would want.

'Here you go, Helen,' Bridget said. 'All there for the poor lad. He's holding up well, considering, don't you think?'

'Yes,' Helen said, looking at the tray. 'Where's the orange juice, Bridget? You know Mick likes a glass of cold juice with his breakfast.'

'Oh, sorry,' Bridget exclaimed, running to the fridge. 'It slipped my mind.' She opened the fridge but then gave a little yelp. 'Oh, feck! I forgot to buy some. I'm so sorry, Helen. I'll text John and he'll get it on his way home from school later today.'

Helen nodded. 'Thank you. But I don't suppose you could go and get it right now? Or maybe Kate could go? I hate for Mick not to have a nice breakfast.'

'I'm sorry,' Kate said, 'but I only have time for a quick bite before surgery starts in about twenty minutes. Pat went out on a call just now. I'm sure Mick will understand.'

'Very well. I suppose he'll cope,' Helen said and walked out with the tray, her shoulders and back telling them she did not approve.

Bridget sighed and shook her head. 'I remember when he was nine and got the chickenpox, she fussed around him like a crazy mother hen and he lost his temper with her. The same will happen again. She only remembers she's his mother when he's sick. She's trying to play the hero.' Bridget continued when she saw Kate's shocked face, 'I know it sounds awful, but between you and me, Mick was better off with me and Pat and John and the people in the village. Kids need consistency. Helen can't help being the way she is.'

Kate nodded. 'I see,' she said. 'Well, I suppose not everyone has that mother instinct.'

'Very true. Helen isn't a bad person, and she supports Mick in other ways. I suppose she felt honour bound to come here and start fussing when she heard about his accident.'

'Maybe she feels guilty,' Kate suggested. 'You know, like she has to put on some kind of show?'

'Could be,' Bridget said as she finished her tea. 'But I think there's another reason she galloped over here in a hurry. Something to do with that place by the tower. I heard her talking to someone on the phone yesterday and telling them to go and investigate. What could that be about, do you think?'

'Not sure,' Kate said, feeling a dart of guilt about telling a fib. But the fewer the people who knew what was going on, the better. *So*, she thought as she went out to the practice, *Helen didn't rush over only to nurse her injured son. She also has a very secret agenda.*

When Helen had left, the whole house seemed to breathe a sigh of relief. The next day, Mick returned to the living room, declaring he needed company and practically ordered Kate to join him during her lunch hour. She happily complied and sat down in the chair by the fireplace while Mick lounged on the sofa, his injured foot on a padded stool.

'Hi there. How's things?' he asked the minute she sat down.

'Fine,' Kate replied. 'Bit busy at the minute with the flu season beginning, and all. But Christmas is coming and then it'll all settle for a bit, I'm told.'

'Until it revs up again after New Year,' Mick said with a grin. 'You ain't seen nothing like the beginning of January around here. I'm happy Dad has you to assist him. I don't want him to keel over just when he's about to retire.'

'Thanks for the cheer,' Kate quipped, biting into the sandwich she had just made herself in the kitchen. 'I only have half an hour,' she explained, 'so this'll have to be a quick chat.'

'Okay.' Mick shifted on the sofa. 'I'll make it snappy, so.'

Kate forgot to chew. 'Make what snappy?'

'Telling you what happened about that phone call from LA.'

'Oh, yes. I had forgotten about that. So?' Kate chewed and swallowed. 'What happened? Did they make you an offer?'

'Oh yeah,' Mick said with a wry smile. 'They sure did.'

'Oh, wow!' Kate exclaimed, feeling excited. 'That's fantastic! So it's going to be a movie, then?'

'No.'

She blinked at him. 'Why not?'

'Because,' Mick said looking glum, 'I turned them down.'

'Turned them down?' Kate said, confused. 'Why?'

'Because of the changes they wanted me to make.' Mick sat up. 'That call was from the Feelgood Channel. They were interested in the play for a miniseries, you see.'

'The Feelgood Channel?' Kate exclaimed. 'You mean the one with the sweet romance miniseries? But that's the wrong genre… I mean your play is…'

Mick nodded. 'Exactly. My agent sent them the pitch by mistake. The producer used to work for Miramax but he had changed jobs for some reason. Anyway, they said they loved the premise, and the title, but that the story was too dark. They said if I rewrote the whole thing and took out the black humour, the sex, the satire, the bad language and… well, practically everything, and made the love story the central theme, then we'd have a deal.'

'Oh, God.'

'Yeah.' Mick regarded Kate. 'So I fell down the stairs for nothing. But the money they offered was good, of course.' He paused. 'You might think I'd be livid about it.'

'I would be in your shoes – shoe,' Kate added, looking at Mick's good foot.

'Nah, I'm not. It has made me look at the play with different eyes. It might be a little too dark and too controversial. Not subtle enough. Plus, our chats before the accident have inspired me to go in a slightly different direction. What you said about your man Cormac made me think.'

'What did I say about him?' Kate asked. 'I can't remember.'

'Something along the lines of him not quite believing in his magic powers himself and that he's a little puzzled by it. Something like that.' Mick looked enquiringly at Kate. 'So how's it going anyway? You and him, I mean.'

'Why do you ask?'

Mick smiled. 'Because I saw the two of you dancing in the pub that night. You looked so incredibly in tune, and then there was the way you looked at each other…'

'I don't know what you mean,' Kate said, feeling her face redden.

'Yes, you do.'

'I don't want to talk about it.' Kate looked away so he wouldn't see the sadness that welled up inside her. 'I have to get back to work in a minute anyway.'

'That bad, eh?'

Kate looked back at Mick. 'We're just not seeing things the same way. It's not working at all between us.'

'And it makes you sad.'

'Yes.' Kate hesitated for a moment. Mick was a true friend who cared about her, and it would be good to share her problems with someone who'd listen. 'He's a wonderful person,' she said. 'Kind and caring. Everyone loves him. But the way he thinks is not at all compatible with what I've been taught. I can't support his methods in any way. We constantly argue about it and I know we'll never agree. And that makes it impossible for us to have any kind of relationship. Except maybe some kind of friendly connection.' She blinked, fighting with tears that had welled up because of the kindness and understanding in Mick's eyes.

'I see what you mean. Must be hard,' he said.

Kate nodded. 'It makes me so sad,' she said, her voice shaking. 'Even though I know we're wrong for each other. But still, I feel so drawn to him despite knowing that we're not compatible. And he doesn't trust me. That's what's making me sad.'

'You don't think you could talk about it?' Mick suggested. 'If you decided to keep all that stuff about healing out of the conversation, maybe…'

'No. That's not possible. It's so much part of who we are and what we care most about.' Kate wiped her eyes with the back of her hand. 'Before I came here, I was working in the A&E department in a hospital in Dublin, which was exciting and challenging. But I found it so frustrating that we couldn't spend any time with patients or make them feel reassured. I thought it was something in me – that I lacked empathy or something.'

'I'm sure that wasn't true,' Mick protested. 'Both Bridget and Dad say you have great people skills.'

'Do they? That's nice to know. I came here to get a break from all of that, but also to learn more about handling patients. Cormac has that wonderful way with people. That's one of the things I like about him, so I'd never want to stop discussing my passions with him. If we could only solve the controversies between us.' She sighed. 'But what's the use? I'll be leaving at the end of April anyway.' She looked at Mick, feeling even sadder.

'I'm sorry,' he said gently.

'Thank you.' Kate checked her watch and got up from the chair. 'Thanks for listening.'

'Any time,' Mick said and waved. 'See you later.'

'Yeah. Later.' Kate walked out and closed the door, ready to tackle the rest of the day, cheered by what Mick had said about her people skills. At least Pat and Bridget believed in her, and that was a huge relief.

Her phone pinged as she walked into the practice. It was a text message from Liz, the microbiologist.

*Have the results. Call me when you can.*

# Chapter Nineteen

It was hard to concentrate on patients, as the text message kept popping up in Kate's mind all through the afternoon. She couldn't wait to hear what Liz had found, and heaved a sigh of relief as the last patients, a mother and baby with a chesty cough, left with a prescription for antibiotics. Kate closed the door behind them and went back to the desk, filed the report into the computer and turned it off, before picking up her phone.

Liz answered on the second ring, 'Hi, Kate. How are you?'

'Fine, thanks,' Kate replied. 'Tiring day, but they all are these days, running up to Christmas.'

'I can imagine.' Liz paused. 'So I got the results of the analysis. I'm sure you're dying to know what that lump of earth contained.'

'Yes,' Kate said. 'Of course I am. What did you find?'

Liz laughed. 'The results were surprising, actually.'

'Really? Why?' Kate asked, her heart beating faster. 'Tell me. I'm going nuts here waiting.'

'Okay. I'll tell you. But I'm sorry to break some bad news to you. That bit of earth didn't actually contain very much. A few minerals and a tiny bit of limestone. But none of the antibiotic properties like the famous Fermanagh discovery.'

'None at all?' Kate asked, incredulously.

'Nope. Sorry to disappoint you.'

Kate didn't quite know what to say. 'But,' she started, 'that ointment made from it has healed some really bad scars. It can't just be this healer's magic hands or something, can it?'

'Not likely,' Liz replied. 'They do say faith can move mountains.'

'Not like this.'

'Hmm.' Liz was silent. 'Did you say it was mixed with something?' she said after a while. 'What was it?'

'Coconut oil and oregano oil,' Kate replied.

'I see. Hmm, well oregano oil has strong antibacterial properties, of course. That's been used since the times of Ancient Greece. Could be that. And combined with coconut oil, it could be something that might be very healing. And that could have had an anti-inflammatory effect on the scar tissue.'

'Yes, maybe,' Kate agreed, her heart sinking. This was disappointing to say the least. It would have been such a boost to patients with bad scarring if there had been some undiscovered ingredient in the earth. 'What about the Fermanagh stuff?' she asked.

'It'll take a year or two before the clinical trials are conclusive, but we're all excited about it. It's a pity that this sample doesn't have any similar antibiotic qualities. Or something new for healing scars. It would have been great if we had found something closer to home.'

'It would,' Kate agreed. 'But maybe it was a good thing in a way. It would have caused problems for the village.'

'It could have stirred things up a bit and ruined the peace, I suppose. But things like that take time, of course. Don't know what's going on with the other stuff in Fermanagh. I think it's going to be big, but we're not there yet.'

'Thank you so much for doing this,' Kate said. 'I really appreciate it.'

'No problem,' Liz said. 'I love doing this kind of thing. And maybe, if you come across something else that occurs naturally in that area that seems to work, give me a shout. Plants, roots, anything.'

'I will,' Kate promised. They said goodbye and Kate stayed at the desk, staring out into the dark garden wondering how she was going to break the news to Cormac. She had wanted to know what was in the soil that had been so healing, and now her curiosity was satisfied. But she didn't quite know what to do with the information. Tell Helen that there was nothing there for her to use? And then tell Cormac? But he would be upset that she had done this behind his back and the rift between them would be greater than ever. And he would be so disappointed that his remedy simply consisted of mud and the few ingredients he had added himself. The fact that the ointment seemed to be so healing was a mystery she couldn't understand. Feeling even more conflicted than before, Kate decided to leave well enough alone. For now.

The landline phone rang downstairs after tea. Bridget went to answer, thinking it was someone needing a doctor. But she came back looking relieved. 'Clodagh O'Meara for you, Kate.'

'Me?' Kate asked, getting up from the kitchen table where they had just finished eating. 'What does she want?'

'No idea,' Bridget said.

'Go and find out and come back and tell us,' Mick suggested. 'She's great craic, that woman.'

Kate went out into the hall and picked up the phone. 'Hello, Clodagh. How are you?'

'I'm grand, girl,' Clodagh replied. 'No problems here at all. I'm calling about the quilt I made for you. I've finished it, and thought you might like to come and collect it.'

'Oh, goodness,' Kate said, crestfallen. 'I had completely forgotten about it. I should have come round to talk about it, but it's been so busy here lately.'

'I know,' Clodagh replied with a laugh. 'That's why I didn't want to bother you. But I think, as the nights are getting chilly, you might need something to keep you warm. So I hurried it up a little.'

'I can't wait to see it. When would it suit you?'

'How about tonight?' Clodagh replied. 'If it's not too late for you.'

'Not at all,' Kate said, feeling excited to see the quilt made just for her. 'It's only half past seven. I'll be up there as soon as I can.' She suddenly looked forward to the evening ahead. It was just the break she needed right now.

'Excellent,' Clodagh said. 'And it'll be just the three of us, of course.'

'Three?' Kate asked. 'You mean with Brian, your dog?'

Clodagh laughed. 'No, I meant you, me and Cormac. He was the one who suggested I ask you up.'

'Oh,' Kate said, the butterflies in her stomach fluttering even more.

'So I'll put the kettle on,' Clodagh's cheery voice said. 'See you in a little while.'

Kate said goodbye and hung up, staring at her face in the mirror. She looked pale and drawn after a long day, and her green cardigan made her look even more drained. She turned and ran up the stairs to her room, rifled through her wardrobe and threw on her red cashmere sweater, the one she had worn that night she danced with Cormac. Then she applied a little foundation, blusher and some mascara, all of which put a little life in her face and lifted her mood. So, she was maybe too dressed up for a cup of tea with an old woman in a cottage, but for some strange reason she wanted to look her very best. She pushed her fingers through her short hair, and silently blessed Gerry at the hairdresser's for the beautiful cut he had achieved.

Grabbing her bag, she ran down the stairs again and pulled on her jacket, shouting a 'Goodbye I'll see you later' in the direction of the living room, where she could hear Pat and Mick talking. Then she ran out of the house, banged the door shut and got into her car. She grabbed the steering wheel and sat there for a moment, gathering her thoughts – and her feelings. She had a strange inkling something was about to happen and she wasn't sure if it would be good or bad. But this something, whatever it was, *had* to happen to change the stalemate she was in with Cormac. *The air needs to be cleared between us*, she thought, *before we can move on*. And that included telling him about the results of the analysis. She swallowed, and nodded, starting the engine, driving off into the darkness and whatever lay ahead.

# Chapter Twenty

Clodagh's cottage glowed with light, both from the windows and the little lamps on a string around the door and in the trees. It was like something from a fairy tale, Kate thought as she parked the car outside the low stone wall. She took a deep breath of the cold, crisp air and looked up at the stars glinting above as she walked up the path to the front door. The quiet was suddenly broken by an owl hooting in a tree somewhere and then Brian the Labrador barked inside just before Clodagh, in an ankle-length green dress, swung the door open.

'Kate!' she said and stepped aside. 'Come in out of the cold. Be quiet, Brian, it's Kate.'

Brian stopped barking and padded forward to sniff at Kate's leg. She patted his head and smiled at Clodagh as she took off her jacket. 'Hello, Clodagh. Your house looks beautiful with all the lights.'

Clodagh nodded. 'Thank you. Please come in. We have both wine and tea, whatever you prefer.' She walked ahead into the living room where a log fire blazed in the fireplace.

Cormac, looking unusually dressed up in a white sweater and blue trousers, rose from the sofa as Kate entered. 'Hello, Kate,' he said. 'I'm glad to see you.'

'Me too,' Kate said. There was an awkward silence while they faced each other, both trying to appear unaffected by the vibes between them. 'You look nice,' she said to fill the deafening silence.

Cormac's eyes softened. 'So do you,' he said. 'It's been a while since we met.'

'But now you're here,' Clodagh said briskly as if she was unaware of what was going on between them – or maybe wanting to defuse the tension. 'Do you want to see the quilt, Kate?'

'Oh yes,' Kate exclaimed. 'Where is it?'

'Over there.' Clodagh gestured at the large work table by the window.

Kate walked over and gasped as she saw the beautiful quilt spread out over the table. It was made of a multitude of colourful squares, forming a stunning picture of the mountains covered in heather against the blue sky. O'Rourke's tower stood at the edge, overlooking the azure sea with swallows gliding around it, and the Arbutus tree covered in white flowers and red berries, just like it had been when Kate first saw it. She touched the soft material. 'It's the most beautiful thing I've seen in my whole life,' she said, looking at Clodagh with tears in her eyes.

'I hope it will give you sweet dreams. I knew you'd like the mountains, and especially the area around the tower. Cormac told me that you love that place especially.'

'You did?' Kate asked, looking at Cormac.

He smiled and nodded. 'Yes. Of course. It's a magical place for you. And for me,' he added. 'Because it's part of our family histories.'

'And because you brought me there,' Kate said softly. She wanted to touch his cheek or just take his hand, but Clodagh being there stopped her. How strange that she should feel such a surge of affection for him. Maybe it was written in those stars she had seen glimmering in the dark sky outside, or the shared history of their families from centuries ago, but she felt the connection to him so strongly at that moment, as if an invisible hand was pushing her towards him.

'Tea,' Clodagh said in a brisk voice. 'And my fruit cake. Or a glass of wine, Kate?'

Kate blinked and moved away from the table, distancing herself from Cormac's troubling presence. 'A glass of wine would be lovely,' she said. 'But just a small one as I'm driving.'

'Grand.' Clodagh moved across the room to the coffee table in front of the sofa that had been laid with cups, glasses and a plate with slices of fruit cake. They joined her and sat on the sofa, stiffly, side by side, eating cake, Kate sipping her glass of wine and Cormac drinking tea from a mug decorated with shamrocks.

'The quilt is gorgeous,' Kate said. 'I'm really grateful to you for taking so much trouble. Must have taken you many hours.'

'Yes, it did,' Clodagh agreed, pouring herself a glass of wine. 'But it was a real labour of love. Not that I'm going to give it away for free,' she added with a laugh. 'But I'll only charge you for the material.'

'Gosh,' Kate said. 'That's very generous. I wouldn't mind paying the full price at all. It's so exquisite. A work of art.'

'Not at all,' Clodagh protested. 'I did put aside a commissioned tapestry to make your quilt, but I'll catch up in no time.' She leaned forward and looked at Kate. 'I'm proud of having made this quilt for our new doctor.'

'And I'll be incredibly happy to sleep under a quilt made by Clodagh O'Meara,' Kate replied, smiling at Clodagh. She took a big bite of the delicious cake and sipped her wine, leaning back into the sofa, suddenly feeling very happy and blessed to be here in this gorgeous cottage with Clodagh and Cormac, and Brian snoring at their feet.

Cormac visibly relaxed as if he could sense a positive shift in her mood. 'It's truly beautiful, Clodagh,' he said. He sipped his tea and glanced at Kate. 'So what else have you been up to?'

'The usual,' Kate replied. 'The practice is very busy, and then Mick has just come home and will probably need to be entertained. He's already getting bored and restless, even though he has his play to work on.'

'I can imagine,' Cormac said. 'But I'm sure you're cheering him up.'

'Mick was always a very lively lad,' Clodagh said with affection. 'I remember him running around the village when he was small, never sitting still, always into one thing or another.'

'Doesn't surprise me,' Kate said, the image of Mick as a mischievous small boy popping into her mind.

They sat in front of the fire and chatted on for a while, Kate telling Cormac about Tara and how much she missed her, and Cormac nodding and saying he understood as he was very close to his own sister. Then Kate announced it was time for her to go. 'I promised to take morning surgery tomorrow,' she said and got up. 'So I'd like to get to bed early.'

'Of course,' Clodagh said and jumped up. 'I'll pack up the quilt in some tissue paper for you.'

Cormac got up and looked at Kate. 'I'd better get going, too. It'll take a little longer to walk down in the dark.'

'Oh, but I can give you a lift,' Kate offered.

Cormac nodded. 'Thank you. That'd be grand.'

'Great. I'll just get the quilt from Clodagh and then we'll be off.' She took the quilt wrapped in tissue paper. 'Thanks again, Clodagh. Tell me how much I owe you.'

'We can settle that later,' Clodagh said. 'I hope you'll be happy with it.'

'I'll always treasure it,' Kate said. 'Thank you for a lovely evening.'

Clodagh hugged both Kate and Cormac in turn. 'Bye, darlings. Be happy and safe.'

Kate smiled at Clodagh, patted Brian on the head and walked out ahead of Cormac.

He caught up with her when she was getting into the car and settled into the passenger seat, taking the quilt from her and putting it on the back seat. Kate started the engine and they drove off down the winding road towards the village. She turned on the radio and a soft Irish ballad helped to fill the silence that was full of tension. The closeness to Cormac in the small car was unnerving and Kate felt her neck and shoulders tense as she stared into the beam of the headlights that illuminated the winding road ahead.

'Cold evening,' Cormac said as they neared the village.

'Yes,' Kate said. 'Is this the lane to your house?' she asked as they reached a fork in the road.

'Yes. Left here.'

'Okay.'

It didn't take long before they reached the little white cottage, where the light had been left on over the front door. Kate pulled up and turned off the engine. 'Here we are,' she said.

'Yes. Thanks for the lift.' Cormac moved to get out, but Kate put her hand on his arm.

'There is something I need to tell you.'

Cormac turned towards her, his face illuminated by the lights on the dashboard. 'What?'

'It's about that soil beside the tower.'

'What about it?' he asked, his voice tense.

'I found something out about it.'

'You did? What would that be?' There was a wary expression in his eyes as he looked at her. 'You said you needed to tell me. Does this mean it's something I won't like?'

Kate looked down for a moment, struggling with the dilemma of how to break the news to him. Not only that she'd had the soil analysed without telling him, but also that there was nothing in it that explained its healing properties. 'Yes, I'm afraid it is. Please don't be upset when I tell you.'

'So it's bad news, then? What could be worse than me losing access to the field beside the tower?'

Kate squeezed his arm. 'Hey, don't gallop ahead like that with your gloom and doom scenario. My news is both good and bad, depending on how you see it.'

'So tell me,' Cormac ordered, staring at her.

Kate nodded, her throat tight with nerves. 'Remember that lump of soil you gave me?'

'Yes?'

'Well, I put it into my pocket that day we were in Wild Rose Bay. I found it there the next day and I decided to have it analysed by someone I trust. I got the name of a microbiologist at Cork University Hospital and sent her the sample.'

Cormac pulled away. 'You sent it away to be analysed behind my back?'

'I didn't see it that way. Just let me finish.'

'What other way is there? You could have told me about this,' Cormac said, his voice cold.

'I'm telling you now. I didn't think there was much point saying anything before I had the result.'

'Why did you do it at all?' He looked away and focused on the view from the window. 'You didn't trust me when I told you about the healing powers of the earth, did you? You had to go and have it analysed before you could believe it.'

'I did trust you, but I wanted to know exactly what was in it,' Kate said, taken aback by the bitter tone in his voice. 'I needed to know what was in it mostly because I was curious. And then I thought I might stop Helen's company from excavating the area. Can't you see that?'

'No.' He shifted in his seat. 'I understand your motives, but not your doing it without telling me.'

'You wouldn't have agreed if I had asked you. Would you?'

'Probably not. But you don't seem to have cared about my feelings at all.'

Kate felt as if she was up against a stone wall. 'Whatever you think, I have to tell you what happened next. I got the results today.'

'You did?' Cormac turned to look at her. 'And what was it?' he urged. 'Tell me. What does that earth contain?'

'Nothing,' Kate said and let go of his arm. 'I mean, of course, all earth has all sorts of things in it, traces of certain minerals, bacteria and so on. But it doesn't have the same healing properties as the earth in County Fermanagh.' She drew breath and looked at him in the dim light. 'I'm sorry, Cormac.'

'Oh,' he said, looking shocked. 'My God. That's…'

'I know. A bit of a shock.'

'But…' he said, sounding utterly bewildered. 'I mean, it's had such an amazing effect on those wounds. How did this scientist explain that? Did you ask her?'

Kate nodded. 'Yes. She said it might be due to the mixture of oregano and coconut oils. Oregano oil can be effective against infection and inflammation, can't it?'

'Yes, so it's thought. But… I mean, that doesn't explain the effect it had.'

'I know. It's very strange. But in one way it's good news, isn't it?'

Cormac let out an ironic little laugh. 'I suppose it is. Helen certainly has no reason to want it now, and the land is safe.'

'Exactly.'

Cormac fixed on Kate as if her news had just sunk in. 'My God,' he said, slowly letting out his breath. 'This is very strange.'

'I know. You must be disappointed.'

He shrugged. 'No. A little shaken, perhaps. But not really disappointed. There is something there, at the tower, but maybe not in the earth the way I thought. Could be some other powers at work. Or – just me.'

'Your healing hands, you mean?'

He looked at his hands. 'No. I don't actually believe in that. But it's something, somewhere that we can't grasp or comprehend. Something special to that place.'

'There is a magical feel to that land, that's true,' Kate admitted. 'A combination of many things. And people around here feel it very strongly. It might be that the effect of the cream is somehow psychosomatic.' She shrugged. 'We'll never know. But in any case, that place seems a little magical to me. It's all so lovely. Ancient history in the walls of the tower, the standing stone, the people who were there nearly a thousand years ago. But trying to capture it is like trying to catch a shadow or a cloud. Or a dream.'

'I know.' Cormac cleared his throat and opened the door. 'I'll say goodnight now. Thanks for the lift,' he added curtly.

'No, wait,' Kate pleaded.

'For what? I think we've said enough.' Cormac got out of the car and closed the door.

Kate scrambled out of her seat and ran to his side as he walked away. 'Please, don't go off like that,' she pleaded. 'We had such a nice evening. It's a pity to ruin it by arguing.'

He stopped walking. 'Isn't it already ruined?'

'Why?' She looked up at him, trying to see his face, but it was too dark. 'I'm sorry I didn't tell you about doing the analysis. I thought it would be better to wait for the result and then tell you.'

'Why does everything have to be analysed?' he asked. 'Why can't things stay as they are? Couldn't you have left it alone?'

'No,' she said. 'I couldn't. I've seen what that ointment can do and I was amazed. I wanted to be able to recommend it. And I couldn't do that until I knew what it was. But I also did this for *you*,

Cormac. I wanted to find a way to save that little field and for you to continue to gather your plants and roots there. And now you can.'

He looked slightly mollified. 'That's a good thing, I suppose. So what are you going to do now?'

'I'll certainly recommend it to my patients and tell them to get it from you.'

'That's such an honour,' he said, his voice full of sarcasm.

Suddenly furious, Kate grabbed his arm. 'Do you have to be so difficult?' she exclaimed, close to tears. 'Can't you see that this is a positive thing, and not some kind of insult? It could be the start of us working together at last. We could begin to see each other's point of view and perhaps even learn from each other. And that would benefit all those people who come to us for help.' She sighed and let go of his arm. 'And maybe,' she whispered, 'we might at last admit how we feel about each other. But I suppose that's impossible now.' She turned away from him and started back to the car.

Cormac turned and followed her, spinning her around to face him. 'No,' he said. 'That's not impossible. Can we talk about that? About you and me, and forget the other stuff for a minute?'

'Of course,' she said, suddenly feeling a ray of hope. She took a deep breath. 'When we were at the tower that day, there was something between us.'

'Yes,' Cormac whispered, taking both her hands in his. 'It was something special, to do with that place. But also… a connection between us.'

'I… yes. The whisper of the past, the…' She stopped, shivering, emotion overwhelming her. 'Oh, I don't know, really. I don't understand what's going on.'

'But I do.' He leaned towards her. 'Kate…' And then he lightly kissed her mouth before he drew back and gazed at her.

Kate looked into his eyes that were so tender and full of love and felt a warmth inside her. She suddenly knew she had been waiting for this to happen all evening. She closed her eyes and he kissed her again, harder, deeper, wrapping his arms around her and holding her so tight she could hardly breathe. Kate gave herself up to his soft lips, his strong arms and the faint scent of herbs and flowers, knowing that this was what she had been dreaming about ever since they met. They broke apart, breathing hard, smiling.

'Cormac,' Kate murmured, tears of joy in her eyes. 'I feel so strange.'

'In a good way?' he asked.

'In a wonderful way.'

'I feel so full of love for you,' he said and kissed her lightly on the cheek.

'I'm sorry to have brought you such bad news,' Kate said, leaning her head against his shoulder. 'I should have told you what I was doing from the start.'

'That doesn't matter.' He looked at her, his eyes blazing. 'If the earth had been proven to contain something that would be groundbreaking for modern medicine, our whole existence would be changed – and not for the better.'

Kate nodded. 'Yes. I see what you mean. Things would change around here. We wouldn't want the peace and tranquillity of Sandy Cove to be ruined.' She sighed. 'This might be a sleepy backwater and the back of beyond and all that. But it's a blessed place that simply has to be protected. So yes, thank God and all the saints in heaven there was nothing in that earth.'

'But Helen will be upset,' Cormac said with pretend sadness.

'I know. But so what?'

'I'll give her the recipe for my goodnight tea. She's been nagging me for it for ages.'

'That's very generous of you.'

'Not really. I will charge a hefty fee and ask for commission. She'll agree, I'm sure.'

'Maybe you should tell her about that as soon as possible?' Kate suggested. 'Before she gets the news about the earth?'

'I suppose you're right. I'll call her first thing in the morning.' Reluctantly, he let her go. 'You know, I've been living with this belief about myself all my life. This conviction that I have some kind of supernatural gift of healing. It was hard to grow up with that. I was ostracised by the other kids in school and didn't have many friends. This made me a very solitary little boy. And then all those sick people who came to ask me to heal them. I was the seventh son of the seventh son, so I had to have what they called "the gift". It was confusing to say the least. It didn't help that my parents believed it, too.'

'Did you believe it?' Kate asked.

'I did in the beginning.' He laughed. 'I thought I was like Superman and that I'd be able to fly when I was older. That maybe I had come from another planet and my parents had adopted me. But then, when I was a teenager, and I started to doubt it all, I realised that it's important for people to have someone to believe in. And if that person was me, I'd do my best to help them.'

'I know what you mean,' Kate said. 'I have sometimes wondered why I wanted to be a doctor. I was inspired by my dad as I grew up, but there was also something in me that made me want to help and heal the sick. I've realised since I came here that there might be something in my genes from ancient times, from those healers in the Middle Ages. It sounds strange in this day and age to feel like that, but I do.'

'I'm glad you do,' Cormac replied, looking at her with his luminous green eyes. 'We both have that gene, but in different ways. I suppose yours is more involved with science than mine.'

'That's very true,' Kate agreed. 'What about the rest of the family? Did they believe that stuff about your healing powers?'

'Not really. My brothers were much older than me and some of them had even left home when I was born. But my sister Mairead was born a year after me and we were very close when we grew up. She thought it was all superstitious rubbish, which was a huge relief. I felt like just a normal kid when I was with her. She was my only friend, really. We used to run wild over the hills in Dingle in the summertime. Barefoot and free. It was wonderful.'

'Where is she now?'

'She married a fisherman and lives in Dingle town. They have three children. Lovely family. You'll like them.'

'I'm sure I will.'

Cormac smiled and put his arms around Kate. 'And now you'll have to go home and go to sleep. We can't burn the candle at both ends, Dr Kate. And we both have work to do.'

She kissed him. 'Yes. We do. What will you do about the ointment?'

'I'll keep using it on bad wounds. It doesn't do any harm, anyway, does it?'

'No, not at all. And who knows? It could be that you do have healing hands. Some things just can't be explained.' Kate took one of Cormac's hands and put it to her cheek. 'Whatever it is, I love the touch and feel of them.'

'And I could stay here with you all night. Or – I could ask you inside, but it's not the right time.'

'Why?' she asked, suddenly longing to see his home.

'Because it's a mess.' He grinned and let go of her, opening the door. 'I'll ask you to come for tea when I've tidied up. My sweet Kate, we have to say goodnight. Tomorrow is another day, as my aunt Clodagh used to say when I was six and didn't want to go to bed.'

'Another day with you, I hope,' Kate said wistfully.

'Yes. That's something to look forward to.' Cormac leaned over and placed a light kiss on her mouth. 'Goodnight. Sweet dreams. I'll be in touch.'

'Goodnight, Cormac,' Kate said, watching him walk down the path to his door. He turned and waved before he disappeared inside.

Kate got back in the car and sat there watching the light in one of the windows being turned on and the curtains pulled. Then all was dark and silent. She sighed happily and turned the car round, driving the short distance home, deep in thought. She knew she was deeply in love with Cormac despite their only having known each other for a few weeks. But the feeling, that connection between them, had been there from the start. It was as if it was meant to happen, and nearly as if they had known each other in an earlier life. A ridiculous idea, of course, but deep down there was something about it that appealed to her. The big problem was the fact that she'd be leaving in a few months. But that was a long way off, and she decided not to worry about that right now.

She parked the car outside the house and got out, closing the door softly so she wouldn't wake anyone. Then she took the parcel with the quilt from the back seat, opened the door and tiptoed in, hanging up her jacket before heading upstairs, thinking everyone was asleep. But as she reached the stairs, she noticed a light under the door to the living room and someone talking and laughing inside. Intrigued, Kate opened the door and peered in, discovering Mick on the sofa in front of the dying embers of the fire, FaceTiming with someone on his phone. She was about to walk away, but he had noticed her and waved at her to come in.

'Hi, Kate,' he said. 'Guess who I'm talking to?'

'I don't know, who?' Kate said and walked inside.

Mick turned the phone so she could see. 'Someone you know very well.'

Kate looked at the phone and did a double take as she discovered who it was. 'What?' she exclaimed. 'How on earth…'

# Chapter Twenty-One

Kate looked at the face on Mick's phone. 'Tara!'

'Yeah, it's me,' Tara chortled and waved. 'Hi, Kate!'

Confused, Kate looked at Mick. 'But how… I mean, why? What's going on?'

'Nothing,' Mick said, looking the picture of innocence. 'This just happened tonight.'

'This?' Kate asked, sinking down on the sofa. 'What do you mean, *this*?'

'We hooked up by accident,' Tara shouted from Mick's phone. 'I was looking at his Instagram pictures and saw the video of your climb in Kerry. So I put in a comment and then he looked up my Instagram profile and then…'

'Then I looked at her amazing photos. I was so impressed I asked if she'd like to chat, and that's how it all started,' Mick said. He paused and looked from Tara's face to Kate. 'Holy mother, you're so alike. Unbelievable.'

'Have you never seen twins before?' Kate asked.

'Yes, but never up close and personal like this,' Mick said.

'This is getting weird,' Kate said and took Mick's phone. 'Tara, I suppose you're back in New York. You haven't been in touch since you came back. How are things?'

Tara beamed. 'Brilliant. But I'll hang up now. Have to go to the office and check in with my boss. I'll call you tomorrow. See yez later, lads.' Tara hung up, leaving Mick and Kate staring at each other, both laughing.

'She's fun,' Mick finally said. 'And not a carbon copy of you, really, except physically.'

'You mean she's fun and I'm not?' Kate asked.

'No, not like that. You're fun, too. But in a different way.' He peered at her as if he had just noticed her. 'You look… flushed. And glowing.' His eyes narrowed. 'What have you been up to?'

Kate got up. 'Nothing. Must be the wine I drank at Clodagh's.' She opened the parcel she had put on the sofa and unfolded the quilt, spreading it out on the coffee table. 'She made me this quilt. Isn't it beautiful?'

'Stunning. Like a painting. I love the colours and the motif. She's such a talented artist.' He felt the quilt with his fingers. 'And this is light, so you can just put it on top of your duvet. It's exquisite.'

'Unique,' Kate said and folded the quilt. 'And now I'm going to spread this out on my bed and get in under it and go to sleep.'

'And dream sweet dreams, I bet,' Mick said with a wink.

'I will,' Kate said smiling. 'And so should you.'

'I'll just send an email, and then I'll head up to bed.' He paused. 'I enjoyed chatting to your sister. She's great gas.'

'What about that girl you flirted with in the pub a few weeks ago?' Kate couldn't help asking.

Mick looked confused. 'Who? Oh, you mean Susie. No, that was a non-starter. She's in some kind of complicated relationship, she told me. On-off kind of thing. So I backed away. Cute girl, though.' He shrugged, looking a little sad. 'Story of my life. Can't find a girl who's truly single. Even your sister seems to be involved with someone. So she'll just be an online friend, I suppose.'

'Tara, involved?'

'Yes, she said something that made me think she was. Do you know anything about that?'

'No idea who that could be,' Kate said. 'Could be someone new. I'll have to ask her tomorrow.' Suddenly exhausted, she stifled a yawn. 'Got to go to bed. 'Night, Mick.'

'G'night, Kate. Sleep tight under that lovely quilt.'

Kate walked slowly upstairs, the quilt under her arm, her mind full of what had happened tonight. *Cormac*, she thought. *How strange and wonderful that we found each other*. She could still feel his kisses on her mouth and his arms around her. The love she felt for him knew no reason and didn't have much to do with her medical training and logical mind. Her heart ruled when it came to Cormac, and her head seemed to have taken a back seat. They would never agree about certain subjects and would probably argue hotly at times. But perhaps some of his beliefs about healing had rubbed off on her. Would this result in making her a better doctor, give her a deeper insight into healing? She was sure it would.

Mick and Tara connecting like that had been a bit of a shock, but it made her smile. They would get on very well, whatever happened between them. Kate would normally be more interested, ask questions, worry about whether it was a good idea, or if they were suited to each other, but her heart was too full of her own feelings, overshadowing her concerns for her twin sister. It made her a little sad that she and Tara hadn't been connecting like they used to, and that Tara didn't seem that interested in Sandy Cove and its connections with their father. But perhaps that was because she was so involved with her own world that was so different to Kate's reality.

Once in her room, Kate spread the glorious quilt over her duvet and got ready for bed. She crawled in under the bedclothes, running her hand over the soft quilt, closed her eyes and drifted off to sleep, walking with Cormac in her dreams through a meadow full of flowers.

# Chapter Twenty-Two

It was hard to concentrate on work, but during the next few days, Kate found herself immersed in patient care as there was a rush of people with flu symptoms, many of them small children. As Pat was no longer there to take morning surgery, Kate was working full time. She also had to make house calls to older people living in isolated areas who were too ill to come to the practice, even after hours. Pat remarked that they weren't strictly speaking obliged to make house calls after surgery hours, but this was the best way to make sure they were seen quickly and were reassured by someone they knew.

Kate didn't mind going out at night, even if it was tiring and gave her little time to see Cormac. She loved calling into the small cottages, where she was greeted with enormous gratitude and often treated to a cup of tea and a slice of cake in front of the turf fire, sometimes cuddling a little dog or a cat. She also enjoyed the chats and the stories of the old days of long ago, and was often told hilarious tales. She slowly began to understand Pat's love of this kind of doctoring and started to wonder if going back to big city medicine was really what she wanted to do. And in her own case, being here had made her feel closer to her father and her roots. She was beginning to see familiar features in some of the people around the village – a kind of kinship she hadn't noticed when she first arrived. It would be hard to leave all of this behind. But she would have no choice. The medical board would never accept her as the sole doctor of this rather busy country practice, as they would say that six months was not enough experience and that she needed to train for at least another year.

She told herself to think positively and looked forward to seeing Cormac at the weekend, when she had Sunday off and the weather forecast was good. They had planned to go for a hike again to Wild Rose Bay and then climb to the tower, where they would have a picnic lunch that Bridget had promised to prepare for them. But would everything be the same as it was the night they kissed? Despite having another four months at the surgery, Kate couldn't help worrying about what would happen next. There was still that niggling fear that Cormac hadn't quite forgiven her for having the sample tested without telling him. And also her own feelings of doubt about their relationship. They had put their concerns aside and let the attraction between them carry them away, but once they sobered up, would their differing opinions break them apart?

And Tara was giving Kate even more cause for concern. She was increasingly evasive about the person Mick said she was involved with. They had a great time joking and laughing, and Tara shared all her amazing photos from her trip down the Amazon, but they never seemed to focus on anything serious any more. She did tell Kate she was in touch with Mick, however, and how he had told her about his play. 'It seems really good,' she said. 'I gave him a few pointers about how to handle the relationship in the story.'

'Did he ask for your opinion on that?' Kate asked, amused by how Tara had a habit of handing out advice even if it hadn't been sought.

'No, but I told him anyway. Isn't it funny how men have no idea what women really want to hear?'

'Some men do, though,' Kate argued, her mind, as always, drifting to Cormac.

'Like that guy you're dating?' Tara said. 'Tell me about him.'

'Oh,' Kate said with feeling. 'It's difficult to describe Cormac. He's not like any man I've ever been involved with. I think you have to come here and meet him.'

'You look completely besotted when you say his name.'

Kate smiled. 'I am. Totally. He has… a kind of aura. He's very good-looking but I don't think he is aware of it. And he's intelligent and gentle and kind, but then he has this fire inside him. I have a feeling he would be very fierce if he got angry. He knows so much about Irish history and folklore, and you should hear him speak Irish. It's so beautiful. And his voice…'

'I get it,' Tara said, laughing. 'Hey, do a selfie with him and send it to me. I want to see this Mr Wonderful.'

'I will,' Kate promised, wondering why Tara was yet again changing the subject. Why was Irish history so boring to her?

'And tell Mick to work on the play,' Tara added. 'I'm off to Denver for Christmas with the crew. And then we're doing a feature on the luxury chalets and all the celebs who own them for *Vanity Fair*. We're sharing this huge chalet ourselves, and Joe will do the cooking. His family is Italian, so that should be fab.'

'You two seem to be getting close.'

'Maybe,' Tara replied airily.

'Are you and Joe dating?' Kate asked, anxious to finally know what was going on in Tara's life.

Tara shrugged. 'Sort of, but not really. I mean, there's this *feeling* between us, but we haven't really spelled it out or done anything about it. Let's just say there's sexual tension. He's my boss, so that makes it complicated. And he's not delighted that my photos get picked sometimes instead of his when they do the layouts for our features. But they have his company stamp on them, so he gets the glory, of course.'

'Doesn't sound fair,' Kate remarked.

'I know. But sometimes you have to take the back seat if you want stuff to work.'

'Stuff?' Kate asked.

'Oh, never mind,' Tara said, resigned. 'It's all a bit complicated, as the saying goes.' She changed the subject and then they had to say goodbye. No more was said about Tara's love life in their subsequent video chat when they wished each other Happy Christmas with tears in their eyes, as this would be the first Christmas apart since… Well, no need to spell that out.

How her life had changed, Kate thought. All to the good, except for her separation from her twin sister, which felt so hard at times. Being apart from Tara had made the grief for her father worse. But in another way, her job as a country doctor had brought him closer. Tara seemed happier these days, as if the distance and the new job had helped her move on. Tara had obviously little interest in history even if it concerned their family. But now Kate could talk about it with Cormac, and that was a huge comfort. He understood a lot of other things, too, without Kate having to explain. He had a way of reading her moods and responded in ways that were incredibly comforting. Even though they'd only known each other a short time, she often wondered how she would ever cope without him. It would be unbearable to have to say goodbye. But if it came to that eventually, they would still have something precious to remember.

# Chapter Twenty-Three

They walked to the tower on a cold, crisp day with brilliant sunshine. Kate watched Cormac climb up the steep slope ahead of her, nimble and steady on his feet, while she struggled to keep up, trying her best not to topple down the slope by digging her walking sticks deep into the ground. She glanced up now and then, Cormac's lithe figure not only reassuring but also giving her a little frisson as she remembered how he had held her and the way he had looked at her that evening when she had driven him home. Their eyes met as he glanced over his shoulder and she knew it had to be on his mind, too. Then he turned and resumed climbing, increasing his speed while Kate's heart beat like a hammer, both from the exertion and the memory of his kiss.

'It's nearly the end of December,' Kate said as they finally neared the tower. 'How time has flown.'

Cormac stopped walking and leaned on his stick. 'It has, but I feel as if I've always known you.'

'That's true.' Kate held out her hand. 'Help me up. This last bit is very steep.'

Cormac pulled her up to where he was standing. She stood beside him and together they gazed out over the bay and the islands in the distance. 'We haven't been here since that day when we had that argument,' he said.

'I know. It seems so long ago, but it's just a little over a week.'

'And we have made a kind of peace.' Cormac looked at her sideways. 'Or have we?'

'Peace, and maybe an acceptance of our differences,' Kate said. 'I think that works, don't you?'

'Yes. For now. But I'd say we'll always have different opinions.'

'Of course we will,' Kate said, knowing he was right. They would always be on opposite sides of healing and she knew they'd argue about it all the time. But it didn't frighten her at all. She squinted against the bright sunlight. 'Has Helen been in touch?'

'Yes, but she didn't mention anything about any analysis. We just talked about the tea and how she's going to market it. They're branching out into the herb and health food market. So she's interested in some of my other recipes.'

'Don't let her grab all your remedies,' Kate warned.

Cormac laughed. 'Don't worry. I will only share the teas and some of the essential oils. She wants to use the herbs and plants that I grow, and she's even said she'll help me with the finance to build a second greenhouse, maybe even hiring staff. So I'll be a lot better off and could take you on a holiday to wherever you want to go.'

Kate gazed out over the blue waters of the Atlantic, the islands shimmering in the distance and the coastline with the jagged peaks of the mountains. 'I don't want to go anywhere but here.' *And I don't want to leave*, she thought. *Oh, God, how will I be able to bear it?*

Cormac touched her cheek. 'Neither do I.'

Kate smiled at him, trying her best not to think about the future.

'You look upset,' Cormac remarked. 'Is there something wrong?'

'No.' She hesitated, not wanting to ruin this perfect day. 'I'm just thinking about the future.'

'Don't think about that,' Cormac ordered. 'I'm worried, too, but I've put it out of my mind. Just concentrate on right now, okay?'

Kate nodded. 'You're right. And at this moment, all I want is lunch. I'd say Bridget packed us a five-star picnic.'

'Judging by all the little packages, I think you're right.' Cormac resumed the climb, and Kate followed. It didn't take long before they were sitting on the steps of the tower, digging into chicken drumsticks, brown bread with salmon pâté, hard-boiled eggs with chives and to finish off, a large slice of chocolate cake.

'It's like those picnics in the Famous Five books,' Kate said as she finished her slice of cake. 'We should have home-made lemonade to wash it down like they did. I used to get so hungry when I read those books.'

Cormac laughed. 'I know what you mean. But they had weird things like potted shrimp and thick slices of ham and pigeon pie as well, didn't they?'

'They did.' Kate laughed and held out her mug. 'Any more coffee in that thermos?'

'A few drops,' Cormac said and poured what was left into her mug.

Kate drank the last of the coffee and glanced at Cormac, who was tidying up the picnic. The mild winds had turned colder and dark clouds gathered above them. The brief respite was over and now they had to hurry home before the rain and the wind turned nasty. But it came as no surprise as it was, after all, late December. Kerry had a mild climate but January could be cold with frequent storms before it turned warmer again in February. Kate was looking forward to Christmas in the old house, even though Cormac would spend it in Dingle with his family. Then she had been invited to dinner at their house in early January, which she was looking forward to. It would be interesting to meet his family, especially his sister to whom he was very close. Another milestone in their relationship, too, even if it would be a while before he met Tara.

They made their way down from the tower, across the little beach of Wild Rose Bay, which Cormac said was lovely in early summer when the roses were in bloom. Then up the slope and down the cliff walk before they reached the village and the main street. By the time they got to the lane leading to Cormac's cottage, Kate was exhausted and just wanted to sit down in front of the fire with a cup of tea.

It was nearly dark when they reached the white cottage on the edge of the cliffs, where they could hear the waves crashing onto the rocks below.

'Here we are,' Cormac said and opened the door, flicking on a light switch. 'My humble abode.'

Kate stepped into the little hall and followed Cormac into a cosy living room, where a red velvet sofa stood on polished floorboards in front of the old fireplace in which some logs waited to be lit. She took off her jacket and looked around as Cormac put a match to the fire. 'This is lovely,' she said, surprised by the tasteful interior, the bookcase crammed with books and the beautiful abstract oil paintings on the walls. There was a sheepskin in front of the fireplace and a small coffee table that looked as if it had been made from driftwood. The room was warm and inviting and far from the messy bachelor pad she had expected.

Cormac pulled the curtains with a Celtic design across the window. 'Sit down in front of the fire,' he said, 'and I'll get you a cup of tea. Or would you prefer wine?'

'Tea sounds great,' Kate replied as she sank down on the sofa and held her hands out to the flickering flames. 'I love this room. Did you do all this?'

'Not entirely,' he replied. 'The sofa belongs to my landlady, but the art is all mine and the curtains were made by Aunt Clodagh. And they're all my books, of course.'

'No TV?' Kate asked.

Cormac shrugged. 'No. Never watch it. But I have a laptop, and I can stream the news or listen to the radio in the kitchen just to keep up with what's going on.'

'Can I help you with the tea?' Kate asked.

'No, just relax and enjoy the fire. I won't be long,' Cormac said and disappeared into the kitchen.

While he was gone, Kate got up and wandered around, looking at the paintings, marvelling at their beautiful colours and shapes. Then she walked to the bookcase and smiled at the array of titles, Jane Austen and the Brontë sisters among them.

'You seem to like historical fiction, just like me,' she said when Cormac came back with a steaming mug of tea.

He handed her the mug. 'Yes, that's my guilty secret. I used to sneak-read my sister's Harlequin romances when I was a teenager. I loved romantic stories set centuries ago. And then I graduated to the Brontës.'

'Just like me,' Kate said sipping her tea. 'How strange.'

'Another thing we have in common.' Cormac gestured at the sofa. 'Sit down and put your feet up while we wait for dinner. I just got it started. Hope you like roast lamb. This fancy cooker Cordelia left behind has a rotisserie spit, so it'll cook perfectly in no time at all.'

'It's smelling delicious already,' Kate said, her mouth watering. She put up her feet and pulled a wool throw over her legs, while Cormac cooked roast potatoes and parsnips in the kitchen. She nearly drifted off to sleep but woke up as a plate with roast lamb was put in front of her on the coffee table. Cormac poured her a glass of wine.

'There,' he said. 'Just let me get a jug of water and we can eat.'

'No wine for you?'

'No,' he replied. 'It's not that I don't like it, but in my misspent youth I liked it a little too much. So I gave it all up.' He stopped on the way to the kitchen. 'I wasn't an alcoholic, but I was afraid it was going that way, so…'

'That was very brave of you,' Kate said. 'I'm guessing you were dependent rather than addicted, but it can easily become a real problem in some cases.'

'That's what I thought.'

'Now I feel a little guilty drinking wine in front of you.'

Cormac laughed. 'Please don't. It doesn't bother me at all watching you enjoy a glass of wine. Especially that wine. I know it's very good.'

'Delicious,' Kate said, taking another sip.

Cormac leaned over and placed a kiss on her mouth. 'Just to taste the wine from your lips.' Then he left to fetch the food and they ate sitting together on the sofa, feeding each other bits of lamb, potatoes and parsnips, finally settling, their arms around each other, looking at the dancing flames around the logs, telling each other things about themselves that they hadn't shared before.

'I'm sad for you,' Cormac said when Kate told him about how her father had died and how she and Tara had had to cope with their grief. 'You don't seem to have had that closure everyone needs after such a tragedy.'

'Not really,' Kate murmured, leaning her head on his shoulder. 'The funeral was a little hasty as Tara and I had to get back to our jobs so it was a kind of quick goodbye and then the sale of the house a few months later. It wasn't until afterwards I felt the shock and the grief. I've had this little pain in my heart ever since. So many regrets, so many unsaid words… And then, every time I try to talk to Tara about it, she refuses to discuss it. I'd love for us to stop being in denial about it.' Kate hadn't realised until now how much she'd wanted to talk about her father, or just how good it might feel to share her grief.

Cormac's arms tightened around her. 'Maybe you should have a memorial service? With your sister. Right here in Sandy Cove? After all, your family originally came from here, so it might be like coming home and connecting with your father's roots.'

'A memorial service?' Kate said. 'I'm not sure how that could be arranged. Tara has such demanding work commitments.'

'You could do it in the spring. That would give her plenty of time to plan.'

Kate nodded, touched both by his concern and the idea of a memorial mass for her father in the little church in Sandy Cove. 'It would be a lovely thing to do. I'll think about it.'

'In the meantime we'll spend as much time together as we can,' Cormac said and got up to put another log on the fire. 'And you'll have to brace yourself for my family. They're a wild bunch and can get rowdy at times.'

Kate laughed. 'I can't wait,' she said, wondering how it was possible that such a gentle, soft-spoken man could come from a family that was wild and rowdy. She felt a dart of nervousness as she thought of meeting them. How would they feel about her, a doctor practising conventional medicine with opinions far removed from their traditions rooted in ancient history and folklore? That might jar with them at the best of times, even if she wasn't in a relationship with their son and brother. But worst of all – she was from Dublin.

Christmas turned out to be a quiet affair with Bridget and John and their two daughters, who both studied in Limerick. Mick and Pat had gone to Killarney to celebrate Christmas with Helen's family as they always did. Bridget cooked a delicious dinner with turkey, ham and all the trimmings, Kate and the two girls assisting, and John laying the table in the dining room.

Kate missed Tara terribly, but had been cheered up by a brief FaceTiming session earlier while Tara pointed the camera at the winter wonderland outside her window. There were no calls, so Kate could continue to enjoy the evening without being asked to tackle any medical emergency. They ended the evening in front of the television watching *The Sound of Music* and everyone singing along with Julie Andrews to all the well-known tunes. A lovely Christmas, which sent Kate to bed in a good mood. After the rather quiet New Year's celebrations at the village pub with Mick, Kate mentally prepared herself for the coming months when she would be running the practice on her own. But she was more nervous about meeting Cormac's family at the weekend. She told herself sternly not to worry. Cormac would still love her even if his family found her wanting. She didn't quite know why she was so worried. Maybe because of the clash of two different worlds, two different ways of thinking. Would she and Cormac be able to bridge that gap?

# Chapter Twenty-Four

The O'Shea family home, a modern house just above Dingle town, had beautiful views of the harbour and the fishing boats moored at the quayside. The town itself was charming with pubs, restaurants and quaint shops selling souvenirs and handcrafted items along the street lining the harbour. The lanes and alleyways going up the hills were lined with a mixture of old cottages, Victorian houses and old churches. The old-fashioned street lights were beautiful and there were candles flickering in all the windows. But Kate found herself too occupied with the thought of meeting Cormac's family to really appreciate it fully. She had on a white embroidered shirt and a blue cardigan, and had put on her black ankle-length skirt and a pair of suede boots, hoping it would be the right outfit for this kind of evening. She parked her car outside the front gate and got out, carefully lifting a basket of flowers she had bought in a flower shop in Killorglin on the way.

Cormac opened the door as she walked up the garden path. 'There you are.' He pulled her into the house and kissed her hard on the mouth before he let her go. 'Good evening, lovely Kate.'

'Good evening,' she replied, breathless from both the kiss and her nerves. She found herself standing in a large bright hall with a gleaming wooden floor and a mahogany hallstand from which hung a variety of coats and jackets. Her face in the mirror was pale, her eyes huge.

Cormac held the basket while she took off her coat. 'Lovely flowers. Mammy will love them.'

'I hope so.'

'Of course she will. And she'll love you, too. You look beautiful.'

'Thank you.' Kate pushed at her hair and straightened her cardigan. 'Okay. I'm ready.'

'Don't look so scared,' Cormac said and took her hand. 'They won't eat you. Come on. Everyone's in the living room waiting for you. Just catch your breath and we'll go inside. How do you like Dingle so far?'

'I love it. Such a gorgeous little town,' Kate replied, knowing he was trying to calm her down.

'It's a grand place,' Cormac agreed. He squeezed her hand. 'Ready?'

She nodded and took the basket of flowers from him. 'Let's go inside.'

'Come on,' Cormac said and led her down a corridor and into a large room with a bay window from where you could see the lights from the town below. There was a piano and an Irish harp beside it, which told Kate that this was a family who loved music. Most of the floor was taken up with a thick Donegal carpet in beautiful hues of blue and green, and the room was furnished with a mix of old and new with a large green sofa piled with embroidered cushions and two leather easy chairs. A group of people consisting of three men and two women were gathered in front of the fireplace, and they all turned round as Cormac and Kate entered. 'Here she is,' Cormac announced. 'My lovely Kate.'

The older of the two women, who was tall and slim with long black hair streaked with grey, stepped forward holding out both her hands. 'Kate,' she said. 'I'm Noreen. Welcome to our house.'

'Thank you,' Kate said and held out the basket. 'I brought this for you.' She was immediately struck by how alike she and Cormac were, as was the younger woman, who must be his sister.

Noreen took the basket. 'Such gorgeous flowers. Thank you so much, Kate.' Her green eyes twinkled. 'Come and meet the rest of the party. Not as many as I'd like, but as children grow up you have to get used to the family shrinking.' She gestured at the men. 'Come and meet Kate, lads.'

A tall, distinguished-looking man with a shock of white hair came forward. 'Hello, Kate. I'm Donncha, Cormac's father. And these lads are Sean and Darragh, my two oldest sons. We have four more, but they're scattered all over the country. And this beautiful young lady is Mairead, the baby of the family.'

Mairead swung her long black hair out of her eyes and smiled at Kate. 'So nice to meet you at last,' she said. 'Cormac has been going on and on about you every time we meet. And you're just as gorgeous as he said.'

'Thank you,' Kate said, feeling suddenly shy. 'And he told me all about you.'

'Oh my God,' Mairead exclaimed. 'Did he, the dirty rascal? What did he say?'

'Just nice things,' Kate assured her.

'Oh, phew,' Mairead said. 'That's a relief. Sorry my husband isn't here tonight but he's minding the kids at home. They're all very sniffly at the moment, so we didn't want them here blowing their noses on the tablecloth and spreading their germs around. But you'll meet them next time you come over to Dingle. If you feel strong enough for three rowdy children who never stop shouting.'

'I'd love to meet them,' Kate replied. 'I adore children, and I bet yours are gorgeous.'

'Of course they are,' Cormac cut in. 'The most beautiful children in Ireland. And the boldest.'

Mairead shoved her elbow into his side. 'Not as bold as you were at that age.'

'Hey, guys,' Cormac called to his brothers, 'come and meet Kate.'

The two brothers, as tall as their father, shook hands with Kate and wished her welcome to the house. 'You're from Dublin, aren't you?' Darragh asked.

'Yes, but please don't hold that against me,' Kate pleaded. 'Our family is originally from Kerry,' she added, hoping that would make her look better.

'Ha, the O'Sheas came to Kerry from Cork, so we're blow-ins as well,' Sean cut in.

'Yes, about two hundred years ago, but that's like yesterday around here,' Darragh remarked.

'Dinner's ready,' Noreen suddenly shouted from the door that led to what Kate discovered was a spacious kitchen-diner, where the long table was laid with a huge array of food with everything from cold chicken and ham, salmon pâté, shrimps, potato salad and both soda bread and baguettes that seemed to be newly taken out of the oven.

'Please sit down and help yourselves,' Noreen said as she placed a jug of water and a bottle of wine on the table.

'What an amazing spread,' Kate said as she heaped her plate with everything.

'Oh, it's just the usual family tea we do when we get together,' Noreen said.

'Delicious.' Kate said, and sat down between Cormac and Mairead.

Sean put a few bottles of beer on the table before he sat down opposite them. 'What do you want to drink, Kate?' he asked.

'A glass of wine, please,' she replied.

When everyone was sitting down, Cormac's father tapped his glass with his fork. 'Silence, please,' he ordered. 'I want to say welcome to Kate.' He raised his glass of beer and smiled at her. 'Welcome to our house, Kate. I hope you will enjoy yourself here tonight.'

'And we hope you've practised your performance,' Darragh cut in, winking at Cormac.

Kate nearly choked on the sip of wine she had just taken. 'Performance?'

'Yes,' Mairead said. 'We always do some kind of party trick after dinner on Saturday nights. All our friends will call in for drinks, tea or coffee later, and then we do something like that for the craic. Singing, dancing, playing an instrument, you know the typical Irish thing.'

'Oh, eh,' Kate stammered. 'I see.' She looked at Cormac. 'But I haven't prepared anything, and I can't sing or play an instrument,' she said, annoyed and embarrassed. 'And Cormac seems to have forgotten to mention this small detail.'

'You could read a poem in Irish, though, couldn't you?' Noreen suggested. Then she laughed. 'Or you could just watch everyone else. Don't worry, Kate, you don't have to perform if you don't want to. Darragh is just trying to scare you.'

Cormac threw a piece of bread at his brother that hit him on the face. 'That's for scaring Kate.'

Darragh threw the piece of bread back. 'That's for not getting the joke.'

Cormac was about to retaliate with his napkin when Noreen shouted: 'Stop it! Behave yourselves, lads. What's Kate going to think?' She shook her head and smiled apologetically at Kate. 'Sorry about this, pet. This always happens with these boys when they get together. Always fighting and arguing. And I can't even say they've had drink taken as an excuse.'

Kate started to laugh. 'Don't worry, Noreen. It's made me feel even more welcome.'

'Yer a grand girl, Kate,' Donncha shouted from the end of the table. 'Can we calm down now and eat?'

And they did. The ice had been broken and everyone started to talk at once, digging into the food, laughing and sharing jokes. Kate found herself deep in conversation with Mairead, who told her about the life of fishermen and her work as a legal secretary. 'But right now I'm taking a break,' she said. 'I have three small children and they need me more than anyone right now. Once they go to school, I'll take it up again. I just feel that I should be there for my kids when they're small. In any case one of them is always sick with one thing or another, especially in the winter. And my husband has to go out with the boats early every morning.' She put her hand on Kate's arm. 'I'm so happy about you and Cormac,' she whispered in Kate's ear. 'He looks so good now. Less tense and worried than he was before. And you're a handsome couple.'

Her words made Kate smile tenderly. 'Thank you. He's good for me, too. I have no idea what the future will bring, but right now everything's perfect.'

'And your job?' Mairead asked. 'You'll stay in Sandy Cove?'

Kate shrugged. 'I'm not sure. But if not, I'll solve it somehow.'

'I'm sure you will,' Mairead said. 'If it's meant to be, it'll all fall into place one way or another.'

When dinner was over they all returned to the living room and later, when a lot of people arrived through the door, the music started and the party was soon in full swing. Donncha played the piano and Noreen sat by the harp and played, singing an Irish ballad in her beautiful voice. Darragh picked up a tin whistle and continued the music, and at the end of the music session, Mairead sang 'Danny Boy' so beautifully that everyone dabbed at their eyes and blew their noses when she had finished. The guests started to take their leave, and Cormac and Kate said their farewells and got into Kate's car for the drive back to Sandy Cove. Noreen gave Kate a loaf of her soda bread and a little pot with salmon pâté. 'I saw how much you enjoyed it,' she said. Then she kissed Kate on the cheek. 'It was so nice to meet you. Thank you for coming.'

'Thank you for a lovely evening,' Kate replied.

'Bye, Mammy,' Cormac said as he got into the car. 'I'll be in touch.'

Then they waved and drove off, back to Sandy Cove, finally alone together.

'Your family is lovely,' Kate said as they turned down the road to Cahersiveen.

'They're a grand bunch. And they loved you.'

'I loved them, too.' Kate stared thoughtfully ahead. 'But it's only the start of the year and I have a tough few months to come.' She turned her head and glanced at him. 'And then I'll be out of a job in April unless I go back to Dublin.'

'I know.' Cormac touched her hand on the steering wheel. 'But I have a feeling it will be solved one way or the other. And that you will stay.'

'How?' she asked, staring into the darkness. 'I wish I was as optimistic as you.'

'It's not optimism, it's a feeling,' Cormac argued.

'I hope you're right,' Kate mumbled, her heart sinking as she thought of what lay ahead. Alone at the surgery, coping with the flow of sick people – how would that affect her? 'You won't see much of me during the next few weeks,' she said.

'I know. But you'll cope. You're strong and will rise to the challenge. In any case, I'll be busy, too. As I told you, Helen asked me to work with her to develop some of my herbal teas for her firm so they can market them.'

'That's brilliant,' Kate said. 'That should be a fun project for you, and it'll help her get over the disappointment of the cream and the lack of a magical ingredient.'

'She seems to have taken that on the chin. Don't worry, Kate,' he added. 'You'll manage very well. You're a good doctor.'

'I'll do my best,' Kate mumbled as they drove through the quiet streets of Cahersiveen and onto the coast road that would take them to Sandy Cove.

The next week was busy, but not as bad as Kate had feared. Everyone seemed to be taking it easy after the New Year's Eve festivities, and there were only a few really bad cases of the flu. Mick came back and picked up the work on his play. Kate and Cormac managed to see each other when Kate was free, and he even came with her on her Saturday rounds. Pat was in touch every day, but there wasn't much to tell him except that everything was ticking over. 'It'll get busy next week,' Pat said. 'It always does. Call me if you need to ask anything. I'll be happy to help out, if only over the phone,' he added wistfully.

Kate felt sorry for him. He missed the practice and his patients. But it was probably the right thing for him to do as his health might have suffered had he continued working those long hours.

'I appreciate your help and advice,' she said. 'Managing the practice on my own is a little daunting, to be honest.'

'Ah, you'll be fine,' Pat soothed. 'You're a good doctor.'

She remembered those words when, only two weeks into January, the flu season finally hit them. Most of the seriously ill patients were old and living on their own, so Kate had to grab her bag and head off into the hills at all hours, trying her best to help and soothe, sometimes having to call an ambulance or even taking someone to hospital herself. She was often exhausted, crawling into bed late at night, sleeping soundly until she was woken up by Bridget, still tired after not getting enough sleep. But despite her exhaustion, she found the challenge exciting and stimulating, as she had to use her diagnostic skills to the max.

There was little time for relaxing, and she didn't even find time to connect with Tara, but she knew she and Mick often chatted online, which made Kate feel oddly left out and even a little envious of the fun they seemed to be having. Pat called every day and his advice and comments were hugely helpful. She knew he longed to be back at her side, but it wouldn't have been wise for him to have to work this hard. 'The stress and long hours would probably kill him,' Mick said, when Kate had come off the phone. 'He nearly collapsed last year after the flu season. I'm glad he's over there in Killarney playing golf and socialising. I'm sure my mother is, too.'

But one dark and wet afternoon, when Kate had just had a quick lunch, she gave a start as she saw someone in the hall. She watched the figure of a man walking towards her. 'Pat!' she exclaimed. 'What are you doing here?'

'I just came back to breathe in the smell of antiseptic,' he said.

Kate laughed. 'You miss the hard work and the long hours?'

'Like crazy. Golf is fun, but not what it's cracked up to be.' He looked at her for a moment. 'You look so tired. Is the flu season bad this year?'

She nodded. 'The waiting room is packed. And I have a few house calls this evening. But we're managing. Bridget is a true star. I think it's easing off a little, too.'

He nodded. 'Yes, it usually does around this time. All the socialising around Christmas means a lot of people sharing their germs, and then we get this huge surge of flu cases and other infections. But it usually calms down towards the end of January.'

'Exactly. More people on trolleys in the hospitals than in the actual wards this week, I believe. I'm hoping to keep most of the older people out of hospital by catching them early, before they get too ill. Lots of antibiotics, unfortunately, but it can't be helped.'

'I know.' He touched her shoulder. 'I'm actually here because I drove Mick to Tralee to go for a check-up. We just came back. He's upstairs having a rest. I'm staying the night, so I'll see you later. I might have some news for you then.'

'About what?' Kate asked, mystified.

'I'll tell you tonight. Now, off you go, back to work.'

Kate shrugged and went into the surgery, knowing Pat was planning some kind of surprise. Whatever it was, she hoped she'd be able to take it. She was too worn out to cope with anything startling. It wasn't only the pressure at the surgery that made her so tired, but also everything else that was happening around her. Mick and Tara connecting, and Tara's new relationship, which she still hadn't shared with Kate, and then there was the idea of the memorial service Cormac had suggested, which needed a lot of thought and planning. She hadn't had the time or the energy to give all of that much consideration, but there was plenty of time, as it wouldn't be happening until the spring. But she felt this was an added burden for her tired brain. Pat's announcement had better be something good.

*

Late that evening, when Kate came back from a gruelling few hours doing house calls, she found Pat and Mick in the living room, having a heated discussion.

Mick looked pleadingly at Kate when she came in. 'Tell him, Kate. He can't do this. It'll kill him.'

'Do what?' Kate asked.

'He's planning to come back to work here,' Mick said, exasperated. 'I've told him he shouldn't, but he won't listen. And my mother is even encouraging him.'

'What?' Kate asked, sitting down on the edge of an easy chair. 'You want to come back, Pat?'

'Don't look so shocked,' Pat said with a laugh. Then he sobered. 'Kate, I can't stand it much longer. I'm going mad being the retired gentleman who plays golf and goes to dinner parties. I have to get back here somehow.'

'Oh,' Kate said, alarmed by his troubled face. 'But how? I thought you had to give up work for your health? The arrhythmia and the blood pressure issue…' Appalled, Kate wondered how this was going to work. She had come here to help out because Pat was winding down. Why was he now going back to square one? She looked at him, feeling more confused than ever.

Pat waved his hand. 'Ah that. All under control. The stress of doing nothing is worse than working.'

'But it's only been three weeks,' Kate protested. 'Maybe you should give it a chance. Get used to your new life?'

'I never will,' Pat said hotly. 'It didn't take me long to realise that.'

'I think Kate's right,' Mick cut in. 'You should give it another month or two.'

'Then I'll be worse,' Pat said. 'It's bad enough right now. I'm feeling depressed, and that has resulted in not being able to sleep and a loss of appetite. And I have apparently been a pain in the neck to my wife. We're constantly bickering, and that's another stress factor. My doctor in Killarney has told me to try to occupy myself with something I enjoy. But apart from golf, which I'm beginning to find boring, medicine is what I love to do.' He let out a laugh. 'I overheard this young woman in a restaurant describing golf as "that game you play before you die".' Pat's eyes suddenly hardened. 'I don't want to play golf and wait to die, I want to *live*, I want to do something useful. And with your help, I know I can.'

'My help?' Kate asked.

'Don't listen to him,' Mick said.

'Shut up, Mick,' Pat snapped. 'Let me explain.' He sat back and cleared his throat. 'I've been in touch with the medical board at the Health Service Executive and we had a long chat. If all goes well and they agree to my plan, it will work very well. I'll be working as much or as little as I want this way. Please listen before you say anything.'

Kate nodded. 'Okay. Go on.'

'So,' Pat continued, 'I've suggested that I come back as the GP here and continue to train you for your full GP qualification. I would unofficially work only in the surgery and you would do both some surgery hours and most house calls. In reality I'd only be working part-time.' He drew breath and looked at Kate. 'How does this sound to you?'

Kate stared at him, trying to take it all in.

She had once had such high ambitions to work at a top-notch GP practice in Dublin, where she would be close to all the big hospitals and have access to the best medical services in the country. Pat's idea put all these notions out of her head, and now she had to consider a whole new way forward. But was this a good idea for Pat? Had he breezed over his medical history and pretended to be in better health than he really was? She looked at Mick's worried face and then to Pat.

'It sounds good, in theory,' she said. 'But I need to think about this before I accept.'

Pat nodded. 'Absolutely. It's not something you decide just like that. Sleep on it and let me know in the morning.'

'I think I've already made my decision, actually,' Kate said, feeling suddenly that there was no need to hang around. 'But I would only do this if you had a full check-up, and not with a doctor who happens to be a pal of yours. A full medical in Tralee hospital. If I'm happy with the results, we can talk about it again and work out schedules and contracts.'

Mick looked at her with relief. 'Great idea about the check-up, Kate. Thank you.'

'Pat?' Kate said.

He nodded. 'I thought you'd say something like that. And I agree. In your shoes, I'd do the same. I'll book a medical examination—'

'No,' Kate said. 'I will. Otherwise I can't be sure it'll be done without pulling strings and a nod and a wink.'

Pat laughed. 'I see you take no prisoners.' He got up and stretched. 'But I agree. I'm off to bed. Let me know when you've made the appointment.'

'I will. And another thing,' Kate said, feeling she was on a roll. 'We'd have to update the surgery, starting with that brown carpet.'

Pat laughed. 'Okay, that's a deal.'

When Pat had left, Mick looked at Kate and shrugged. 'He's such a stubborn auld geezer. But if he really can still work, I think it's the right decision. For him and for my mother. They're happier seeing each other part-time like this. And if you're sharing the workload, I think he'll be fine.'

Kate nodded cheerfully. 'Oh yes, he will. And I'm sure the results of the check-up will be good. He looks perfectly healthy to me. And,' she added, feeling a dart of happiness, 'it might also solve the problem of what to do with my career.'

'He knows that, too, the auld fox,' Mick said. 'That was part of his plan.'

Kate felt a surge of joy as she went over her options and weighed them together, knowing she had made the right decision. There was no doubt that her Dublin plans would have worked out brilliantly in the end, but the road to get there would have been long and hard and full of obstacles. And she would have had to do it all alone. The more she considered it, Pat's idea shone like a bright beacon of light in a dark tunnel, at the end of which was not only a great position as a country GP, but also her love life resolved in a wonderful way. Only a fool would give all that up.

Later that evening, Kate called in to Cormac. 'Hi,' she said when he opened the door. 'Sorry to call so late, but would you like to hear some good news?'

'Yes,' Cormac said, pulling her inside. 'Even though just seeing you is very good news. But what did you want to tell me?'

'Just that I think I'll be staying around for a long time to come,' Kate said, smiling at him as he put his arms around her.

Cormac pulled away. 'Oh? What makes you say that?'

Kate leaned against him. 'Just something in the wind,' she murmured, her cheek against his chest. 'A feeling in my heart. And knowing that I have to stay here no matter what. I belong here. I feel I've come back to where my family began. And to you, who have been waiting for me all my life.'

'Have you been drinking?' Cormac asked, laughing as he tightened his arms around her. 'You don't sound like yourself.'

'This is my new self,' Kate said softly. 'The me who's looking forward instead of back. It's all going to work out.'

'Your work, you mean?'

'And you and me. We were just getting to know each other. I thought we would have to say goodbye. But now we have the time to keep going, to take it slowly and find out where we want to go. How does that sound?'

'Like a dream come true,' Cormac said.

# Epilogue

Late May in Sandy Cove was truly magical, with all the whitethorn bushes in full bloom, hedges of fuchsia lining every road and warm winds blowing through the little village and across the beaches where surfers and sunbathers were enjoying the sunshine.

'Heavenly,' Tara said as she and Kate walked arm in arm the short distance to the church where the memorial mass for their father would be taking place. 'I can see why you love this place so much.'

'Pity you have to go back so soon,' Kate said wistfully. 'I'd love you to stay longer.'

'Me too. But I'll come back in the summer,' Tara promised.

'Of course you will,' Kate said, laughing. 'You have to meet Mick, as you missed him this time.'

'Yes, that was a real bummer,' Tara complained. 'Just my luck that he had to go to London this week.'

'Well, as you know, his play will be going up in the West End in September, so he had to go and meet the director and help out with casting,' Kate remarked. 'Otherwise he'd be here. But at least you'll be meeting Cormac.'

'I can't wait,' Tara said. 'I want to see if he's as wonderful as you've said.'

'He is,' Kate declared. 'I dare you not to like him.'

'I'm sure I will. But will he like me?' Tara asked.

'He will.' Kate squeezed Tara's arm. 'I can't believe you're here at last, even for a few days.'

'I'm so glad I came.'

'Me too,' Kate said. 'And having the mass for Dad here, where his family lived so many years ago, is perfect.'

'I suppose it is,' Tara said. 'But… I don't feel that connected to this place. I know Dad told us about it when we were kids, but it seemed more like a story and not something I could relate to.'

'I've tried to tell you,' Kate said, disappointed that Tara didn't share that amazing feeling of being in touch with their roots.

'I know, but there was so much going on in my life. And I wasn't here, walking around, hearing the stories and meeting the people.'

'No, that's true,' Kate said. 'But maybe one day you'll come here and spend some time with me, won't you?'

'I'd love to,' Tara said. 'I'll see if I can organise some time off, and then I'll come back. I really want to. We need to be together.'

'We do.' Kate sighed and looked up at the blue sky. 'He's up there, smiling.'

'Oh yes, he is. That is something I can feel. And I think I'm beginning to accept that he's gone.'

'Me too. We didn't really give ourselves time to grieve properly when he died, did we? I think we were in too much of a hurry, trying to get back to our lives and maybe thinking that if we hurried on, everything would be okay again. But it never was, was it? Completely, I mean.'

'No,' Tara said softly. 'It wasn't. But now, doing this, feels right.'

'Yes,' Kate agreed. 'It's as if we're confronting our grief, looking it in the face and not saying goodbye to Dad, but just showing him how much we love him. Not living in denial like we have been.'

'Yes, we've been running away without getting anywhere.'

'That's so true,' Kate agreed as they neared the gate to the churchyard. 'Here we are,' she said, just as the bells started to ring.

'What a beautiful little church,' Tara said. 'And look, is that Cormac waiting on the steps?'

Kate smiled as she saw Cormac's tall figure. 'Yes. That's him.'

'He's gorgeous,' Tara said and walked swiftly forward. She grinned and held out her hand. 'Cormac,' she said. 'I'm Tara. So nice to meet you at last.'

'Hello, Tara.' Cormac took her hand and then kissed her on the cheek. 'I'm so happy to meet you.' He held out his other hand to Kate. 'Come, let's go inside. Everyone's here.'

They walked into the church and Kate saw what Cormac meant. The church was packed with many of her patients, but also, apart from Pat, Helen, Bridget and John, Cormac's family, his Aunt Clodagh and most of the population of Sandy Cove. Kate was suddenly overwhelmed with emotion and tears blurred her vision as Cormac led her and Tara to their pew.

The music was beautiful, all organised by Cormac's mother and sister, most of the hymns in Irish. It really felt as if their father was being returned to his roots, to the very origins of his family and the land they had come from. Both Kate and Tara found it impossible to hold back their tears. They held each other tightly, smiling at the end of the mass as the priest came forward to offer them words of comfort. Then they walked out into the glorious spring sunshine, meeting everyone and thanking them for coming.

Finally, there was tea at the Wellness Centre organised by Sally, which turned into a party that lasted well into the night, with food and drink from the nearby pub. By that time, Tara had met everyone and been charmed and flirted with by various handsome Kerrymen, which, she declared, meant she simply had to get back as soon as she could.

'I never knew the men in Kerry were so hot,' she said to Kate as they walked back to the house. 'They have that wild, cheeky way about them.'

'What about Joe?' Kate asked.

Tara laughed. 'Yeah, what about him? He's very attractive, and we have this thing going, but I have a feeling it won't last. But time will tell. We work well together, and he's asked me to go on a photo shoot in Arizona all on my own, so that means he likes what I do. But it's tricky him being my boss and everything.'

'I can see that,' Kate replied.

'But I'm glad you have your life all sorted,' Tara said. 'You look so happy.'

Kate smiled. 'I am. Very happy. I didn't go for the glamorous medical career I thought I wanted, but this is far more rewarding.'

Tara looked at Kate and nodded. 'And you found the love of your life.'

'Yes, I did. I had to come here to find him.'

Tara laughed. 'And now your life will be here in this little village in the back of beyond.'

'No better place to be,' Kate said.

# A Letter from Susanne

I want to say a huge thank you for choosing to read *Memories of Wild Rose Bay*. I began writing this novel at the very start of the coronavirus pandemic. As it went on, I found escaping to Sandy Cove a huge comfort. I hope it gave you an opportunity to escape the troubling times for a while, too. The village, with its quirky characters, is not far removed from the reality of a small village in the west of Ireland, and I'm looking forward to going back there for more inspiration. This particular story has been such a pleasure to write, and I found that the characters somehow took over and steered me through the story, doing their own thing at times, strange as that might sound! I hope you liked the twists and turns. If you did enjoy it, and want to keep up to date with all my latest releases, just sign up at the following link. Your email address will never be shared and you can unsubscribe at any time.

*www.bookouture.com/susanne-oleary*

I hope you loved *Memories of Wild Rose Bay*, and if you did, I would be very grateful if you could write a review. I'd love to hear what you think, and it makes such a difference helping new readers to discover one of my books for the first time.

I love hearing from my readers – you can get in touch on my Facebook page, through Twitter, Goodreads and Instagram, or my website.

Thanks,
Susanne

f authoroleary

@susl

837027.Susanne_O-Leary

www.susanne-oleary.co.uk

@susanne.olearyauthor

# Acknowledgements

Huge thanks again to my editor Jennifer Hunt for her inspiring work and support. I couldn't wish for a better editor! Many thanks also, as always, to all at Bookouture, the best publishing team ever to work with! To family and friends, who cheer me on, read my books and listen to my adventures in writing and publishing, thank you all so much.

Made in the USA
Las Vegas, NV
04 November 2022